'What ex⬛⬛⬛⬛⬛⬛⬛⬛⬛⬛end
giving the⬛⬛⬛⬛⬛⬛⬛⬛⬛my
presence, ⬛⬛⬛⬛⬛⬛⬛⬛ked
across at h⬛⬛⬛⬛⬛⬛⬛all,
she will know that I am not your
ward.'

He quirked dark brows. 'Why not simply tell her the truth, Jane? That you begged to be allowed to come away with me?'

She gaped at him.

'Do not look so concerned, Jane,' he taunted as he lounged back on the seat. 'No one, not even my sister Arabella, would dare to question what position I intend you to occupy in my household.'

And what position was that? Jane wondered dazedly.

Had she misunderstood the Duke the previous evening, when he had been so insistent she would travel under his protection? Despite what he had said to the contrary, was he now saying he expected her to become his mistress as payment for that protection?

Author Note

This last year has been an absolutely wonderful one for me, in that I celebrated my 30th Anniversary of writing for Harlequin Mills & Boon in their Modern™ Romance series and, to date, have succeeded in having published over 140 books and a dozen or so novellas. To now have this, my very first Regency romance, published too is fantastic!

The Regency period is one that has always been very close to my heart, and with Hawk and Jane's story I have realised my dream of writing about a time that I consider to be one of the most romantic. The other good news is that this is the first of a quartet featuring the St Claire family, so look out for Lucien, Sebastian and Arabella's stories, coming soon.

I hope you have as much fun reading their stories as I am having writing them!

THE DUKE'S
CINDERELLA BRIDE

Carole Mortimer

MILLS & BOON
Pure reading pleasure™

First published in Great Britain 2009
Harlequin Mills & Boon Limited,
Eton House, 18-24 Paradise Road, Richmond, Surrey TW9 1SR

© Carole Mortimer 2009

ISBN: 978 0 263 86773 2

Set in Times Roman 10½ on 12¾ pt.
04-0409-73463

Printed and bound in Spain
by Litografia Rosés S.A., Barcelona

THE DUKE'S
CINDERELLA BRIDE

Carole Mortimer was born in England, the youngest of three children. She began writing in 1978, and has now published over one hundred and forty books with Harlequin Mills & Boon. Carole has four sons, Matthew, Joshua, Timothy and Peter, and a bearded collie called Merlyn. She says, 'I'm happily married to Peter senior; we're best friends as well as lovers, which is probably the best recipe for a successful relationship. We live in a lovely part of England.'

This is Carole's first Historical novel!
Look out for more fabulous Regency tales from her
in
The Notorious St Claires

Coming soon in Mills & Boon®
Historical Romance

Meanwhile, you can read Carole's
latest Modern™ Romance
PREGNANT WITH THE BILLIONAIRE'S BABY
in May 2009!

Chapter One

1816, St Claire House, London

'I have no immediate plans to marry, Hawk. Least of all some chit barely out of the schoolroom that you have deigned to pick out for for me!'

Hawk St Claire, the tenth Duke of Stourbridge, viewed his youngest brother's angrily flushed face across the width of the leather-topped desk that dominated the library in the St Claire townhouse, his mouth twisting slightly as he noted the glitter of rebellion in Sebastian's dark brown gaze. 'I was merely suggesting that it is past time you thought of taking a wife.'

Lord Sebastian St Claire felt the flush deepen in his cheeks under the steely gaze of his eldest brother. But this awareness of Hawk's displeasure in no way lessened his own determination not to be coerced into a marriage he neither sought nor wanted.

Although it was a little difficult to maintain that

stand, Sebastian acknowledged inwardly, in the face of his brother's piercingly intense gaze. A chilling gaze from eyes the colour of gold and ringed by a much darker brown, and one that had been known to almost reduce the Duke's valet to tears on occasion, and to cause lesser peers of the realm to quake in their highly polished boots when Hawk took his place in the House.

'Do not take that insufferably condescending tone with me, Hawk, because it won't wash!' Sebastian threw himself into the carved chair, facing his brother across the desk. 'Or is it only that you have decided to turn your attentions to me because Arabella failed to secure a suitable match during her first Season?' he added slyly, knowing that his eighteen-year-old sibling had stubbornly resisted accepting any of the marriage proposals she had received in the last few months.

He was also completely aware that Hawk had hated his role as occasional escort for their younger sister. It had resulted in the marriage-minded debutantes and their ambitious mamas seeing the unusual occurrence of the Duke of Stourbridge's presence at balls and parties as an open invitation to pursue him!

Until, that was, Hawk had made it known, in his chillingly high-handed manner, that none of those young women met the exacting standards he set for his future Duchess!

Hawk's mouth tightened. 'We were not discussing a match for Arabella.'

'Then perhaps we should have been. Or possibly Lucian?' Sebastian mentioned their brother. 'Although it really should be you, Hawk,' he continued tauntingly. 'After all, you are the Duke, and of the four of us surely the one most in need of an heir?'

At one and thirty, and over six feet tall, his brother Hawk had powerful shoulders and an athletic body that was the pride and joy of his tailor. Today he wore a black jacket which fit snugly across wide shoulders, a pale grey waistcoat and paler grey breeches above highly polished Hessians. His thick dark hair, streaked with gold, was styled with casual elegance, and beneath a wide, intelligent brow were intense golden eyes, the straight slash of a nose between high cheekbones, and a thin, uncompromising mouth above a square jaw. All spoke of his arrogant and determined character.

Even without his title, Hawk was undoubtedly a force to be reckoned with. As the powerful Duke of Stourbridge he was formidable.

Hawk looked completely bored by this particular argument. 'I believe I have made it more than plain these last months that I have yet to meet any woman who is up to the arduous task of becoming the Duchess of Stourbridge. Besides,' he continued, as Sebastian would have argued further, 'I already have two obvious heirs in my younger brothers. Although, going on your more recent behaviour, I would not be happy to see either you or Lucian becoming the next Duke of Stourbridge.' He gave Sebastian a silencing glower.

A glance Sebastian totally ignored. 'If either Lucian or I *were* to become the next Duke of Stourbridge, you can depend on it that you would not be around to see it, Hawk!'

'Very amusing, Sebastian.' The Duke's dismissal was absolute. 'But following the…events of last month, I realise I have been somewhat remiss in not settling your own and Lucian's future.'

'Last month? What did Lucian and I do last month that was so different from—? Ah.' The light finally dawned. 'Can you possibly be referring to the delectable and recently widowed Countess of Morefield?' he challenged unabashedly.

'A gentleman does not discuss a lady by name, Sebastian.' Hawk eyed his brother disapprovingly. 'But now that you have brought the incident to my attention…' he steepled slender fingers '…I could indeed be referring to your reprehensible behaviour concerning a certain lady of our mutual acquaintance.' His voice was icy.

Sebastian grinned unapologetically. 'I can assure you that no one, least of all the Countess, took our interest seriously.'

Hawk looked down the long length of his nose. 'Nevertheless, the lady's name was bandied about at several clubs—my own included. Many of your friends were making wagers, I believe, on which one of you would be the first to oust the Earl of Whitney from the Coun—from the lady's bedchamber.'

Sebastian looked unrepentant. 'Only because they were all aware that we were both totally in ignorance of the other's interest in the lady. Of course, if you had cared to confide in either of us that *you* intended taking up residence in that particular bedchamber, then Lucian and I would simply have backed off and left you and Whitney to decide the outcome!' He eyed Hawk challengingly.

Hawk's wince was pained. 'Sebastian, I have already had occasion to warn you of the…indelicacy of your conversation!'

'So all this talk of the parson's mousetrap is because Lucian and I inadvertently stepped on your toes last month?' Sebastian could barely restrain his humour. 'Or possibly it was another part of your anatomy we intruded upon? Although I do believe,' he continued, as Hawk looked in danger of delivering another of his icy setdowns, 'that you have also now tired of the lady's… charms…?'

The slight flaring of the Duke's nostrils was the only outward sign of his increasing displeasure with the trend of the conversation. 'After the attention you and Lucian brought to that unfortunate lady I deemed it necessary to withdraw my attentions so as not to add further speculation to the impending scandal.'

'If you were not so damned secretive about your mistresses the whole incident could have been avoided.' Sebastian shrugged dismissively. 'But I do assure you, Hawk, I am not about to marry just to appease your outraged sensibilities!'

'You are being utterly ridiculous, Sebastian—'

'No, Hawk.' Sebastian's humour faded. 'I believe if you were to give this subject more thought, you would realise that *you* are the one who is being ridiculous in trying to choose my wife for me.'

'On the contrary, Sebastian. It is my belief that I am

only acting in your best interests. In fact, I have already accepted an invitation on our behalf from Sir Barnaby and Lady Sulby.'

'I take it they are the parents of my intended bride?'

Hawk's mouth tightened. 'Olivia Sulby is the daughter of Sir Barnaby and Lady Sulby, yes.'

Sebastian gave a derisive shake of his head as he stood up. 'I am afraid that whatever invitation you have accepted on my behalf you will just have to unaccept.' He moved to the library door.

'What are you doing?' The Duke frowned at him darkly.

'Leaving.' Sebastian gave him a pitying look. 'But before I go I have a proposition of my own to set before you, Hawk…' He paused in the open doorway.

'A proposition…?' Hawk found himself so deeply disturbed by his brother's stubbornness that—unusually—he could barely hold his temper in check.

Sebastian nodded. 'Once you are married—happily so, of course—I promise I will give serious consideration to the parson's mousetrap for myself!' His step was jaunty as he closed the library door softly behind him.

Hawk sat back heavily in his chair as he contemplated the closed door for several long seconds before reaching for the decanter of brandy that stood on his desktop and pouring a large measure.

Damn.

Damn, damn, *damn*.

He made a point of never attending house parties in the country once the Season had ended and the House had dispersed for the summer. He had only committed himself to spending a week in Norfolk with the Sulbys for the sole purpose of introducing Sebastian to the young woman he had hoped would become his brother's future bride.

His own acquaintance was with Sir Barnaby Sulby—the two of them having dined together at their club several times. There had been no opportunity for Hawk to meet the other gentleman's wife and daughter during the Season, the Sulby family not having received an invitation to the three balls at which Hawk had been Arabella's escort, but Hawk knew from his enquiries that on her father's death Olivia Sulby would inherit Markham Park and its surrounding thousand acres of farmland. As the younger brother of a duke such a match could be considered perfect for Sebastian.

Except Sebastian had now told Hawk—all too succinctly!—that he had no intention of even considering taking a wife until Hawk had done so himself. Leaving Hawk committed to spending a week in Norfolk—a county of flat fenland so totally unlike his own beloved Gloucestershire.

It had all the appeal of a walk to the gallows!

'There you are, Jane. Do stop your dawdling on the stairs, girl.' Lady Gwendoline Sulby, a faded beauty in her mid-forties, glared her impatience as the object of her attention came to a halt neither up nor down the wide staircase. 'No, do not come down. Proceed back up to my bedroom and collect my shawl for me before our guests start to arrive. The silk one with the yellow rosebuds. I do believe the weather might be changing, Sulby.' She turned worriedly to her portly husband as he stood beside her in the spacious hallway in anticipation of the arrival of their guests.

Jane knew that Sir Barnaby was twenty years older than his wife, and he was looking most uncomfortable in his high-necked shirt and tightly tied necktie. His yellow waistcoat stretched almost impossibly across his rounded stomach, and his brown jacket and cream breeches were doing little to hide that strain.

Poor Sir Barnaby, Jane mused as she turned obediently back up the stairs to collect the requested shawl. She knew her guardian would so much rather have been out on the estate somewhere with his manager, wearing comfortable old clothes, than standing in the draughty hallway of Markham Park, awaiting the first dozen or so house guests who would shortly arrive for the start of a week's entertainments and gentile frivolity.

'Bring down my white parasol, too, Jane.' Olivia frowned up at her, a young replica of her mother's earlier beauty, with her fashionably rounded figure, big blue eyes, and golden ringlets arranged enticingly about the dewy beauty of her face.

'Do not shout in that unladylike manner, Olivia.' Lady Gwendoline looked scandalised by her daughter's behaviour. 'Whatever would the Duke think if he were to hear you?' She gave an agitated wave of her fan.

'But *you* shouted, Mama.' Olivia pouted her displeasure at the rebuke.

'I am the mistress of this house. I am allowed to shout.'

Jane smiled slightly as she continued on her way back up the stairs, knowing that the illogical bickering between mother and daughter was likely to continue for several more minutes. The arguments had been constant and sometimes heated during the last week as the household prepared for the arrival of the Sulbys' house guests, and most of them had the phrases 'the Duke' or 'His Grace' in their content.

For the Duke of Stourbridge was to be the Sulby's guest of honour this week—as every member of the overworked household had been constantly made aware, as they cleaned and scrubbed and polished Markham Park in preparation for 'His Grace, the Duke's' arrival.

Not that Jane expected to be included in any of the planned entertainments, or even to meet the illustrious Duke in person. She was only a poor relation. Jane Smith. A distant relation that the Sulbys had taken pity on and charitably offered a home to for the last twelve of her two and twenty years.

Markham Park had seemed rather grand and alien to Jane when Sir Barnaby and Lady Gwendoline had first brought her here, her childhood having been spent in a tiny south coast vicarage, being lovingly cared for by her widowed father and Bessie, his elderly but motherly housekeeper.

But Jane had consoled herself with the fact that at least Markham Park was within walking distance of the sea—allowing her, during the brief times she was able to escape the seemingly ever-watchful gaze of Lady

Sulby, to go down to the rugged shoreline and enjoy its wild, untamed beauty.

Jane had quickly discovered that she liked Norfolk winters the best—when the sea would seem to rage and fight against the very restrictions of nature as an inner part of her longed to fight against the ever-increasing social strictures that were placed upon her. For, after she had shared the nursery and schoolroom with Olivia, until she reached the age of sixteen, she had stopped being treated as Olivia's equal and had become more maid and companion to the spoilt and pampered daughter of the house.

Jane paused as she passed the cheval mirror in Lady Sulby's bedroom, studying her reflection critically and knowing as she did so that she was everything that was not fashionable. She was tall, for one thing, with long legs and a slender willowy figure. She wished she could say that her hair was an interesting auburn, but instead it was a bright, gleaming red. And, although her complexion was creamy, she did have that unattractive sprinkling of freckles across the bridge of her tiny nose. Plus, her eyes were green.

None of this was complemented in the least by the gowns Lady Sulby had made up for her. They were always of a pastel shade that did nothing for Jane's vibrant colouring. Her present one, of the palest pink, was so totally unflattering with the red of her hair.

Of course it was very doubtful that Jane would ever meet anyone who would want to marry her. Unless the local vicar took pity on her and made an offer. And as he was a middle-aged widower, with four unruly young children all under the age of eight, Jane did so hope that he would not.

She gave a weary sigh as she collected the requested silk shawl from Lady Sulby's dressing table, noticing as she did so that Lady Sulby's jewellery box had not been returned to its proper place in the top drawer.

But Jane's attention was diverted from the jewellery box as she heard the sound of a carriage outside, travelling down the yew-lined gravel driveway to Markham Park.

The Duke and his brother Lord Sebastian St Claire at last? Or one of the Sulbys' other guests?

Curiosity impelled Jane to move quickly to the window to look outside. A huge, magnificent black carriage, pulled by four of the most beautiful black horses Jane had ever seen, was being driven down the driveway by a black-liveried groom. Two other servants dressed in black perched upon the back, and a ducal crest was visible on the door.

It was indeed the Duke, then.

He did seem to like black, didn't he? Jane mused, even as she gave in to further temptation and gently moved the brocade curtain to one side, the better to be able to see the Duke himself when he stepped down from the carriage.

A groom had hopped nimbly down from the back to hold the door open for him, and for some inexplicable reason Jane's heart seemed to have increased in tempo. In fact it was beating quite erratically, she noted frowningly. Just in anticipation of the sight of a Duke? Was her life really so dull?

She gave a rueful smile as she acknowledged that it would indeed be exciting to at last see the much-talked of Duke of Stourbridge.

Her breath caught in the slenderness of her throat as first a booted foot descended onto the lowered step, quickly followed by the ducking of a head as the Duke of Stourbridge stepped completely out of the carriage and then down onto the gravel driveway, straightening to take his hat from the waiting servant before lifting his haughty head to take in his surroundings.

Goodness, he was tall, was Jane's first breathless realisation. Quickly followed by the acknowledgement that, with hair the colour of mahogany shot through with streaks of gold, and those powerfully wide shoulders and athletically moulded body, he was also the most handsome man she had ever set eyes on. His features were severe, of course, as befitted a duke who looked to be in his thirtieth year at least, but there was such hard male beauty in that austerity that just to look at him took Jane's breath away.

In fact she did not seem able to stop looking at him.

There was intelligence as well as arrogance in that wide brow, though the precise colour of his eyes was something of a mystery as he viewed his surroundings with unmistakable disdain, looking down his nose at the scene before him. The sculptured mouth had narrowed, and dark brows were rising in haughty surprise as he turned to see his hostess hurriedly descending the steps towards him, rather than waiting inside Markham Park for him to be formally announced.

'Your Grace!' Lady Sulby swept him a low curtsey and received a haughtily measured inclination of that arrogant head in return. 'Such an honour,' she fluttered. 'I— But where is your brother, Lord St Claire, Your Grace?' Lady Sulby's voice had sharpened to an unbecoming shrill as she realised there was no one else inside the Duke's carriage.

Jane could not discern the Duke's reply—could only hear the deep rumble of his voice as he obviously made his hostess some sort of explanation for his solitary state.

Oh, dear. Everything did not appear to be going to plan. Lady Sulby's plan, that was. And an already thwarted Lady Sulby was not to be displeased further by the delay of the delivery of the shawl she had requested Jane to bring to her almost ten minutes ago.

Jane moved quickly down the hallway to Olivia's room to collect the parasol before hurrying to the wide staircase with the required items, aware of the rumble of voices below as Sir Barnaby engaged his guest in conversation.

Lady Sulby had previously expressed high hopes of Olivia making a favourable impression on the Duke's youngest brother, Lord Sebastian St Claire, and now that the young lord had failed to arrive Lady Sulby would no doubt be in one of the spiteful moods that usually had the servants running downstairs to the sanctuary of the kitchen at the first opportunity. Jane knew she wouldn't be allowed the same privilege until after she had helped Olivia change into her dress for dinner and styled her hair.

When the family were at home Jane was usually allowed to dine with them in the evenings, but Lady Sulby had informed her only that morning that once their guests had arrived she would be expected to take her meals downstairs with the other servants.

Which would not be any hardship at all, when Jane considered the few dresses she had in her wardrobe. None of them was in the least suitable for dining with a duke, she acknowledged ruefully as she hurried to the staircase. And if she could deliver the shawl and parasol while the Duke still engaged the attention of his host and hostess, then she would perhaps manage to avoid the rebuke Lady Sulby was otherwise sure to make concerning her tardiness.

Jane could never afterwards explain how it happened. Why it happened. She was only aware that the staircase was no longer firm beneath her slippered feet, and that instead of hurrying down the staircase she instead found herself tumbling forwards.

Or at least she would have tumbled if a pair of strong hands hadn't reached out and grasped her upper arms to halt her.

She found herself instead falling forward into a hard, immovable object. A man's chest, Jane quickly realised, as she found her nose buried in the delicate folds of an impeccably tied, pristinely white necktie, her senses at once assailed by the smell of cologne and clean male flesh, both mingling with the faint smell of a cigar.

The Duke of Stourbridge's clean, male chest. The Duke of Stourbridge's perfectly tied cravat too, Jane discovered seconds later, as she struggled to right herself and looked up into that aristocratically austere face and discovered that his eyes—those eyes whose colour she had been unable to discern earlier, as she had looked down at him from the window of Lady Sulby's bedroom—were of the strangest, most intense shade of gold. Not brown, not hazel, but pure, piercing gold, rimmed with a much darker brown that somehow gave him the appearance of a large bird of prey. The mesmerising appearance of a large, dangerous bird of prey…

Hawk's mouth tightened at the unexpectedness of this physical assault. Having spent the last two days confined to his carriage, the comfort of which had nevertheless not been enough to prevent him from being rocked and bumped about on the sadly uneven roads, he wished only to be shown to his rooms and provided with hot water for a bath before he had to present himself downstairs, in order that he might be introduced to his fellow guests before they dined.

The hostelries at which he had dined along the way, and the inn he had had perforce to stop at the previous night, had been far beneath his usual exacting standard. And minutes ago his hostess, until then a woman totally unknown to him, had shown such want of breeding as to almost accost him as he alighted from his carriage.

Hawk had reflected long and hard as to the advisability of coming to Markham Park at all during the two days preceding his departure from London, as well as during the long, interminable hours it had taken to arrive here, and this latest incident of having one of the Sulby household servants actually throw herself into his arms only served to prove how correct had been his misgivings.

'I am so sorry, Your Grace.' The maid's voice was slightly breathless, her expression stricken as she glanced warily down into the hallway, where Sir Barnaby and Lady Sulby could still be seen and heard engaged in conversation with Lord and Lady Tillton. The other couple had arrived with their son Simon just as Hawk was being taken up to view his suite of rooms by the footman, who had now fallen discreetly back from this unexpected exchange.

Hawk's gaze narrowed and his mouth tightened as he detected a look of apprehension in the shadowed green eyes the maid turned back to him. He certainly wasn't accustomed to having anyone, least of all a servant, accost him in this way, but he realised now that the girl must have tripped—that as he had ascended the stairs he had merely been standing in the way of her tumbling unchecked to the hallway below. Certainly there was no need for her to look quite so apprehensive on his account.

Although that glance down at Sir Barnaby and Lady Sulby seemed to imply that it was not his own displeasure this young girl feared…

Hawk's mouth thinned even more at the realisation. He had always found Sir Barnaby to be a pleasant, even jovial companion on the few occasions they had dined together, so he could only assume that it was from Lady Sulby that the maid feared retribution for her ill-timed actions.

'I really am sorry, Your Grace.' The young girl moved to pick something up from the stairs that she seemed to have dropped when they collided. 'I— Oh, I am so sorry, Your Grace!' The girl gasped her dismay as she poked him in the stomach with the parasol she had just retrieved from the stair.

Hawk drew in a sharp breath at this second unexpected attack, and wondered incredulously if the last few minutes were going to be indicative of this week's stay in what he had discovered on the drive here was indeed a flat, uninteresting fenland, with little to recommend it.

Including the delivery of letters. His own missive explaining that his brother Sebastian would be unable to attend after all had clearly not arrived, resulting in Hawk having to make Sebastian's excuses verbally to his host and hostess.

In light of the ill-bred behaviour of Lady Sulby on his arrival, and the fact that Olivia Sulby, when introduced, had all the indications of being exactly the type of simpering miss Hawk found irritatingly exhausting, he could not help but frown as he wondered if perhaps Sebastian had been privy to some insight about the Sulby household that he had not.

Jane gave an inward groan as she saw the visible signs of the Duke's displeasure, sure that such an illustrious person was completely unaccustomed to being physically accosted in this way.

Not only had she almost knocked him down the stairs, but now she had actually poked him in that flat, manly stomach with a parasol.

None of which Lady Sulby or Olivia seemed to have witnessed, thank goodness, as they still conversed with the Tilltons in the hallway below. But it could only be a matter of time before one or both of them looked up and became aware of the debacle taking place on the staircase above them.

Jane gave the patiently waiting footman a desperate look of pleading as he stood silent witness to the encounter—although she had to look hastily away again when she thought she detected a glint of laughter in John's otherwise deadpan expression.

'If you would come this way, Your Grace? I will show you to your rooms.' John stepped sideways to allow the Duke to move around the obviously mortified Jane and so precede him up the wide staircase.

Some of Jane's tension eased, and she gave John a grateful smile as the Duke did exactly that—only to once again find herself the focus of those all-seeing gold-coloured eyes as the Duke paused briefly and gave her one last narrow-eyed frowning glance.

Her smile faded, and she clutched the parasol and shawl to her bosom as she found herself held mesmerised by that penetrating gaze for several long, heart-stopping seconds. He took in her appearance from red hair to slippered feet, before those thin, chiselled lips tightened once more and the Duke turned to continue his gracefully elegant way up the stairs.

Jane breathed shakily as she found herself continuing to watch him, her breasts quickly rising and falling, her cheeks feeling uncomfortably hot, and her pulse racing as she stared at the broadness of the Duke's shoulders in that perfectly tailored jacket, admired the slight curl in the darkness of his fashionably styled hair…

'For goodness' sake, Jane. I said my shawl embroidered with the pink roses, not the yellow.' Lady Sulby finally seemed to have seen her on the staircase. 'Really!' She turned confidingly back to the Tilltons. 'I declare the girl does not understand even the simplest of instructions.'

Jane knew, as she turned to go back up the stairs and saw Olivia's expression of derision, that she had understood Lady Sulby's instruction perfectly—that it was Lady Sulby who was being deliberately awkward. But it would serve no purpose to contradict Lady Sulby. Especially not in front of her guests.

The blush intensified in Jane's cheeks as she reached the top of the stairs and saw that the Duke had once again paused on his way to his rooms, on the gallery overlooking the hallway this time. His top lip was now curled back in cold disdain as he stood witness to Lady Sulby's waspish set down.

'Your Grace.' Jane gave a polite inclination of her head as she approached, and then hurried past him down the hallway, knowing that the blush on her cheeks would clash horribly with her red curls, and that the unattractive freckles on her nose would be rendered more visible by her high colour.

Not that it particularly mattered what the Duke of Stourbridge made of *her*. He was far, far above her precarious social station, and as such would have no further reason to even notice her existence.

If, that was, for the rest of his stay Jane desisted from falling down the staircase into his arms or attacking him with a parasol!

How could she have been so ungainly, so inelegant, so utterly without grace? Jane wondered as she sat down shakily on the side of Lady Sulby's four-poster bed, dropping the shawl and parasol on the bedcover beside her as she put both her hands against her hot and flustered cheeks. The Duke, as had been obvious from that last disdainful glance in her direction, had obviously been wondering the very same thing.

Oh, this was dreadful. Too horrible for words. She just wanted to curl up in a ball of misery in the window-seat in her bedroom and not appear again until that beautiful black carriage, with its ducal crest and its illustrious guest inside, had rolled back down the driveway and disappeared to London, whence it came.

'Whatever are you doing, Jane?' A stunned Lady Sulby came to an abrupt halt in the doorway to her bed-chamber, and a guilt-stricken Jane rose from her sitting position on the side of her silk-covered bed.

The older woman's gaze moved critically about the room, a frown marring her brow as she saw the jewellery box on the dressing table. Jane had earlier intended returning it to the still open top drawer, but had totally forgotten to do in the excitement of the Duke's arrival.

'Have you been looking at my things?' Lady Sulby's demand was sharp as she swiftly crossed the room to lift the lid of the jewellery box and check its contents.

'No, of course I have not.' Jane was incredulous at the accusation.

'Are you sure?' Lady Sulby glared.

'Perfectly sure.' Jane nodded, stunned by her guardian's suspicions. 'Clara must have left the box out earlier.'

Lady Sulby gave her another searching glare before replacing the jewellery box in the drawer and closing it abruptly. 'Where is my shawl, girl? And you have failed to bring Olivia's parasol down to her,' she added accusingly.

'Which I need if I am to accompany Lady Tillton and Simon Tillton into the rose garden.' Olivia smiled smugly as she stood in the open doorway.

Jane had not even noticed the younger girl until that moment, and avoided meeting Olivia's triumphant gaze as she hurriedly handed her the parasol, her own thoughts still preoccupied with Lady Sulby's earlier sharpness concerning the jewellery box.

Why would Lady Sulby even suspect her of doing such a thing? As far as Jane was aware the box contained only the few costly jewels owned by the Sulby family and several private papers, none of which was of the least interest to Jane.

'It really is too bad of Lord St Claire not to have accompanied His Grace after all,' Lady Sulby murmured distractedly once Olivia had departed for her walk in the garden. 'Especially as it has caused me to rearrange all my dinner arrangements for this evening. Still, the influenza is the influenza. And I do believe that the Duke was rather taken with Olivia himself,' she added with relish. 'Now, would *that* not be an advantageous match?'

Jane was sure that she was not expected to make any reply to this statement—that Lady Sulby was merely thinking out loud while she plotted and planned inside her calculating head.

But Jane's silence on the subject did not mean that she had no thoughts of her own on an imagined match between Olivia and the Duke of Stourbridge. Her main one being that it was ludicrous to even think that a man as haughtily arrogant as the Duke would ever be attracted to, let alone enticed into marriage with, the pretty but self-centred Olivia.

'Why are you still standing there, Jane?' Lady Sulby demanded waspishly as she finally seemed to notice her again. 'Can you not see that my nerves are agitated? I shall probably have one of my headaches and be unable to attend my guests at all this evening!'

'Would you like me to send for Clara?' Jane offered lightly, knowing that Lady Sulby's maid, a middle-aged woman who had accompanied Gwendoline Simmons from her father's home in Great Yarmouth when she had married Sir Barnaby twenty-five years ago, was the only one who could capably deal with Lady Sulby when she was beset by 'one of her headaches'.

A regular occurrence, as it happened, but usually relieved by a glass or two of Sir Barnaby's best brandy. For medicinal purposes only, of course, Jane acknowledged with a rueful grimace.

'I do not know what you can possibly find to smile

about, Jane.' Lady Sulby threw herself down onto the chaise, her hand raised dramatically to her brow as the sun shone in through the window. 'You would be much better served returning to your room and changing for dinner. You know I cannot abide tardiness, Jane.'

Lady Sulby's comment on Jane changing for dinner caused her to frown. 'Did you not tell me earlier that I was to dine belowstairs this evening—?'

'Have you not been listening to a word I said, girl?' Lady Sulby's voice had once again risen shrilly, and she glared across at Jane, not even her faded beauty visible in her displeasure. 'The Duke has arrived without his brother, leaving me with only thirteen to sit down to dinner. A possibility I cannot even contemplate.' She shuddered. 'So you will have to join us. Which will make an imbalance of men to ladies. It will not do, of course, but it will have to suffice until our other guests arrive tomorrow.'

Jane's own face had lost all colour as the full import of Lady Sulby's complaints became clear. 'You are saying, ma'am, that because Lord St Claire is indisposed you wish me to make up the numbers for dinner this evening?'

'Yes, yes—of course I am saying that.' The older woman glared at her frowningly. 'Whatever is the matter with you, girl?'

Jane swallowed hard at the mere thought of finding herself seated at the same dinner table as the formidable Duke of Stourbridge, sure that after their disastrous meeting on the stairs earlier it was probably his fervent wish never to set eyes on her again!

As Lady Sulby had already remarked, it really would not do.

'I am sure I do not have anything suitable to wear—'

'Nonsense, girl.' A flush coloured Lady Sulby's plump and powdered cheeks as she bristled at this continued resistance to her new arrangements. 'What of that yellow gown of mine that Clara altered to fit you? That will do perfectly well, I am sure,' Lady Sulby announced imperiously.

Jane's heart sank as she thought of the deep yellow gown that Lady Gwendoline had decided did not suit her after all, and which had been altered to fit Jane instead.

'I really would not feel comfortable amongst your titled guests—'

'I am not concerned with *your* comfort!' Lady Sulby's face became even more flushed as her agitatation rose. 'You will do as you are told, Jane, and join us downstairs for dinner. Is that understood?'

'Yes, Lady Sulby.' Jane felt nauseous.

'Good. Now, send Clara to me.' Lady Sulby lowered herself down onto the cushions once again, her eyes closing. 'And tell her I am in need of one of her physics,' she added weakly, as Jane moved obediently to the door.

Jane waited until she was outside in the hallway before giving in to the despair she felt just at the thought of going down to dinner wearing that horrible yellow gown. Of the arrogantly disdainful but devastatingly handsome Duke of Stourbridge seeing her in that bilious yellow gown.

Chapter Two

'Is this some new sort of party game? Or is it just that you are contemplating what singular delights you might have in store for me later this evening?' Hawk mused derisively to the woman standing—hiding?—behind the potted plant at his side. 'Perhaps you intend spilling a glass of wine over me during dinner? Or maybe hot tea later in the evening would be more to your liking? Yes, I am sure that hot tea would cause much more discomfort than a mere glass of wine. That potted plant really is an insufficient hiding place, you know,' Hawk added, when his quarry made no response to any of his mocking barbs.

His humour had not been improved when he'd come downstairs to the drawing room some minutes ago, to meet and mingle with his fellow house guests before dinner. His bath water had been hot, but of insufficient quantity for his needs, and his valet, Dolton, was no happier with his present location than Hawk. In his agitation he had actually caused the Duke's chin to bleed whilst shaving him, an event that had never happened before in all his long service.

But Hawk had found his darkly brooding mood lightening somewhat a few minutes later when, while in polite conversation with Lady Ambridge, an elderly if outspoken lady he was long acquainted with, he had spotted what appeared to be an almost ghostly yellow being flitting from behind one oversized plant pot to another. He had assumed it was in an effort not to be noticed, but it had actually achieved the opposite.

It was testament to how bored Hawk already was by the conversation of his fellow guests that he had actually excused himself from Lady Ambridge's company to stroll across the room and stand beside the plant at that moment hiding the elusive creature.

A single glance behind the terracotta pot had shown her to be the earlier perpetrator of the painful bump in his chest followed by the even more painful dig in his stomach with a parasol. Hawk's surprise that she was not a maid after all but was obviously a fellow guest was completely overshadowed by the strangeness of her behaviour since entering the drawing room.

He was also, Hawk realised with not a little surprise, more than curious to know the reason for it. 'You may as well come out from behind there, you know,' he advised, even as he continued to gaze disdainfully out at the room rather than at her, impeccable in his black evening clothes.

This time, at least, he did receive an agitated reply. 'I really would rather not!'

Hawk felt compelled to point out the obvious. 'You are only drawing attention to yourself by not doing so.'

'I believe you are the one drawing attention to us both by talking to me!' Her voice was sharp with indignation.

He probably was, Hawk acknowledged ruefully. The fact that he was the highest-ranking person in the room, and so obviously the biggest feather in Lady Gwendoline Sulby's social cap, also meant that he was attracting many sidelong glances from his fellow guests while they pretended to be in conversation with each other.

As the Duke of Stourbridge, he was used to such attention, of course, and had learnt over the years to ignore it. Obviously his quarry did not have that social advantage.

'Perhaps if you were to explain to me why it is you feel the need to hide behind a succession of inadequate potted plants…?'

'Would you just go away and leave me alone? If you please, Your Grace,' she added with guilty breathlessness, as she obviously remembered exactly who she was talking to, and in what way.

For some inexplicable reason Hawk had the sudden urge to laugh.

And, as he rarely found occasion to smile nowadays, let alone laugh with a woman, he noted it with surprise. Women, those most predatory of beasts, as he had found during the ten years since he had inherited the title of Duke following the death of both his parents in a carriage accident, were no laughing matter.

He sighed. 'You really cannot hide away all evening, you know.'

'I can try!'

'Why would you want to?' His curiosity was definitely piqued.

'How can you possibly ask that?'

His brows rose. 'Perhaps because it seems a reasonable question in the circumstances?'

'The gown,' she answered tragically. 'Surely you have noticed the gown?'

Well, yes, it would be difficult *not* to notice such a violent yellow creation, when all the older ladies present were wearing pastels and Miss Olivia Sulby virginal white. The colour really was most unbecoming with the vivid red of this girl's hair, but...

'Please do go away, Your Grace!'

'I am afraid I really cannot.'

'Why not?'

Hawk, having no intention of admitting to an interest he himself found unprecedented, chanced another glance at her. That gown was most unattractive against the red of her hair and the current flush to her cheeks, and the matching yellow ribbon threaded through those vibrant locks only added to the jarring discord.

'Did your modiste not tell you how ill yellow would suit your—er—particular colouring when you ordered the gown?'

'It was not I who ordered the gown but Lady Sulby.' She sounded irritated that he had not realised as much. 'I am sure that any modiste worthy of that name would have the good sense never to dress any of her red-haired

patrons in yellow, giving the poor woman the appearance of a huge piece of fruit. Unappetising fruit, at that!'

This time Hawk was totally unable to contain his short
bark of laughter, causing the heads of those fellow guests
closest to him to turn even more curious glances his way.

Jane, aware of the curious glances of the other Sulby
guests, really did wish that the Duke would go away.

The gown, when she had put it on, had looked even
worse than she had imagined it would, and the yellow
ribbon Lady Sulby had provided to dress her hair only
added to the calamity.

But Jane had known that Lady Sulby would only
make her life more unbearable than usual if she did not
go down to dinner as instructed, and so she really had
had no choice but to don the hated gown and ribbon and
enter the drawing room—before trying to make herself
as inconspicuous as possible by moving from the shelter
of one potted plant to another, hoping that when she
actually sat down at the dinner table the gown would not
be as visible.

But she hadn't taken into account the unwanted curiosity and attention of the Duke of Stourbridge. And
his laughter, at her expense, was doubly cruel in the
circumstances.

'You really should come out, you know,' he drawled.
'I am sure that there cannot now be a person present who
has not taken note of my conversation with a very
colourful potted plant!'

Jane's mouth firmed as she accepted the truth of the
Duke's words, knowing he had been the focus of all

eyes for the last five minutes or so as he apparently engaged in conversation—and laughter—with a huge pot of foliage. But it really was too bad of him to have drawn attention to her in this way when she had so wanted to just fade into the woodwork. Not an easy task, admittedly, when wearing this bilious-coloured gown, but she might just have succeeded until it was actually time to go in to dinner if not for the obvious attentions of the Duke of Stourbridge.

In the circumstances she had little choice but to acknowledge and comply with his advice, stepping out from behind the potted plant and then feeling indignant all over again as the Duke made no effort to hide the wince that appeared on his arrogantly handsome face as he slowly took in her appearance—from the yellow ribbon adorning her red hair to the lacy frill draping over her slippers.

'Dear, dear, it is worse even than I thought.' He grimaced.

'You are being most unkind, Your Grace.' Her cheeks had become even redder in her indignation.

He gave an arrogant inclination of his head. 'I am afraid that I am.'

Jane's eyes widened at the admission. 'You do not even apologise for being so?'

'What would be the point?' He shrugged those powerful shoulders in the black, expertly tailored evening jacket that somehow emphasised the width of his shoulders and the lean power of his body. 'I am afraid you also have me at something of a disadvantage…?'

Jane drew in an agitated breath. 'On the contrary, Your Grace. I am sure that any disadvantage must be mine!'

Hawk's gaze was drawn briefly to the swelling of creamy breasts against the low bodice of her gown—enticingly full breasts, considering her otherwise slender appearance—before his narrowed gaze returned to her face. Like her colouring and her figure, it was not fashionably pretty. But the deep green of her eyes, surrounded by thick, dark lashes, was nonetheless arresting. Her nose was small, and covered lightly with the freckles that might be expected with such vibrant colouring, and her mouth was perhaps a little too wide—although the lips were full and sensuous above a pointedly determined chin.

No, he acknowledged, she did not possess the sweetly blonde beauty that was currently fashionable— the same sweetly blonde beauty he found so unappealing in Olivia Sulby!—but this young lady's colouring and bone structure were such that she would remain beautiful even in much older years.

All of which Hawk noted in a matter of seconds, which was surprising in itself.

Women, to the Duke of Stourbridge, had become merely a convenience—something to be enjoyed during the few hours of leisure that he allowed himself away from his ducal duties.

His alliance with the Countess of Morefield had been brief and physically unsatisfactory, and had only served to convince Hawk that the demands a mistress made on his time were invariably unworthy of the effort expended in acquiring that mistress.

Surprisingly, Hawk recognised that this young woman—for she was much younger than the women he usually took as mistress—if dressed and coiffured properly, could, in the right circumstances, be worthy of his attention.

Except that he still had no idea who or what she was. She was several years older than those 'simpering misses' of which Olivia Sulby was such a prime example. But, from the way Lady Sulby had spoken to her earlier, she did appear to be part of the Sulby household. Although in what capacity Hawk could not guess. Olivia Sulby, as he already knew, was an only child, so this interestingly forthright creature could not be Sir Barnaby's daughter.

Perhaps Lady Sulby's daughter from a previous marriage? His hostess had certainly spoken to her sharply enough for such a relationship to exist, although Hawk could see absolutely no resemblance between the plump, faded beauty of Lady Sulby and the strikingly beautiful redhead standing before him.

But if she was a young, unmarried lady of quality Hawk knew he could not take her as mistress—no matter what his unexpected interest. That he had even been thinking of doing so was reason enough for him to maintain a distance between them. And sooner rather than later.

Before he could effect a gracious withdrawal, a flustered and obviously disapproving Lady Sulby bustled over to join them. 'I see you have met my husband's ward, Jane Smith, Your Grace.   Dear Jane came to us from a distant relative of Sir Barnaby's. An impoverished parson of a country parish,' she added dismissively, shooting a censorious glance at the object of her monologue, a hard glitter in her eyes. 'You look very well in that gown, Jane.'

Hawk's brows rose at the insincerity behind the compliment even as he shared a look of sceptisism with the young lady he now knew as Jane Smith. Jane Smith? The blandness of the name did not suit this vibrant young woman in the least.

'Miss Smith.' He bowed formally. 'Might I be permitted to escort Sir Barnaby's ward in to dinner, Lady Sulby?' he offered, as the dinner bell sounded.

As hostess, Lady Sulby naturally would have expected this privilege to be her own, for some inexplicable reason—despite his earlier decision to distance himself from Jane Smith—Hawk now felt a need to thwart his hostess.

Maybe because she had—deliberately?—drawn attention to the gown that was making Jane so unhappy. Or maybe because of the way she had spoken so condescendingly of Jane's impoverished father. Whatever the reason, Hawk found himself unwilling to suffer Lady Sulby's singularly ingratiating attentions even for the short time it would take to escort her to the dining room.

Although the stricken look on Jane Smith's face as she became the open focus of the angrily hard glitter of Lady Sulby's gaze told him that it had perhaps been unwise on his part to show such a preference.

A realisation that was immediately confirmed by Jane Smith. 'Really, Your Grace, you must not.'

Hawk gave her a hard, searching glance, noting the slight pallor to her cheeks and the look almost of desperation now in those deep green eyes. Jane Smith, unlike almost every other woman of Hawk's acquaintance, most definitely did *not* want the Duke of Stourbridge to single her out for such attention. In fact, those green eyes were silently pleading with him not to do so.

'In that case…Lady Sulby?' He held out his arm, the polite smile on his lips not reaching the icy hardness of his eyes.

His hostess seemed almost to have to drag her attention away from Jane Smith before turning an ingratiating smile in his general direction. 'Certainly, Your Grace.' She placed her possessively grasping hand on his arm before sweeping regally through the room ahead of her other guests.

Jane stood back and watched them, her heart beating erratically in her chest, having easily recognised the look of promised retribution in Lady Sulby's gaze before she had turned and graciously accepted the Duke's arm.

Why had the Duke offered to escort Jane in to dinner? He of all people had to know that as the Sulbys' principal titled guest, etiquette demanded that he escort Lady Sulby. To do anything else would cause something of a sensation.

But, oh, how Jane wished she could have accepted. How—despite the cruelty of his laughter at her expense—

she would have loved to be the one who was swept regally from the room on the arm of the aristocratic Duke of Stourbridge. He was so haughtily attractive, so powerfully immediate, that Jane had no doubt those austere and yet mesmerising features would appear in her dreams later tonight.

'What do you mean by making such a spectacle of yourself, Jane?' Olivia had appeared at her side, her fan raised so that her acerbic tone and disdainful expression could not to be observed by the other guests as they prepared to follow Lady Sulby and the Duke through to the dining room. 'Mama is going to be absolutely furious with you for deliberately attracting the Duke's attention in that way.'

Jane gasped at the unfairness of the accusation. 'But I did nothing to—'

'Do not lie, Jane. We all saw you making a fool of yourself by openly flirting with the man in that shameless way.' Olivia glared, the tightness of her mouth giving her a look very much like her mother's at that moment. 'Mama is going to be very angry if your behaviour has caused the Duke any embarassment,' she told Jane warningly. 'That gown looks absolutely horrid on you, by the way,' she added cuttingly, before walking away to smilingly take the arm of the waiting Anthony Ambridge, the elegible grandson of Lady Ambridge.

Dinner was, as Jane could have predicted, an absolutely miserable time for her. Lord Tillton sat to the left of her, and constantly tried to put his hand on her thigh until she put a stop to it by digging her nails into his wrist, and a deaf and elderly woman sat the to her right, talking in a monologue that thankfully required no response on Jane's part—because she was sure she would not have heard her even if she had attempted a reply.

To make matters worse, the Duke, on Lady Sulby's right, with Olivia seated next to him—two blonde sentinels guarding a much valued prize—proceeded to ignore Jane completely and so succeeded in increasing her misery.

By the time Lady Sulby signalled for the ladies to retire and leave the men to their brandy Jane's head was pounding. She longed for nothing more than to escape to her room, where she might at last take the pins from her hair before bathing her heated brow and hopefully alleviating the painful throbbing at her temples. After Olivia's earlier comments it would merely be postponing the inevitable confrontation with Lady Sulby, of course, but Jane hoped that even a short delay might be advantageous.

'I think you are being very wise, Jane.' Lady Sulby, talking to Lady Tillton in the drawing room, paused and gave a terse inclination of her head when Jane asked to be excused because of a headache. 'In fact, I think it would be beneficial to everyone if you were to keep to your room until we can be sure that you are not the carrier of anything infectious.'

Jane's face whitened at the deliberate insult—did it promise retribution?—before turning to lift the hem of her gown and almost run from the room.

'*That you are not the carrier of anything infectious.*'

Lady Sulby could not have told Jane any more clearly that she considered Jane's very presence to be a dangerous source of infection to her guests—but no doubt especially where the Duke of Stourbridge was concerned!

Hawk was sure he had never spent an evening of such boredom in his entire life, knowing after only two minutes in the company of Lady Sulby and the vacuously self-centred Olivia that the older lady was everything he disliked, in that she was a gossipy small-minded, social-climbing woman, with not a kind word to say for anyone or anything, and that in twenty years or so—if not sooner!—her daughter would be exactly like her.

But the dinner fare, unlike the company he had been forced to endure, had been surprisingly excellent, with each course seeming to outdo the last, to such a degree that Hawk had wondered if, before taking his leave at the end of the week, he might not be able to persuade the Sulbys' cook into joining one of his own households.

And of course there had been that strangely memorable incident with Jane Smith earlier. Although, with hindsight, Hawk had decided that even there he had been unwise—that the eligible Duke of Stourbridge should not have engaged a young unmarried lady to whom he had not even been formally introduced at the time in conversation of any kind. The fact that she was, despite Lady Gwendoline's obvious sharpness to her, Sir Barnaby's ward, meant that no doubt she had ambitions of her own concerning advantageous marriage.

His wariness had been confirmed when he had observed her from between narrowed lids for several minutes at the start of dinner. She had proceded to flirt outrageously with James Tillton—a man Hawk knew to keep two mistresses already, in different areas of London—constantly turning in his direction whilst completely ignoring the poor woman seated at her other side, as she'd gallantly attempted to engage her in conversation.

'What do you think, Stourbridge?'

He turned his attention to the other gentlemen seated around the table, partaking of the surprisingly excellent brandy. 'I agree with you entirely, Ambridge.' He answered the elderly gentleman—he believed was the matter of horseflesh—before moving languidly to his feet, carrying his glass of brandy with him. 'If you will excuse me, gentlemen? I believe I will partake of some of this brisk Norfolk air our hostess was in such raptures about earlier.' He strolled across the room to open one of the French doors before stepping outside onto the moonlit terrace, relieved to step out of the room and away from the banality of the conversation.

How was he possibly to stand another six days of this? Hawk asked himself wearily. Perhaps he could arrange for Sebastian to have a 'relapse', and so excuse himself on the pretext of brotherly concern? Such a course presented the problem of arranging to have a letter delivered to himself, of course, but surely that was preferable to the prospect of dying of boredom before the week was out?

Although there really was something to be said for

the bracing Norfolk air, he discovered, as he drew in a deep breath and felt his head immediately begin to clear. Perhaps he would consider an estate in Norfolk, after all. Just not this one.

Having now met and spent time in the company of Olivia Sulby, his marital plans regarding that young lady and his brother Sebastian were definitely cancelled. For one thing he loved his youngest brother far too much to inflict that simpering chit on Sebastian and the rest of the St Claire family, let alone her social-climbing mother. It really—

Hawk's attention had been caught, and held, by a movement to the left of the moon-dappled garden—a slight deviation in the shadows beside the tall hedge that told him he was no longer alone in his enjoyment of the bracing air. He had been joined by a fox, perhaps. Or maybe a badger.

But, no, the moving shadow was too tall to be either of those nocturnal animals. The intruder into his solitude was definitely of the two-legged variety, and it moved purposefully along the hedge towards the gate that Dolton, a dedicated city-dweller, had shudderingly informed his employer earlier led down to a beach and the open sea.

It was a man, then. Or perhaps a woman. On her way to some romantic tryst, maybe? Or could it be something slightly more serious, such as smuggling? Hawk believed that it was still as rife here in Norfolk as it was reputed to be in Cornwall.

While actively fulfilling his role as a justice of the

peace in Gloucestershire, Hawk did not consider it any of his business—but his attention sharpened as the breeze gusted strongly, lifting the dark shielding cloak that encompassed the prowler and revealing something much lighter in colour worn beneath.

Such as a gown of vivid yellow…?

Could that possibly be Jane Smith moving stealthily away from the house in the direction of the beach? And, if so, for what purpose?

Hawk told himself again that it was none of his business what Jane Smith did. She was the unmarried ward of Sir Barnaby, and Hawk would be well advised to keep well away from her for the remainder of his visit here, or risk finding himself manoeuvred into the parson's mousetrap—a fate he had no intention of succumbing to until he had seen all of his siblings happily settled, and certainly not with the impoverished ward of a minor peer. When the time came Hawk fully intended marrying a woman of suitable breeding—one who would quietly and efficiently provide the heirs necessary for the Duke of Stourbridge but would make no other demands upon his time or his emotions.

To deliberately seek out Jane Smith, a young woman who had already caused him to act completely out of character earlier this evening, would be decidedly unwise. He would be better served by rejoining the other gentlemen and forgetting even the existence of Jane Smith.

But the impulse—madness?—which had afflicted him earlier, when his curiosity had first been piqued enough to engage Jane Smith in conversation, did not seem to have dissipated, and rather than rejoining the gentlemen inside the house Hawk instead found himself placing his brandy glass down on the balustrade and moving down the steps into the garden, with the sole intention of following to see exactly where Jane Smith was going alone so late at night.

And why.

Chapter Three

'Are your tears because your lover has failed to arrive for your tryst, or because as yet there is no lover?'

Jane stiffened as she easily recognised the Duke of Stourbridge's deep, slightly bored voice coming from above and behind her as she sat among the dunes. Her chin was resting on her drawn-up knees, the hood of her cloak having fallen back to reveal the wildness of her hair, now free of the confines of its pins, as she stared out at the wildly beating waves upon the shore, tears falling unchecked down her cheeks.

She pulled her cloak more firmly about her before answering him. 'The reason for my tears is not your concern, Your Grace.'

'And if I choose to make it my concern?'

'Then I wish you would not. In fact, I would prefer it if you left me.' She was too miserable at that moment to even attempt to be polite. Even—especially?—to the exalted Duke of Stourbridge. Though polite was not a word she would have used to describe any of their encounters to date!

'You are ordering me to leave, Jane? Again?' he mocked lightly.

Jane was dimly aware of his having now moved to stand beside her in the shelter of the dune, probably ruining his evening slippers in the process. But she did not care. She was too unhappy, too desperately low, to consider the Duke's discomfort at that moment. After all, she had made no invitation for him to join her here.

'I am, Your Grace.' She nodded tersely.

'I am afraid that will not be possible, Jane.' He gave a sigh as, completely careless of his expensively tailored clothing, he lowered his considerable length to sit down on the dune at her side. 'It would be most ungentlemanly of me, having discovered a lady in such distress, to simply walk away and leave her here, where anyone might come along and, discovering that she is alone, attempt to take advantage of the situation.'

Jane glanced at him frowningly in the darkness. 'Even if she has asked you to do so? Even if she is not a lady?' She turned her face away so that he wouldn't see the anger that was quickly replacing her tears.

'Is this about the gown, Jane?' Impatience edged his voice now, and he continued with disdain. 'Because if it is then you only have to look at Lady Sulby, to engage her in a moment's conversation, to know that a fine gown does not make a lady.'

Jane made a choked sound, caught somewhere

between a sob and a laugh. 'That remark is certainly not that of a gentleman, Your Grace!'

The Duke gave another sigh. 'I am finding it increasingly difficult to behave like a gentleman since arriving here in Norfolk.'

Jane gave him another sideways glance. The moonlight was throwing into stark relief the sharp edges of his aristocratic profile, his high cheekbones, his strong and determined jaw.

He was dressed meticulously in black again this evening, with a high-collared white shirt and his cravat tied neatly at his throat, a pale grey satin waistcoat beneath his jacket. But the force of the wind had ruffled the dark thickness of his hair into disarray, giving him a somewhat piratical appearance and, strangely, making him appear less like the haughty and unapproachable Duke of Stourbridge who had arrived at Markham Park earlier this afternoon.

But she must not forget that was exactly who he was, Jane reminded herself firmly, and that no matter how disconsolate she might feel, however much he might appear in sympathy with her plight at this moment, at the end of his week's stay he would leave to return to his privileged life in London—while she would still be here under the tyrannical rule of Lady Sulby.

Just the thought of that was enough to cause the now angry tears to fall anew.

'Come now, Jane.' The Duke turned to her. 'Whatever is wrong? It really cannot be so bad—'

'And how can you possibly know that, Your Grace?'

Misery and, yes, a certain despair gave her the courage to lift her head and glare at him. 'You are not the one who has been made to feel unwanted and less than you know yourself to be!'

Hawk stared at her. The moonlight chose that moment to come out from behind a cloud, clearly illuminating the tangled wildness of her hair, the deep sparkling green of her eyes, and the full sensuality of those pouting lips.

Dear God, he wanted to kiss those lips!

He did not just want to kiss them, he wanted to devour them!

Such an uncontrolled longing shocked Hawk intensely, as he had not felt it once since assuming the title of the Duke of Stourbridge ten years ago, all of his actions and words since that time had been measured and well thought out as he thoroughly considered and weighed any possible repercussions.

But at this moment Hawk found he could not think of anything else but kissing the lush ripeness of Jane Smith's inviting lips, of crushing the slenderness of her body to his, under his, as his mouth plundered hers and his hands became entangled in the thick fire of her unconfined hair before he explored the creamy swell of her full breasts, that slender waist and curvaceously welcoming thighs. Hawk realised with even more shocking clarity that, to him, Jane Smith was neither unwanted nor less than she knew herself to be. In fact, he could not remember ever wanting any woman as hotly, as immediately, as he now wanted the inadequately named Jane Smith!

Instead of acting on that impulse, and shocked at the intensity of his sudden desire to taste and hold Jane Smith, he moved abruptly to his feet and stepped away from her. 'I will leave you to your solitude, then, Jane.'

'I hope I have not offended you, Your Grace…?' She grimaced as she too rose to her feet, her cloak falling back further to reveal that she did indeed still wear the detested yellow gown. The gusting wind moulded its thin material to that slender waist, and the long, shapely length of her legs.

'I am not in the least offended.' Hawk stood rigidly, a nerve pulsing in his tightly clenched jaw as he kept his gaze averted from the temptation she represented to his normally rigid control. 'I am merely acknowledging my intrusion—'

'I did not—'

'Do not come any closer, Jane!' Hawk found himself warning her from between clenched teeth as she reached out a hand towards him, the heat in his body, the throbbing of his loins, telling him just how dangerous this situation had become.

Had he been so long without the warm comfort of a woman—that brief, physically unsatisfying liaison with the Countess of Morefield excluded—that he was in danger of forcing his attentions upon a vulnerable and unprotected young girl? Was this what years of restraint and enforced solitude as Duke of Stourbridge had brought him to? If so, it was intolerable, and Hawk made a vow to see to the tiresome business of taking a mistress as soon as he returned to London.

Jane had come to a stricken halt as she heeded the Duke's warning, staring up at him in the darkness. Did he too think that because she was only the orphaned daughter of an impoverished country parson she was unworthy of his notice? That she was beneath even the politeness of the high and mighty Duke of Stourbridge?

'Go then, Your Grace.' She faced him proudly, her head back defiantly. 'And I will endeavour to ensure that you are not bothered any further by my unwelcome presence for the remainder of your stay at Markham Park!'

'Jane, you misunderstand me—'

'I do not think so, Your Grace.'

'Jane, you will cease "Your Gracing" me in that contemptuous tone.'

'I most certainly will not!' She was beyond reason, beyond caution, wanting only to hurt as she was being hurt.

'Jane, you are playing with fire,' the Duke warned harshly, his hands now clenched at his sides.

'Fire, Your Grace?' Jane echoed tauntingly. She was tired, so very tired. For the last twelve years she'd always been meek and submissive, never being allowed to have a mind or will of her own. 'What would *you* know of fire? You, who are cold and haughty and look down your disdainful nose at everyone. What are you doing, Your Grace?' She gasped incredulously as the Duke moved to grasp her arms and began to pull her forcefully towards him.

'Hawk, Jane.' His face was only inches away from hers now, his breath warm against her cheek, those haughty features hard and predatory in the moonlight. 'My name is Hawk,' he explained harshly.

She looked up at him questioningly.

Hawk?

The Duke of Stourbridge had been named for a bird of prey?

A dangerous bird of prey. Jane dazedly recalled her assessment of him earlier today even as she stared up at him in shocked fascination.

'A fanciful notion of my mother's.' His tone was grim as he held Jane easily against the hard strength of his body.

Jane didn't care at that moment how he had come by his unusual name. She was only concerned with the fact that the Duke of Stourbridge—the haughty and arrogantly aloof Duke of Stourbridge—was holding her tightly in his arms as he moulded the softness of her curves against his much harder ones and his gaze became fixated on her mouth.

In fact, everything about the high and mighty Duke of Stourbridge gave every indication that he was about to kiss her!

It was unthinkable.

Unimaginable…

And yet Jane found she *could* imagine it. Could already feel the hardness of those perfectly moulded lips on hers as his mouth plundered and claimed. Possessed. For surely any woman the Duke of Stourbridge chose to kiss would know the full force of the ardour he was normally at such pains to hide from his fellow beings, but which Jane could now see so clearly in the fierce glitter of his eyes? Just as clearly she could feel the tense hardness of his body as it pressed intimately against her own…

'You should not have come here alone, Jane.' The Duke's gaze, that fiercely golden gaze, moved searchingly, hungrily, over the pallor of her face. 'You should not, Jane!' He began to lower his head towards hers.

Jane was held in motionless fascination for several long seconds as her lips parted instinctively to receive his.

A kiss.

One kiss.

Her first ever kiss.

Surely it was not too much to ask? To take for her own? After twelve long years of being denied the touch, the warmth, of another human being?

But a deeper, more knowledgeable instinct told her that Hawk St Claire, the powerful and forceful Duke of Stourbridge, would not stop at one kiss. His years and experience would demand he take more, much more. He was a man who would take and take again, while giving nothing of himself in return.

'No!' She turned her head away to avoid his kiss and at the same time pushed against his restraint, fighting to escape the steely band of his arms, but only succeeding in pressing herself more intimately against him. 'No!' Again she protested, fearing the desire that she could clearly see still held him in its grip. 'You must not! Please, Hawk, you must not…!'

Her pleas pierced the fierce desire that raged through

Hawk's body, causing him to pause, to blink dazedly as he stared down at her in stunned disbelief.

This woman—this girl—was the ward of his host. The *unmarried* ward of his host.

He released her abruptly to step back, jaw tight, eyes gleaming a glittering, inflexible gold. 'You should not have come here alone, Jane,' he repeated harshly.

Her throat moved convulsively in the moonlight. 'No, I should not. But I had not expected anyone to follow me—'

'No, Jane?' Hawk's voice was hard, inflexible. 'Are you sure that your present indignation is not due to the fact that it was the wrong man who responded to your invitation?'

She looked bewildered by his accusation. 'The wrong man? I do not understand—'

'Was it not James Tillton who was supposed to attend you here tonight rather than myself?' Hawk had realised belatedly, as he remembered the flirtation he had witnessed during dinner, that this must be the case—that Jane's dismay when he had joined her here had really been due to the fact that her lover—James Tillton?—had not arrived for their arranged tryst.

'Lord Tillton?' Jane gasped at his accusation. 'I detest Lord Tillton! He behaved most disgracefully towards me during dinner—to such a degree that in the end I had to pierce his wrist with my fingernails in order to stop his pawing of me beneath the table. Besides which, he is a married man!' she added frowningly.

Hawk's mouth twisted scathingly. 'Summer house

parties like this one are notorious for the night-time assignations of people who are indeed married—but not to each other.'

'Indeed, Your Grace?' Her voice was icily cold. 'And which female guest's bed have you chosen to grace with your *own* illustrious presence tonight?'

Even now, in her pride and anger, Hawk could appreciate how beautiful, how tempting the inaptly named Miss Jane Smith truly was. Admittedly, her years spent under the guardianship of the forceful Lady Sulby seemed to have cowed the more spirited parts of her nature, but they were still there nonetheless—in the way that Jane challenged him, in the way that she never flinched from contradicting him. Two things that rarely, if ever, happened to the Duke of Stourbridge.

Jane Smith was unusual in that she did not seem to see him as just a duke. She saw past his title to the man beneath, and it was to that man that she spoke during her moments of rebellion. It was to that man that her beauty appealed. To such a degree that Hawk had briefly forgotten all the caution that had served him so well these last ten years.

It would not—it *must* not!—happen again.

'I have no interest in bedding any of the ladies now residing at Markham Park,' he said disdainfully, knowing by the way Jane stiffened that she had heard his intended rejection of her own charms in that carefully worded dismissal. 'Now, if you will excuse me, I believe I will make my excuses to the Sulbys before retiring to my bedchamber for the night.' He bowed abruptly before turning to leave.

'Not without first making me an apology, Your Grace!'

Hawk turned slowly back to her, his narrowed gaze taking in the taut lines of her body and the challenge in her defiantly raised chin.

'For almost kissing you…?'

She gave him a contemptuous glare. 'For wrongly accusing me of encouraging Lord Tillton!'

Was it possible Hawk had mistaken the events he had witnessed earlier at the dinner table? Had Jane not been encouraging Tillton after all, but rather, as she claimed, fighting off the other man's unwanted attentions? Attention towards a young woman about whom it was obvious her guardians did not care, let alone offer protection to?

'If I was mistaken—'

'You were!'

'If I was mistaken then I apologise.' Hawk nodded abruptly. 'But in future I would advise you not to come here alone. You might find yourself in much graver danger another time than you have this evening.'

'Until now these dunes have always been my place of refuge!'

Until Hawk had intruded.

Until he had held her in his arms and attempted to kiss her.

But that was a temptation she had not demanded apology for…

She was magnificent. Hawk could acknowledge that

even with his inner determination not to initiate any further intimacy between them. Her unconfined hair blew in the wind, a thick curtain of flame, her eyes were wide and challenging, and those perfectly pouting lips were set defiantly.

All of those things told Hawk that she would be a formidable lover. That this woman was more than capable of matching the depths of his own passion, which he was always at such pains to hide from others and which Jane, instinctively, was able to touch and ignite.

Jane Smith, he decided determinedly, was a definite danger to the icy reserve of the Duke of Stourbridge.

Jane Smith was even more of a danger to the inner man that was still, at heart, the sensual Hawk St Claire.

'They obviously no longer offer such refuge,' he pointed out coldly, unpityingly. 'I will bid you goodnight, Miss Smith.' He turned away, and this time he did not look back, did not hesitate as he strode purposefully back to Markham Park.

Jane watched him go—a tall, forbidding shape that finally disappeared into the darkness—knowing that it wasn't only the refuge of the dunes that the Duke of Stourbridge had invaded this evening. When he had touched her, when he had looked in danger of kissing her, he had awakened a hunger deep inside her, a desire she had never known before, which had caused her breasts to swell and harden, and which had ignited a fiery warmth between her thighs that had made her want to forget all caution as she met and matched the passion she had been sure would be in his kiss. At that moment Jane knew she had wanted to lie down with him amongst the sand dunes, to strip away every vestige of the haughty coldness of the Duke of Stourbridge even as they stripped away their clothing, to explore, to kiss, to caress—

There Jane's heated thoughts came to an abrupt halt. Because she had no idea what came after the kissing and caressing!

She did remember Lady Sulby's cautions to Olivia at the start of her Season concerning her behaviour with the more roguish members of the ton—the main one being, 'A lady may take as many lovers as she wishes after she is married, but not a single one before she has the wedding ring upon her finger.'

Did Jane's wanton longings concerning the Duke of Stourbridge mean that she was not, after all, the lady she had always thought herself to be…?

'You sent for me, Lady Sulby?' Jane stood obediently in front of the other woman the following morning as Lady Sulby sat at the table in her private parlour, reading through the correspondence strewn across the table in front of her.

The blue gaze was ice-cold as Lady Sulby swept her a disparaging glance before answering. 'You are completely recovered this morning from your headache, Jane?'

Her tone and demeanour were surprisingly mild. Instantly increasing Jane's wariness. She had been expecting further retribution for what Olivia had warned her Lady Sulby perceived as Jane's 'flirtatious behaviour' with the Duke of Stourbridge the evening before. The mildness of the older woman's tone now did not in the least deceive her into dropping her guard.

'I am quite recovered, thank you, Lady Sulby.'

The older woman gave a gracious inclination of her head. 'You slept well?'

'Fitfully.' As expected, Jane had found her dreams full of images—not of the Duke of Stourbridge, but of the man who had held her in his arms and ordered her to call him Hawk. Those images had been so erotically arousing that she had awoken suddenly in the darkness, gasping, her body shaking, her nipples hard and aching to the touch, and an unaccustomed dampness between her thighs.

'Indeed?' Lady Sulby sat back in her chair, the once beautiful face hard and unyielding as she looked at Jane from between narrowed lids. 'Could that possibly be because you failed to sleep alone…?'

Jane gasped at the accusation even as she felt the colour drain from her cheeks. Surely Lady Sulby had not misunderstood Jane's response to Lord Tillton's advances towards her the evening before in the same way the Duke had?

Or could Lady Sulby possibly be referring to the Duke himself…?

Coming so soon after the memory of Jane's erotic dreams about him, the thought made her cheeks now suffuse with colour.

'Do not trouble yourself to answer, Jane,' Lady Sulby snapped, before Jane had recovered sufficiently to refute the accusation. 'It will serve no purpose for me to hear any of the sordid details—'

Jane's shocked gasp interrupted her. 'But there *are* no sordid details—'

'I said I did not wish to hear!' The older woman looked at her with unguarded dislike. 'It is enough that, despite all our efforts, all the guidance and care that Sulby and I have so generously given you these last twelve years, you have still grown into a woman exactly like your wantonly disgraceful mother!'

Every drop of blood seemed to drain from Jane's head and she felt herself sway dizzily. 'My—my mother…?'

Lady Sulby's top lip curled back disgustedly. 'Your mother, Jane. A woman much like yourself. That is, completely lacking in morals and—'

'How dare you?' Jane had known when the maid had informed her that Lady Sulby wished to see her that she was about to bear the brunt of that lady's displeasure, but she had been in no way prepared for the vitriol of this attack on her mother and herself. 'My mother was good and kind—'

'And who told you *that*, Jane?' The other woman eyed her with scorn. 'That fool of a parson who married her?' She shook her head contemptuously. 'Joseph Smith—like every other red-blooded man, it seems!— never could see any fault in his beautiful Janette. But I knew. I always knew that she was nothing but a shameless wanton.' Her eyes glittered fanatically. 'And in the end was I not proved correct about her immoral character?' Lady Sulby surged to her feet, her face twisted and ugly in her fury.

Jane staggered back from the attack, all the time

shaking her head in denial of the dreadful things Lady Sulby was saying about the woman who had died shortly after giving birth to her. 'My mother was sweet and beautiful—'

'Your mother was a harlot! A temptress and a whore!'

'No…!' Jane recoiled as if from a physical blow.

'Oh yes.' Lady Gwendoline glared at her contemptuously. 'And you are exactly like her, Jane. I warned Sulby when he insisted we take you into our household. I told him what would happen—that you would only disgrace us as Janette disgraced us. And last night I was proved correct in my misgivings.'

'But I did nothing last night of which I am ashamed!' Jane attempted to defend herself, totally stunned at the things Lady Sulby was saying to her, and shocked to the core by the raw hatred she could clearly see in the other woman's face.

'Janette was not ashamed, either.' Lady Sulby shook with rage, that wild glitter in her eyes intensifying. 'She did not even apologise for being three months with child when she married her gullible parson!'

Jane really felt as if she were going to faint dead away at this last accusation. Her mother had been with child when she had married her father? With Jane herself?

But that did not make her mother a harlot or a whore. It only meant that, like many couples before them, her parents had precipitated their marriage vows. Jane was far from the first child to be born only six months after the wedding…

She shook her head. 'The only person that should concern is me, and I—'

'You *would* think that.' Lady Sulby glared at her. 'You who are just like her. With never a thought for the disgrace you bring on this family with your wanton actions.'

'But I have done nothing—'

'You have most certainly done *something*!' Lady Sulby's hands were clenched at her sides. 'The Duke's valet has informed Brown, the butler, that they are leaving this morning, and—'

'The Duke is leaving…?' Jane repeated hollowly, surprised at how much this knowledge managed to distress her when the rest of her world appeared to be falling apart—when she already felt as if she were in the middle of a nightmare without end.

'Do not pretend innocence with me, Jane Smith,' Lady Sulby told her sneeringly. 'We all witnessed the way in which you deliberately set out to attract the Duke yesterday evening—to tempt him to your bed, no doubt with the intention of trapping him into marriage. But if that was your hope then his hasty departure this morning must tell you that it was a wasted effort. The Duke is not a man to be trapped into anything—least of all marriage to a wanton chit like you. Oh, you are a wicked, hateful girl, Jane Smith!' Lady Sulby's voice rose hysterically. 'A veritable viper in our midst! But I see from your rebellious expression that it bothers you not at all that you have totally ruined any chance of Olivia becoming the Duchess of Stourbridge!'

Jane very much doubted, after the Duke's comments

yesterday evening concerning Lady Sulby, that there had ever been the remotest possibility of Olivia finding herself married to the Duke, and was sure that any hope that Olivia would do so had only ever been Lady Sulby's own misguided fantasy after Lord Sebastian St Claire had failed to arrive.

'I want you out of this house today, Jane,' Lady Sulby told her shrilly. 'Today—do you hear?'

'I have every intention of going.' After this conversation, and the things Lady Sulby had said about her mother, Jane knew that she could not stay here a day, an hour, a moment longer than absolutely necessary.

'And do not imagine you can come crawling back here if, like your mother, you find yourself with child!' Lady Sulby scorned. 'There is no convenient parson here for you to marry, Jane. No besotted fool you can beguile into marrying you in order to give your bastard a name!'

Jane became very still, all the pain she had felt at the unfairness of Lady Sulby's accusations concerning the Duke fading, all emotion leaving her as she stared at the other woman as if down a long grey tunnel.

Lady Sulby's eyes narrowed with spite as she saw the shocked disbelief Jane was too stunned to even attempt to hide. 'You did not know?' She trilled her triumph at having shaken Jane's composure at last. 'Even after she died giving birth to you Joseph Smith could not bear to sully the memory of his beloved Janette by telling you he was not your real father!'

'He *was* my father!' Jane's hands had clenched at her sides. 'He was...' Tears of anger blurred her vision at the terrible things this dreadful woman was saying about her mother and father.

She had never known her mother, but her father had been everything that was gentle and kind. Jane did not believe he could have been that way with her if he had not been her real father.

Could he…?

'He most certainly was not.' The older woman looked at her with triumphant pity. 'Your mother seduced your real father, a rich and titled gentleman, into her bed, hoping that he would become so besotted with her he would discard the woman who was already his wife. Something he refused to do even when Janette found herself with child!'

'I do not believe you!' Jane shook her head in desperate denial. 'You are simply trying to hurt me—'

'And *am* I hurting you, Jane? I hope that I am,' Lady Sulby crowed triumphantly. 'You look very like Janette, you know. She had that same wild beauty. That same untameable spirit.'

And suddenly Jane saw with sickening clarity that Lady Sulby had spent these last twelve years trying to break that spirit in Janette's daughter. She had belittled the physical likeness she perceived to Janette by dressing Jane in gowns that did absolutely nothing to complement her. Lady Sulby hated Jane as fiercely as she had hated her mother before her…

'Janette was spoilt and wilful,' Jane's nemesis continued coldly. 'She had the ability to twist any man around her little finger in order to persuade him into doing her bidding. But she made a terrible mistake in judgement in her choice of lover,' Lady Sulby sneered. 'A mistake immediately brought home to her when he did not hesitate to dismiss her from his life when she told him of the child she was expecting. You, Jane.'

'You are lying!' Jane repeated forcefully. 'I have no idea why, not what Janette was to you, but I do know that you are lying!'

'Am I?' Lady Sulby eyed her derisively even as she reached out a hand to her desk and plucked up one of the sheets of paper lying there. 'Perhaps you should read this, Jane?' She held up the page temptingly. 'Then you will see exactly who and what your mother really was!'

'What is that?' Jane eyed the letter warily. Who could be writing to Lady Sulby now, twenty-two years after Janette's death?

'A letter written twenty-three years ago by Janette to her lover. Never sent, of course. How could she send it when her lover was already married?' Lady Sulby sniffed disgustedly.

'How do you come to have her letter?' Jane shook her head dazedly.

Lady Sulby gave a taunting laugh. 'Think back to twelve years ago, Jane. Surely you remember that I came with Sulby when he came to collect you after Joseph Smith died…? Of course you remember,' she scorned, as Jane flinched at the memory. 'Just as I remember going through Janette's things and finding letters she had written to her lover but never sent. Vile, disgusting letters—'

'There was more than one letter?' Jane felt numb, disorientated.

'There are four of them.' Lady Sulby snorted. 'And in each one Janette talks to her lover of the child they have created together in sin—'

'Give that to me!' Jane snapped warningly, snatching the letter from Lady Sulby's pudgy hand to hold it fiercely against her breast. 'You had no right to read my mother's letters. No right! Where are the others?' She moved to the desk, sifting agitatedly through the papers there, easily finding the other three letters written in the same hand as the one she already held. Letters which Lady Sulby had obviously been reading when Jane came into the room. 'Does Sir Barnaby know about these letters…?'

'Of course he does not.' Lady Sulby sniffed scornfully. 'I have kept them hidden from him these last twelve years. Why do you think I was so concerned when I saw you with my jewellery box yesterday?'

Because the letters had been hidden there!

'How dare you?' Jane turned fiercely on the other woman, cheeks flushed, her eyes glittering deeply green. 'You are not fit to even touch my mother's things, let alone read her private letters!'

Lady Sulby recoiled from that fiery anger, her hand held protectively against her swelling breasts. 'Stay away from me, you wicked, wicked girl.'

'I have no intention of coming anywhere near you.' Jane faced the older woman unflinchingly. 'I would not want to soil my hands by so much as touching you. I have tried so hard to like you but never could. Only Sir Barnaby has ever been kind to me here. Now I can only feel pity for him, kind and loving man that he is, in having such a vicious and vindictive woman as his wife.'

'Get away from me, you horrible girl!'

'Oh, I am going—never fear.' Jane's head was up as she walked to the door, her spine proudly straight. 'Let me assure you that I shall leave here as soon as I have packed the few things that truly belong to me.' Including her mother's letters!

Jane knew, as she hurried down the hallway to her tiny bedroom at the back of the house, that she was glad—relieved!—to at last have reason to leave Markham Park.

No matter what the future held for her—where she went, what she had to do in order to survive—Jane knew it could never be as awful as the years she had spent at Markham Park under the knowing and cruel hatred of Lady Sulby.

Chapter Four

⟨⚬⟩

Hawk luxuriated in the heat of his bath, relaxing back in water that today was pleasurably hot and shoulder-deep—compliments of the fastidious Dolton, he felt sure.

Hawk had risen early and dressed before going down to the stables to mount the horse he had instructed Dolton to have saddled for him, surprisingly enjoying the ride across the sandy beach, his mood lightening as the salty breeze whipped through his hair and drove the cobwebs from his brain.

He had even allowed himself, briefly, to think of Jane Smith. The early-morning light had helped to put their encounter late the previous evening into perspective, thus making a nonsense of it—and of the sudden desire Hawk had felt for her. He had been bored—extremely so—and not a little irritated, and Jane, with her curvaceous body and sharp tongue, had presented a diversion from that boredom and irritation. Not necessarily a welcome one, he had acknowledged with a frown, but a diversion nonetheless.

Hawk's mood had been further lightened when he had returned from his ride to Markham Park and read the letter that had been delivered in his absence. It was only a weekly missive forwarded from his man of business in London, Andrew Windham, but the Sulbys could not know that. Without knowing the contents of the letter they had readily accepted Hawk's explanation that they necessitated he leave immediately.

Or at least as soon as he had bathed, Hawk acknowledged with a satisfied sigh as he sat forward to pick up the jug beside the bath and tip its hot contents over his hair, before washing it, musing as he did so on the fact that he would be away from Markham Park within the hour. The arrival of Andrew's letter—a letter Hawk had so wanted to arrange himself—could not have been more fortuitous.

He could be at Mulberry Hall by tomorrow. Back in Gloucestershire. In control of his surroundings and the people who inhabited them.

And safely removed from that brief lapse of control he had known last night with Jane Smith…

Hawk banned Jane Smith and her bewitching green eyes firmly from his thoughts as he stepped out of the bath to wrap a towel about his waist and use another to dry his hair. He would ring for Dolton so that he might help him dress and shave before being on his way. He would not even delay his own departure until Dolton had packed his belongings into the second coach, preferring to be away from here, from the Sulbys—from the temptation of Jane Smith?—as soon as was possible.

It was not cowardice on his part but self-defence that made him so determined not to see or speak to Jane Smith again before he left. Desire was something one felt for a mistress, not a young, unmarried woman—in this particular case the orphaned daughter of an impoverished country parson, who would surely have marriage rather than bedding in mind.

A bedding was definitely what he was in need of, Hawk mused as he strolled through to his bedroom. A good, satisfying tumble in bed with a woman of experience who would expect nothing from him in return but a few expensive baubles. Yes, that would dispel any lingering thoughts of Jane Smith firmly from—

He turned incredulously in the direction of the bedchamber door as, after the briefest of knocks, it was flung open. The subject of his thoughts came hurtling through the doorway, her face flushed, her eyes over-bright, and that glorious red hair dishevelled, with wisps trailing loosely against her cheeks and down her creamy throat.

'Oh!' Jane Smith came to an abrupt halt, the colour deepening in her cheeks as she obviously took in Hawk's state of undress.

His first instinct was to pick up and quickly don the robe that lay waiting on a bedroom chair. His second instinct was to ask why should he? He was in the privacy of his bedchamber—a privacy Jane had rudely intruded upon—so why should he concern himself with her obvious embarrassment at his semi-nakedness?

He raised one disdainful brow. 'I trust you have good reason for interrupting my ablutions in this abrupt manner?'

Jane stared at him. *Did* she have good reason? She couldn't think—had no idea why she was even here. And Hawk—most definitely not the Duke of Stourbridge!—was standing there looking so—so—

His shoulders had appeared wide and powerful in those superbly tailored jackets, but the naked flesh was so much more immediate. His arms were muscled, a dark smattering of hair grew on his tanned chest, and down below the towel wrapped about his tapered waist...

Her startled gaze returned to his face, and just as instantly became aware of the disarray of his recently washed hair as it curled, as yet ungroomed, across his brow, taking away much of his austerity and giving him a youthfully rakish appearance.

Minutes ago it had seemed vitally important that Jane speak to the Duke before he left. Now she could not even remember what she had wanted to speak to him about!

That dark brow rose even higher. 'Jane?'

She swallowed, frowning as she tried to remember.

'I wish you to take me with you when you leave today, Your Grace!' The words tumbled from Jane unchecked as she finally remembered her purpose for being here.

She had gone back to her bedroom after leaving Lady Sulby in order to read her mother's letters. Not 'disgusting and sinful' letters at all, but those of a woman pouring out her heart to her lover as she told him of the child she carried—the child they had created in love—assuring him that she loved their child as she still loved him. Whoever he was. Because all four of the letters had begun simply, 'My dearest love', and ended with, 'Ever yours, Janette'.

Jane had sat and cried after reading them. For Janette. For Joseph Smith, whom her mother had obviously felt a deep affection for but had never loved in the way she had her married lover. For the real father Jane had never known…

But once the tears had ceased Jane had remembered her vow to leave here today. And that there was someone else leaving Markham Park this morning who, if asked, might take her with him.

The Duke of Stourbridge.

Except this morning he did not look anything like the Duke of Stourbridge, with his hair still damp and dishevelled after bathing, and only a towel draped about those powerful thighs!

'You wish me to take you with me when I leave…?' He spoke softly, incredulously, those sharply etched features revealing nothing of his inner thoughts at her request.

Jane nodded. 'If you would not mind, Your Grace.'

If he would not mind!

This girl burst into his bedchamber, unannounced and with complete disregard for his privacy, and then proceeded to ask if she could accompany him when he left here today!

With what purpose in mind?

Yes, Hawk accepted that he had behaved with reckless impulsiveness the previous evening, when he had taken Jane into his arms and attempted to kiss her. But that really did not give her the right to think he might possibly want to pursue a relationship with her. Certainly not to assume he would want to take her with him when he left today!

His mouth twisted derisively. 'Jane, can you be under the delusion that I wish to make you my mistress?'

'No, of course not!' She recoiled at the suggestion, her face paling, her eyes turning a deep, appealing green.

They had an appeal that, even in his wariness over her exact intentions, Hawk found he was not immune to. Irritatingly.

He lifted the towel from his shoulders to absently dry his hair. 'Then what do you want from me, Jane?'

She blinked. 'Merely to ride in your carriage with you when you leave here today. I have a small amount of money saved, if you require payment—'

'No, I do not require payment, Jane! Not of any kind.' Ice edged his voice. 'Because you will not be coming with me.' He threw the towel impatiently down on a chair before donning his robe after all, a dark scowl creasing his brow. 'How old are you, Jane?' he demanded as he tied the belt tightly about his waist.

She looked dazed by the question. 'How—? I am two and twenty, Your Grace.'

'Indeed?' Hawk nodded abruptly. 'Old enough by far to know that you do not burst unannounced into a gentleman's bedchamber and then, finding him in a state of undress, proceed to ask him to take you away with him!'

Put like that, perhaps his assumption that she wished to become his mistress was understandable, Jane acknowledged ruefully. If completely wrong. She simply wanted to leave here as quietly and as speedily as possible.

She grimaced. 'I do not wish you to take me away with you, Your Grace. I merely wish to share your coach with you when you leave.' She also wished she'd had the forethought to wait until he had invited her to enter before bursting into his bedchamber in this way. She would certainly have saved them both embarrassment if she had done so.

Although the Duke didn't exactly *look* embarrassed as he began to pace the room restlessly. Even dressed only in the black silk robe, he was still possessed of that supreme self-confidence that seemed such a natural part of him it surely had to be inborn.

Deservedly so, Jane acknowledged as she found herself remembering the lean strength of his body. Muscles rippled in those long legs even now as he walked, and the defined muscles in the chest she had viewed earlier were something she dared any woman to resist. And especially a woman who had already found herself dreaming about him quite shamelessly the night before.

Jane felt her nipples swell and harden against the softness of her drab-muslin gown, her breasts rising and falling beneath the bodice. She suddenly found it difficult to breathe, and that strange warmth was back between her thighs.

She did not believe the accusations Lady Sulby had made about her's mother wantonness. Those letters she had read seemed to confirm that her mother had loved only one man: her married lover, Jane's natural father. But as Jane looked at the Duke of Stourbridge—at Hawk—she could not help wondering if she might not herself be a wanton. She had dreamt of this man last night. Hot, erotic dreams. And she was so physically aware of him now that she once again felt an unaccustomed ache low in her stomach.

'You have no idea what you are asking, Jane!'

She raised her eyes to meet the Duke's glittering golden gaze as he glared at her. 'I assure you I would try not to be any trouble—'

Hawk interrupted with a humourless laugh. 'Believe me, Jane, you do not have to try!' He could not spend hours, days, confined in his coach with a woman he had already physically responded to so uncharacteristically.

Damn it, he might respond in that way again, once alone in his coach with her, and take her on one of the seats!

'Why the urgency, Jane? What has happened since yesterday evening to make you so determined to leave here?'

She turned away so that he could no longer read the emotions in her eyes. 'I have decided I can no longer reside under the same roof as Lady Sulby. That is all.'

No, damn it. It was not all. What had that witch done to Jane to create the desperation he sensed in her? What could Lady Gwendoline possibly have said or done to Jane this morning to precipitate her immediate flight from Markham Park?

It was none of his business, Hawk reminded himself sternly. He did not like Lady Sulby, and had found her to be a pretentious and spiteful woman, but she was nevertheless the wife of Jane's legal guardian, and as such Hawk knew he had no right to interfere.

No matter how disturbed he was by the haunted look he had perceived in Jane's eyes a few minutes ago. Even if the thought of leaving her here to the continued coldness of Lady Sulby brought the bile rising to the back of his throat.

If Jane left her guardian's home with the Duke of Stourbridge—a single gentleman—then without a doubt the Duke of Stourbridge would be forced into marrying her.

Something Hawk did not intend to happen!

He turned away from the renewed appeal in those expressive green eyes. 'No, Jane. I am afraid it will not be possible for you to travel in my coach with me today. Whatever disagreement you have had with Lady Sulby, you must face it and deal with it. Running away from your problems solves nothing.' Hawk knew that what he was advising was the correct and only course in the circumstances, but inwardly he could not help but feel appalled as he listened to his own pomposity.

What other choice did he have? None that he could see.

But he could have wished that Jane did not look at him so disappointed before she turned her head away and her slender shoulders slumped defeatedly.

He drew in a sharp breath. 'Perhaps if you were to tell me exactly what has occurred to cause this distress—'

'Thank you, no, Your Grace.' Her shoulders were tensed proudly now. 'It only remains for me to wish you a safe journey.' She walked towards the door.

'Jane!'

'Goodbye, Your Grace.' The quiet dignity of her voice cut through him like a knife.

Hawk crossed the room in long, forceful strides to press his hand against the closed door. 'Jane, surely you must see how unsuitable it would be for you to travel anywhere alone with me?'

'I understand completely, Your Grace—'

'Jane, I have warned you about "Your Gracing" me in that dismissive way!' Hawk reached out to grasp her shoulders with both hands. 'I can see that you are upset, Jane.' His voice gentled. 'But can you not see it is an upset that will quickly pass? Lady Sulby does not mean to be cruel, I am sure—'

'You know nothing of the sort!' The defeated air had completely left Jane as she glared up at the Duke, her hands clenching at her sides. 'She is a bitter, hateful woman, full of viciousness for those she considers beneath her. I do not believe you would treat even one of your dogs in the cruel way that she has dealt with me!'

She wrenched out of the Duke's restraining grasp before turning to leave, aware of his golden gaze following her frowningly as she let herself out of the his apartments to hurry back down the hallway to her own room.

The Duke might have refused her passage in his coach, but that made little difference to her decision to leave. In fact, she refused to remain here for even another day!

If she could only get to London she could then take

a public coach to Somerset—could find Bessie, her father's old housekeeper, who she believed now resided with her married son in a village only two miles from where they had all used to live.

Bessie had known both her mother and her father before Jane was born. And household servants, as Jane well knew from her position as neither a family member nor quite a servant in the Sulby household, often knew more about their employers than those employers might have wished.

Bessie would perhaps know more about Janette's lover than Lady Sulby, in her vindictive prying into Janette's personal letters, had ever been able to learn.

Once Jane's tears had stopped after she had read her mother's achingly emotional letters—letters that had never been sent to her married lover—she had come to a decision. Her real father might never have wanted her, might have callously cast off his lover once he knew she carried his child, but that did not mean that child could not now come back to claim *him*.

As a married man, it might not be comfortable for him to suddenly be presented with a daughter of two and twenty—but how much care had he given for Janette's comfort when he had denied both her and their unborn child?

None, as far as Jane could see.

Yes, the Duke might have refused to allow Jane to accompany him when he left later this morning. But her resolve was now such that Jane knew she would walk to London if she had to!

* * *

'More wine, Your Grace?' The serving girl at the inn in which Hawk had decided to spend the night hovered expectantly beside the table, holding up a jug of wine.

Hawk nodded distractedly, having touched little of the food that had been served to him along with the wine in this private dining room. Not because there was anything wrong with the food, but because wine alone served him better in his darkly brooding mood.

He had left Markham Park shortly after that unsatisfactory conversation with Jane, any relief he had expected to feel at his release from the Sulbys' oppressive company—Lady Sulby especially—completely overshadowed by that last haunted look in Jane's eyes as she had turned away from him. As the distance between the ducal coach and Markham Park had increased Hawk had found those inner shadows deepening. Until now, ten hours later, he was beset with such feelings of guilt at leaving Jane to her fate that he could think of little else.

But to have brought Jane away with him would have compromised her as well as himself. Totally.

Perhaps that was what she had wanted?

Somehow he did not think so. Her despair this morning had been too intense, too overwhelming to be anything but genuine in her desire to get as far away from Lady Sulby's viciousness as was possible.

That he was partly to blame for that viciousness Hawk did not doubt, having been totally aware of his hostess's fury the evening before, when he'd singled

Jane out for his attentions. And that lady's ambitions concerning her daughter and himself had become apparent during the long, tortuous dinner, when he'd had Lady Sulby seated on one side of him and the fair Olivia on the other.

As if that had ever been even a remote possibility!

But Hawk was haunted by the accusations he had himself hurled at Jane the previous evening, concerning her behaviour at dinner with Lord Tillton. Accusations he now knew to be unfounded.

Having failed to see James Tillton again before retiring yesterday evening, Hawk had deliberately sought him out this morning, when taking leave of his fellow guests, and had noted grimly the half-crescent indentations in the older man's wrist. Indentations very like the piercing of neatly trimmed fingernails. *Jane's* neatly trimmed fingernails.

There had also been nothing of the siren about Jane when she had appeared so suddenly in Hawk's bed-chamber that morning—none of the beguiling seductress using her persuasive skills in order to entice him into taking her away with him. There had been only the paleness of her cheeks and that haunting look of desperation in her eyes.

Damn it, there was nothing he could have done!

And yet that he had done nothing at all did not sit well with Hawk, either...

'Can I get you anything else, Your Grace...?'

He looked up at the frowning serving girl, realising by the uncertainty of her expression that she had taken his scowl of frustration as a personal comment on the inn's fare.

'No.' He sighed, nodding as she offered to remove his almost untouched plate of food from the table. 'Except perhaps another jug of wine. Also…' He halted her at the door. 'Send my manservant to me here as soon as he arrives, will you?'

Much to Hawk's added displeasure, his own departure from Markham Hall had been so precipitate that Dolton had not yet arrived at the inn with the second coach conveying Hawk's clothes.

What was keeping the man? He might have news of Jane—might be able to report that when he'd left she had been smiling and happy…

No, he would not. Hawk instantly rebuked himself heavily. Any more than Dolton would be able to tell him that Lady Sulby had suddenly become a lady of grace and beauty! By even hoping Dolton would be able to tell him of anything pleasant left behind at Markham Park. Hawk was merely trying to appease his own conscience, for abandoning Jane in the way that he had after she had asked for his help.

What would Jane do now? Would she still go ahead with her decision to leave the only home she had known for the last twelve years? If so, where would she go? And to whom?

'Your Grace?'

Hawk had been so deep in thought that he had totally missed Dolton's arrival. He smiled at the sight of a friendly face before Dolton's look of surprise made him realise that he was not usually so familiar with his valet. 'Dolton.' He sobered. 'I trust you had an uneventful journey?'

'Er—not exactly, Your Grace.' The other man frowned uncomfortably. He was a small, slender man of middle years, his blond hair slightly thinning, his eyes a watery blue. Eyes that at this moment seemed to be evading his employer's.

'No?' Hawk arched surprised brows. His question had been a politeness only. He expected that any problems Dolton might have encountered along the way would have been dealt with without the necessity of informing his employer of them.

Dolton still avoided meeting Hawk's piercingly questioning gaze. 'No, Your Grace. I—perhaps we could discuss this upstairs in your room, Your Grace?' he added awkwardly, as the serving girl bustled back into the parlour with the second jug of wine Hawk had requested.

Hawk's brows rose even higher at the strangeness of Dolton's behaviour. 'As you can see, I have not yet finished dining.'

'No, Your Grace.' Dolton chewed on his bottom lip. 'It's just that I really would like to talk to you in private. If you please, Your Grace?' He shrugged uncomfortably.

'Leave us, please.' Hawk dismissed the serving girl as she still hovered, probably with the intention of seeing to Dolton's dinner requirements. 'Now,' he turned musingly to the other man once they were alone, 'kindly tell me what has thrown you into such confusion, Dolton?'

His manservant drew in a deep breath before grimacing. 'I would much rather show you, Your Grace.'

'What can possibly have happened to disturb you so, Dolton?'

Hawk shook his head bemusedly as he stood up. 'Have you discovered a stain on one of my jackets you cannot remove? Or perhaps a scuff on one of my best boots?' It had been known for Dolton to be thrown into a paroxysm over just such an occurrence.

'Nothing so simple, I am afraid, Your Grace.' Dolton shook his head mournfully before opening the door for the Duke to precede him out of the room.

'A wheel has fallen off the coach, perhaps?' Hawk continued to dryly ridicule the man as he ascended the narrow stairway that led to the bedchambers above.

This inn was no better than the one Hawk had stayed at on his journey to Markham Park, but he had consoled himself with the realisation that at least this time he was on his way to his own home, rather than facing the unpleasant prospect of a week spent amongst virtual strangers.

'No, Your Grace.' His valet sighed as he mounted the stairs behind him.

'For God's sake, man—will you stop shilly-shallying and tell me what all this is about—?'

Hawk had opened the door to the bedroom allocated to him but came to an abrupt halt in the doorway to stare uncomprehendingly at the bonneted and cloaked figure that stood so demurely in the centre of the sparsely furnished room.

Jane Smith raised her lashes to look at him with green eyes that were far from demure.

'What is the meaning of this?' Hawk breathed chillingly, unable to remember when he had last felt so angry. If ever.

'I only left the coach unattended for a minute or so, Your Grace. When I went to collect the picnic lunch the cook had prepared for our journey.' Dolton launched into defensive speech as he stepped around the Duke to enter the room, his expression imploring as he looked up at his employer. 'She must have slipped inside the coach while I was in the house. As you know, Your Grace, I always travel outside, with Taylor, so we were unaware of Miss Smith's presence inside the coach until an hour ago, when it became rather cold and I had the coach stopped so that I could get my cloak. I discovered Miss Smith hiding amongst your trunks, Your Grace,' he concluded unhappily.

Hawk did indeed know of Dolton's preference for sitting up with the coachman. His valet suffered from motion sickness if confined inside the coach for any length of time.

None of which altered the fact that Jane Smith should not be here.

At the inn.

Once again in his bedchamber.

'You seem to be making a habit of this, Miss Smith.' His tone was icy.

'So I do, Your Grace.' She met his gaze unflinchingly.

Hawk drew in a sharply angry breath as he easily recognised her challenging look of defiance. 'I should have you beaten and taken back to Markham Place immediately!'

Jane's chin rose. 'I invite you to try, Your Grace.'

His mouth thinned. 'I was not intending to apply the beating myself, Jane.' He gave his valet a steely glare from beneath ominously lowered brows.

Jane tried, and failed, to suppress her laughter as she saw the look of obvious dismay on Mr Dolton's face at the thought of his employer ordering him to beat her.

'It really is too cruel to tease Mr Dolton in that way, Your Grace.' She shook her head, the heavy weight of Lady Sulby's hatred having lifted as each mile passed, taking her farther away from Markham Park. In fact, apart from the obvious precariousness of her future, Jane was feeling more light-hearted than she had done for some years.

'And what makes you think I was teasing?' The Duke raised haughty brows.

'The fact that I am perhaps two inches taller than Mr Dolton—and possibly stronger, too?' The laughter still gleamed challengingly in her eyes as she easily met the Duke's forbidding gaze.

Not that she did not sympathise with the frustrated anger he must be feeling. Having left Markham Park, he must have assumed he had seen the last of her.

The glittering gold gaze swept over her from head to foot before the Duke turned to spear his still-quaking valet with it. 'Miss Smith will not be staying,' he said ominously.

'Miss Smith most certainly *will* be staying.' As if to prove the point, Jane reached up and untied her bonnet, before removing it completely and placing it on a chair, then turned her attention to her cloak. 'Perhaps not in this exact room,' she allowed, with a mocking inclination of her head. 'But I am sure that the innkeeper will have another room in which I might spend the night.' Her cloak joined the bonnet on the bedside chair.

'And then what?' The Duke glared at her stonily. 'Is it your intention to walk the rest of the way to your destination?'

'If necessary, yes.' Jane perched herself daringly on the edge of the four-poster bed to look up at him with cool deliberation.

His mouth tightened. 'You are without doubt the most irresponsible, stubborn—'

'I think you may excuse yourself from the Duke's displeasure now, Mr Dolton.' Jane turned to smile warmly at the nervously hovering man.

It had perhaps been unfair of her to involve the Duke's valet in her escape from Markham Park and the Sulby family, but the opportunity to slip inside the unattended coach this morning had been too tempting to resist. And the fact that Mr Dolton had then elected to sit up with the driver meant she had managed to remain undetected for hours. Far too many hours for the valet— or the Duke—to consider returning her to Markham Park tonight.

Neither did Jane intend being bullied into returning there tomorrow by the obviously infuriated Duke of Stourbridge.

'Yes, you may leave us, Dolton.' The Duke coldly echoed her instruction. 'For now,' he added gratingly.

'Please go down and have some dinner, Mr Dolton.'

Jane gave the valet another encouraging smile. 'I shall join you shortly.' It had been a long day—a day without any food or water—and Jane felt very much in need of both. But not, of course, until she had finished her conversation with the Duke of Stourbridge.

'I do not believe I gave you leave to issue instructions to members of my staff.'

Jane turned her attention back to the Duke now that Mr Dolton had left the room and closed the door softly behind him. 'You were simply tormenting the poor man—'

'Miss Smith!'

She quirked auburn brows. 'Your Grace?'

Hawk found that his anger had not abated in the least since he had walked into the room and seen her standing there so unexpectedly. In fact, he would have dearly loved to pull her to her feet and give her a good shaking.

Except that he did not trust himself to touch Jane at this moment. He had no idea, if he did, whether he would shake her or kiss her!

He had spent hours tormenting himself with thoughts of having left Jane to the untender mercies of Lady Sulby, only to find that she was no longer at Markham Park after all, but cosily ensconced in his second-best coach as it travelled along some distance behind his own.

His gaze narrowed as he saw her smile. 'I suppose you are congratulating yourself on managing to defy my instructions so effectively?'

Jane was not sure that 'congratulating' herself exactly described it, but she was feeling rather pleased with herself for having so successfully removed herself from Markham Park.

'I am not sure that your instructions came into my thinking when I climbed inside your coach this morning—'

'I am certain they did not!' He glared coldly.

'However,' Jane continued undaunted, 'I cannot deny I am pleased to be away from the Sulby household.'

The Duke's mouth thinned. 'You do realise that your disappearance, and the coincidence of my own departure this morning, will be noticed? That Sir Barnaby will send someone after you?'

She thought of Lady Sulby's deliberate viciousness this morning—of the fact that she had ordered Jane to leave. 'Somehow I do not think so, Your Grace.' She gave a firm shake of her head.

'Jane, do you not see how reckless your behaviour is?' The Duke crossed the bedroom to stand beside her, looking directly into her face. 'You are a young woman alone—an unmarried woman. If anyone should find you at this inn with me—'

'Do not concern yourself, Your Grace.' Jane stood up abruptly to move away, slightly disconcerted by his close proximity. 'If it became necessary I am sure that Mr Dolton could be persuaded into claiming me as a relative.'

He scowled. 'Just how long did you and Dolton spend together inside the coach?'

Jane turned to look at him, suspecting yet another accusation of flirtation but instead finding only grudging humour lurking in the depths of those mesmerising gold eyes.

Some of the tension left her shoulders. 'Only an hour or so. But I believe he likes me well enough to claim me as his niece if anyone should ask.'

'I am sure that he does.' Hawk straightened, finding his temper somewhat abated. He was under no illusion whatsoever that Dolton would voice his protest most strongly if his employer should attempt to cast Jane out into the night.

As the Duke of Stourbridge, he knew that he should demand that Jane return to her guardians immediately—that not to insist on that was madness on his part. But he could not deny that Jane's desperation earlier today to escape those guardians, and his own refusal to help her, had been haunting him all day. Too much so for him to now demand that she return to them.

Instead he sighed wearily. 'Are you hungry, Jane?'

'Ravenous!' she acknowledged ruefully.

'Very well, Jane.' He gave a terse inclination of his head. 'We will have dinner—'

'Oh, thank you, Your Grace.' She stood up to cross the room and clasp both his hands in hers. She looked up at him with glowing green eyes. 'Thank you. *Thank you!*' She punctuated her words with kisses placed upon his hands, finally laying her cheek against one of them with warm gratitude.

Hawk had stiffened at her first touch, needing all of his will-power at that moment not to snatch his hands from the soft feel of her skin against his as she pressed his hand to her cheek. It was such a creamy softness. A sensual softness.

His thumb seemed to move of its own volition in order to stroke that silky warmth, and Hawk hesitated only slightly before he allowed his thumb to touch the rosy pout of her lips. Lips that parted slightly at his touch. The warmth of her breath against his skin was a caress in itself as she looked up at him with those trusting green eyes.

What Hawk would do next hung finely in the balance. His gaze remained on those softly parted lips, a nerve pulsing in his tightly clenched jaw as he fought the need he felt to taste those lips. To taste all of her. From her creamy brow to her dainty feet. He was sure that at this moment, being her reluctant saviour, Jane would deny him nothing.

But if he were to take advantage of her gratitude what would that make him? Beneath contempt—and in his own eyes no better than the people she was so desperately trying to escape!

'Stop it, Jane!' His voice was harsh as he pulled his hands from hers, turning sharply away from the hurt that now shadowed those expressive green eyes. 'I suggest that you wait here while I go in search of Dolton and instruct him to arrange overnight accomodation for my ward—'

'Your ward, Your Grace…?' Jane echoed faintly, sure that she could not have heard him correctly.

His mouth thinned disapprovingly. 'I can think of no other explanation for the presence of a young and single lady, travelling alone in the company of the Duke of

Stourbridge. I am sure that Dolton, with his new penchant for subterfuge, will have no trouble at all in thinking of an excuse for your lack of maid,' he continued dryly. 'Perhaps he could invent an unexpected illness that has prevented her immediately accompanying us to Gloucestershire?'

'Gloucestershire?' Jane said dazed, suddenly very still. 'But I thought— You are not returning to London, Your Grace?' she prompted sharply.

'No, Jane, I am not,' he confirmed mockingly. 'Mulberry Hall, principle seat of the Duke of Stourbridge, is in Gloucestershire. My plan had always been to go there for the rest of the summer. As I have no intention of allowing you to travel anywhere unchaperoned, you will obviously have to accompany me there.'

Jane stared at the Duke disbelievingly, too shocked at that moment to argue.

She had believed the Duke of Stourbridge to be returning to London from where she would be able to buy passage on a public coach to Somerset. And to the warm, comforting bosom of Bessie.

Instead, it seemed Jane now found herself forced to accompany the Duke—a man who had already induced the most erotic longings inside her—to his estate in Gloucestershire…

Chapter Five

'You are very quiet this morning, Your Grace.'

There was no response to Jane's soft observation except the sound of grinding teeth. The Duke's teeth.

It was a sound she had heard several times during the two hours they had shared the ducal coach as it travelled to the Duke's family seat in Gloucestershire. It was rather irritating coming from a man who normally displayed such an air of control and good breeding. Perhaps it was a habit he was unaware of…?

The silence that had beset him since the two of them had parted the previous evening, following a shared dinner downstairs in the inn's parlour, was also unsettling.

They had disagreed throughout most of the meal, of course, as Jane had continued to protest vehemently at the Duke's assertion that she would accompany him to Gloucestershire. The Duke had remained equally adamant, especially in view of her refusal to share her future plans with him, that he would not even consider leaving her at a coaching inn along the way, so that she might make her own way to London.

Jane had thought the awkwardness between them at least partially resolved when she had been forced to back down in the face of the only alternative the Duke would consider to his own plans, which Jane liked the sound of even less than accompanying him to his estate in Gloucestershire—that of being returned to Markham Park and her guardians forthwith!

Admittedly, their goodnights to each other had been a little frosty, but Jane had felt slightly mollified when she'd found that, along with a second bedchamber for the Duke's 'ward', Mr Dolton had also engaged the services of the daughter of the innkeeper to act as Jane's temporary maid, and a steaming hot bath had been there for her enjoyment.

After a good night's rest, Jane had risen from her bed this morning, determined to make the best of her situation. After all, although the Duke was completely unaware of it, Gloucestershire was in fact much closer to her real destination of Somerset than London…

Mary, the innkeeper's daughter, had returned to Jane's room shortly after she had completed her ablutions, carrying a breakfast tray. So Jane had no occasion to see or speak to the Duke again before joining him inside the ducal coach to resume their journey.

As expected, the coach was as magnificent inside as out, with seats upholstered in such a way as to afford them the maximum comfort. Even the sun had come out mid-morning to cheer her. In fact, it would have been a very pleasant journey indeed if not for the noticeable silence of the Duke.

And the grinding of his teeth, of course…!

Now Jane risked a glance at the Duke from beneath her lashes, at once seeing the reason for those grinding teeth: his jaw was clenched so tightly the bones there looked in danger of actually snapping beneath the pressure.

She had tried several times to engage him in conversation these last two hours. She had remarked on the weather as she removed her cloak, and her increasing nervousness at his continued silence had caused her to explain that the green gown she wore today—a particular favourite of hers—had been a birthday gift from Sir Barnaby the previous year. On both occasions she had received only a scowl and a grunt in reply, and she had not felt brave enough since to attempt further conversation.

She sat forward slightly now. 'Have I done something to disturb you this morning, Your Grace?'

'Have I not told you—repeatedly—to stop "Your Gracing" me with every other word?' He glared darkly.

Jane blinked at the fierceness of his expression. 'I do not know what else to call you, Your—sir…' she amended hastily, as he breathed so heavily down his nose it sounded almost like an unbecoming snort.

'Have I not invited you to call me Hawk?' His scowl darkened.

'You have,' Jane confirmed softly, her cheeks feeling slightly warm as she remembered the occasion on which he had done so. 'But while that may do when we are alone, it will hardly suffice when we are in the company of others.'

'It cannot have escaped your notice, Jane, that we are not at this moment in the company of others!' he bit out tautly.

He was being boorish, Hawk knew. But he could not seem to stop himself. As he had already surmised the previous day, when Jane had first asked to accompany him and he had refused, travelling alone with her in the confines of his coach was pure torture!

For one thing she looked so damned happy this morning. Totally unlike the cowed creature he had met for the first time two days ago on the stairs at Markham Park. Was it really only two days since this young woman had literally launched herself into his presence? It seemed much longer! Her eyes shone with excitement today, her cheeks were flushed, and her lips seemed to be curved into a constant smile of contentment.

To Hawk's way of thinking Jane had no right to look so happy when she had thrown his own normally peaceful existence into such disarray!

Her earlier remark about the weather being warm had been accompanied by the removal of her travelling cloak. A move that had revealed she wore a pale green gown beneath that lent her skin a creamy hue while at the same time intensifying the colour of the fiery red curls piled upon her head. Her explanation that the gown had been a gift from Sir Barnaby had at least restored Hawk's faith in his own judgement of the older man; it seemed that Sir Barnaby's only lapse in good taste had occurred twenty-five years ago, when it had come to the choosing of his wife!

But as Jane sat opposite Hawk, looking so relaxed and beautiful, it was impossible for him not to notice that the gown also revealed the bare expanse of her breasts. That creamy swell moved enticingly every time his coach ran over a rut in the road, causing Hawk to shift uncomfortably in his seat as his body hardened in awareness.

Hawk knew that his tailor in London took great delight in fitting his clothes precisely to the muscled width of his shoulders, his tapered waist and powerful thighs—but at this particular moment Hawk could have wished that the man had allowed him a little more room for manoeuvre in the cut of his breeches!

Jane, still an innocent despite her claim of being two and twenty, remained completely oblivious as to the reason for his discomfort.

Hawk scowled anew. 'You dare to rebuke me for my silence, Jane?'

The colour warmed Jane's cheeks as she guessed the reason for his accusation. The Duke had tried repeatedly during dinner yesterday evening to encourage Jane to tell him of her reasons for leaving Markham Park so abruptly had been, and of exactly what she intended doing once she reached London. It had been encouragement Jane had very firmly resisted.

For how could she possibly tell the Duke of Stourbridge—a man who no doubt knew each and every one of his antecedents reaching back several centuries at least—that her only reason for going to London had been to find further transport to Somerset, all with the intention of discovering who her real father might be?

Jane simply could not tell him that. Not only would the Duke question the wisdom of even associating with one such as her, but it would also be disloyal to the mother Jane had never known, who had married a man she did not love in order to give her daughter a name.

And so, much to the Duke's obvious chagrin, Jane had remained stubbornly silent concerning her reasons for travelling to London.

It was a silence that obviously still displeased him.

'I did not rebuke you, Your Grace.' Jane chose to ignore his impatient snort. 'I merely remarked upon the fact that you seem unusually uncommunicative this morning.'

'Unlike some people, Jane, I do not feel the need to spend my every waking moment prattling on about innocuous or—even worse—irrelevant subjects.'

She drew in a sharp breath at his deliberately insulting tone. 'In that case, Your Grace, I will allow you to return to your solitude.' She turned away from him to stare sightlessly out of the window beside her, blinking back unexpected tears as she did so.

Was she wrong not to confide in him?

If he had been just Hawk St Claire, the man Jane had talked to amongst the sand dunes two evenings ago, perhaps she might have felt able to talk to him about such a personal matter. But it was impossible to forget he was also the Duke of Stourbridge, a rich and powerful peer of the realm, a man Jane simply could not tell of her mother's relationship with a married man which had resulted in her own birth.

No matter how much it displeased the Duke, she simply could not!

Hawk's heart clenched in his chest as he saw Jane blink back the tears obviously caused by his impatient anger.

Since the death of his mother ten years ago the only female to have been a constant in his life had been his young sister, Arabella. As a child, Arabella had been engagingly charming, but during the last few months spent at her first London Season she had shown herself to be as wilfully determined to have her own way as her two older brothers, causing Lady Hammond, their amenable aunt and Arabella's patroness, to pronounce her completely unmanageable. Which meant that Arabella was currently unchaperoned, his aunt having taken to her bed in her London home to recover from the rigours of chaperoning a young girl through the Season.

Jane, as Hawk knew from the fact that she was here in his coach with him at all, could be equally stubborn when the occasion warranted. She just went about achieving her objective without his sibling's penchant for confrontation. No doubt her years of being subjugated at every turn by the sharp-tongued Lady Sulby were responsible for her more restrained defiance. At best she had been treated as a poor relation in the Sulby household. At worst—as Hawk had disapprovingly witnessed for himself on the day he'd arrived at Markham Park—as little more than a servant.

He sighed heavily. 'I believe I owe you an apology, Jane.'

She turned to give him a surprised look, those suppressed tears giving an extra sheen of brightness to the green of her eyes. 'An apology, Your Grace?'

He chose to ignore her formal address this time. 'My mood is—churlish.' He nodded. 'But I really should not take out my bad temper on you.'

Jane gave him a rueful smile. 'Not even if I am the reason for that bad temper?'

'But you are not. At least, not completely,' he allowed derisively, as he saw a teasing look of sceptisism enter her eyes. 'You do not have any siblings of your own, do you, Jane?'

'I do not, Your Grace,' she confirmed huskily.

What had he said to make Jane suddenly lower her lashes and clench her hands so tightly together in her lap? He had talked only of siblings, something Jane obviously did not have, and yet curiously the mention had caused her previous air of contentment to fade.

Much as Hawk found it irksome that Jane stubbornly refused to discuss with him her last interview with Lady Sulby, he also found himself most unhappy at being the one to cause her further distress.

He shook his head. 'Jane, you have no idea how lucky you are to be an only child.' He watched intently this time for Jane's reaction—if any—to his remark.

But in the few seconds during which Hawk had noted and questioned her earlier response Jane had somehow drawn upon hidden reserves, and her expression was one of cool interest now. 'Lucky, Your Grace?'

He grimaced. 'I have two younger brothers and an even younger sister—all of whom, it seems, are trying to age me before my time!'

Jane smiled at the image his words projected. 'In what way, Your Grace?'

'In every way!' He gave an impatient grimace.

At that moment he had such a look of a man weighed down by his family responsibilities—an expression so at odds with the arrogantly imperious Duke of Stourbridge—that Jane could not help smiling. 'Tell me about them,' she invited softly.

He sat back on the seat. 'Lucian is eight and twenty, and morose and unapproachable since he resigned his commission in the army following Bonaparte's defeat. Sebastian is six and twenty. He enjoys nothing more than involving himself in every scandal you could think of and some I would rather you could not.' He grimaced with distaste. 'As for Arabella…! My sister is eight and ten in years, and recently attended her first London Season.'

There was such a wealth of feeling in his last statement that Jane had no doubt that Lady Arabella's first Season had not been the success the Duke had hoped it would be.

'She is still very young, Your Grace. There will be plenty more opportuny, I am sure, to receive the required marriage proposal.' Jane attempted to placate him, sure that, as the sister of the Duke of Stourbridge, Lady Arabella St Claire must be a very eligible young lady indeed.

The Duke's mouth twisted ruefully. 'You misunderstand me, Jane,' he drawled. 'My sister has received numerous offers of marriage in the past few months—she has steadfastly refused to accept any of them!' he added hardly.

The fact that the Duke had allowed his sister to do so was very telling indeed, and indicated an indulgence for his younger siblings that had not been apparent in his initial comment about them.

Jane shrugged. 'Perhaps Lady Arabella felt unable to love any of those men—'

'Love, Jane?' he interrupted scornfully. 'What does love have to do with marriage?'

'Oh, but—' Jane broke off her exclamation to bite her bottom lip as she recalled that even her own mother had not married for love but to give her unborn child a name.

Was that really all marriage amounted to? Merely a necessary requirement for the sake of having children, made out of duty rather than love?

Was that what the Duke of Stourbridge would require in his own marriage? A woman to bear him legitimate children, necessary heirs to the dukedom, while he no doubt supported a mistress in town and continued to live his life as he chose?

Was that what all men of the ton required in marriage?

If so, then Jane was glad she had no part of it.

She had already spent too much of her two and twenty years knowing what it was like to be unloved to ever contemplate deliberately committing the rest of her life to such an emotionless state. Better to remain an old maid than to be merely suffered in a loveless marriage.

Besides, who would ever want to marry her now anyway? The daughter of a single woman abandoned in her pregnancy by her married lover!

'Jane…?'

She had allowed her guard to drop, her thoughts to wander, Jane realized as she looked across at the Duke with a guilty start. And the illustrious Duke of Stourbridge was too astute a man, those strange gold-coloured eyes of his too all-seeing to allow such a lapse to pass unnoticed.

He did look so handsome this morning, in a jacket of royal blue, his shirt a snowy white, his waistcoat of pale blue satin and cream breeches worn above highly polished Hessians. But it really would not do, when Jane had just reasoned for herself how small were her own marriage prospects, for her to notice how strikingly handsome the Duke of Stourbridge looked today!

Jane forced a dismissive smile to her lips before answering him. 'Your brothers and sister do not sound so bad, Your Grace.'

He grimaced. 'That is because you do not know them.'

Hawk, although unaware of the reason for it, had been completely aware of the shadows that had briefly claimed Jane's expressive green eyes. That she was hiding something more from him than a disagreement with Lady Sulby he did not doubt. That Jane intended to keep hiding it from him was also not in doubt; he knew, even on such a brief acquaintance, that Jane was possessed of a stubborn need for privacy that almost, but not quite, matched his own.

He eyed her speculatively. 'But you will. At least you will have occasion to meet Arabella,' he added with a frown, not sure that he at all liked the prospect of Jane being introduced to the handsomely brooding Lucian or the mischievous Sebastian.

Despite what Sebastian might have assumed to the contrary during their conversation the previous week, Hawk was in fact very fond of his younger brothers. But he also knew their natures much better than they would perhaps have wished. And the thought of either of those handsome scoundrels taking a fancy to the innocently beautiful Jane was not a comfortable one.

She gave a puzzled frown at his comment. 'How so, Your Grace...?'

Hawk was still scowling at the thought of Jane becoming the object of either of his brothers' romantic interest. 'Now that the Season has ended for the summer my sister Arabella has returned to Mulberry Hall, of course.'

Jane's eyes widened. Lady Arabella St Claire would be in residence at Mulberry Hall when they arrived? Was already there eagerly awaiting her eldest brother's arrival?

Well...no. From the little Hawk had said of his strong-minded young sister, Jane did not think the other girl would be waiting in the hallway of Mulberry Hall eager-eyed and breathless in anticipation of the Duke's arrival!

But eager-eyed or not, Lady Arabella would be at Mulberry Hall when the Duke arrived there with Jane at his side. How did he intend to explain the presence of Jane, a young lady completely unknown to Lady

Arabella, who had obviously accompanied the Duke completely unchaperoned on the long coach journey to his Gloucestershire home?

'Of course,' Jane acknowledged quietly, her lashes lowered onto creamy cheeks. 'I...' She paused to moisten suddenly dry lips. 'What explanation do you intend giving Lady Arabella for my presence, Your Grace?' She looked across at him anxiously. 'After all, she will know that I am not your ward.'

He quirked dark brows. 'Why not simply tell her the truth, Jane? That you begged to be allowed to come away with me.'

Jane gaped at him.

She had given little thought to what explanation the Duke would give his staff for her having accompanied him to his home. If she had thought of it at all, she had assumed that none of the staff employed on the Stourbridge estate would dare to question the Duke concerning his actions. But she doubted a young and headstrong sister would as readily accept Jane's unaccompanied presence.

Ah—at last he seemed to have shaken Jane from the cool reserve she had assumed minutes ago, which had so irritated him, Hawk noted with satisfaction. Although it was highly insulting to realise, from the consternation he could now see in Jane's expression, that she now wondered at his motive for allowing her to travel to Mulberry Hall with him. That she believed his young sister might make assumptions about that motive also!

Before inheriting the title of Duke of Stourbridge, Hawk had been as much of a rakehell as Sebastian now was—had for years enjoyed the same carousing and wenching with his own reckless friends. But the last ten years had necessarily seen a change in Hawk's life. His nature had become outwardly coolly reserved, and, as Sebastian had complained only days ago, any relationships of an intimate nature kept discreetly hidden away from public scrutiny. That Jane could even suspect him of being thought to take a mistress to Mulberry Hall—to the St Claire family's principal seat, the home where his sister was also in residence—was unacceptable. So unacceptable that Hawk could not repress his instinct to make Jane suffer a little for even entertaining such a suspicion.

'Do not look so concerned, Jane,' he taunted as he lounged back on the seat. 'No one, not even my sister Arabella, would dare to question what position I intend you to occupy in my household.'

And what position was that? Jane wondered dazedly. Had she misunderstood the Duke the previous evening when he had been so insistent she would travel under his protection? Despite what he had said to the contrary, was he now saying he expected her to become his mistress as payment for that protection?

'Come, Jane.' He sat forward to take both her tightly clenched hands in one of his. 'When we were together in the dunes two evenings ago you did not give the impression that you found my...attentions repulsive.'

In truth, Jane did not find anything about the Duke of Stourbridge repulsive. In fact, just having him touch her hands in this way had reawakened those feelings of longing that had so disturbed her that night amongst the sand dunes. An experience she had found herself dreaming of repeating ever since.

More than repeating!

This man—Hawk—had awakened longings inside her that she had not even known existed, and even now she could feel herself being drawn towards him, found herself held captive by the intensity of that golden gaze.

He should stop this right now, Hawk knew. Should release Jane's hands, distance himself from her, before explaining exactly what role he intended her to take up at Mulberry Hall.

And yet as he gazed upon the temptation of her softly parted lips, felt the silkiness of her skin beneath his fingertips, he was aware of a desire to reach out and take her fully into his arms and taste her. The hard throb of his body echoed that need. It was a need that Hawk had firmly resisted two evenings ago, but which he now succumbed to. His gaze hooded, he effortlessly pulled her across the small distance that separated them to settle her light weight comfortably on his knee as his arms moved about her and his mouth claimed hers.

Her lips felt as soft and silky beneath his as Hawk had imagined they would, and the smooth skin of her bare arms was like satin to his touch. He moved his hand to curve about her nape and pull her deeper into the kiss.

Fire blazed through him, deep and hot, his mouth hardening against hers before he parted her lips with his tongue and sought the moist heat within.

Her skin exuded the exotic perfume of flowers mixed

with that of sexual arousal, telling Hawk that Jane was not averse to his attentions at all—that in fact she more than returned the desire that raged through him.

He groaned low in his throat, his lips devouring hers as he sipped and tasted the nectar to be found there. One of his hands caressed restlessly down the slender length of her spine before moving to curve possessively about a thrusting breast.

Jane felt drugged from Hawk's kisses. Then, as if she had died and gone to heaven, she felt his hand cup her breast—one of those same breasts that seconds ago had seemed to swell and harden as he kissed her. Her breath caught in her throat as he touched the hardened tip, sending that now familiar heat spiralling between her thighs.

Jane had no idea what took place between a man and woman once they were in bed together—knew only from Lady Sulby's advice to Olivia concerning any future marriage that it was something she would just have to lie back and suffer on the occasions her husband demanded it of her. But this—being in Hawk's arms, having him kiss and touch her in this intimate way—did not feel like suffering. In fact, she felt weak with wanting!

Did that mean that Jane was really not destined for the marriage bed? Her mother's letters to her lover had indicated that she had enjoyed their intimate relationship. Was Jane also one of those wanton women who actually *enjoyed* having a man make love to her?

No, it could not be!

Jane was not any of the things Lady Sulby had accused her of being. She was not!

Even as desire clouded Hawk's mind, and the heated throb of his body made him ache to lie Jane on the seat and ravish her totally, he sensed—knew—the moment Jane was no longer a willing recipient of his attentions.

At the same time he also knew that if he were to uphold any authority as the Duke of Stourbridge, as well as being Jane's proxy guardian, he must be the one to put an end to this. And in such a way that there would be no danger of it happening again.

His mouth had a deliberately cruel twist to it as he raised his head to look down at her, his gaze hard and mocking as she lay limply in his arms. 'Do you see, Jane, how true was my warning of the danger you put yourself in when you chose to travel alone in a gentleman's carriage with him?' he taunted scornfully, even as he lifted her bodily and placed her back on the seat opposite his own.

Her face had become very pale, her eyes wide with shock. 'You—you kissed me only in order to teach me a lesson, Your Grace?'

Hawk steeled himself not to show how the hurt in her eyes and the trembling of her slightly swollen lips affected him. 'Partly,' he confirmed coldly. 'But I also wished you to know, no matter what you may have been thinking to the contrary—' his tone hardened icily '—that the Duke of Stourbridge has no need to use blackmail in order to seduce comely wenches fresh from the country into his bed. I have no need to bother with such persuasion when such women obviously fall into my bed all too willingly!' he added with scathing scorn.

Jane gasped at the accusation even as she knew that the Duke only spoke the truth. She *was* fresh from the country, and she had—momentarily—been all too willing a recipient of his lovemaking.

'That is what you thought I was about, was it not, Jane?'

If anything his voice had become even icier. At that moment he looked every inch the arrogantly self-assured Duke of Stourbridge of their first meeting—his eyes narrowed with ominous intent, those sculptured lips thinned to cruel mockery.

That his accusations had some merit caused Jane to straighten proudly, and she met his gaze unflinchingly, already knowing the Duke well enough to realise that he showed nothing but contempt for people who lacked the courage to stand up to his dictatorial arrogance.

'I was not about to succumb to your bed, Your Grace.'

'All evidence to the contrary, Jane!'

Her brows rose coolly. 'I am not a liar, Your Grace.'

The Duke gave a mocking shake of his head. 'Did no one tell you that self-deception is a form of lying, Jane?'

At that moment Jane's fingers itched to wipe the arrogant smile of satisfaction from the sneeringly curved lips that only minutes ago had so capably devoured her own!

'I would not advise it, Jane.' The Duke's voice had softened warningly as he obviously observed that instinct in the clenching of Jane's hand. 'You have already presented enough of an inconvenience to my peaceful existence without adding striking me to your list of offences!'

She was breathing hard in her agitation. 'Might I remind Your Grace that it was your decision, not mine, that I accompany you to Gloucestershire!'

'So it was.' He nodded dourly. 'A decision I have already come to regret, I do assure you!'

Jane bristled indignantly. 'The remedy to the inconvenience of my company can be easily found, Your Grace.'

His mouth tightened. 'If you are once again suggesting that I allow you continue on to London alone—'

'I am.'

'Then I advise you to put such a thought completely from your mind, Jane,' Hawk continued frostily over her interruption. 'The only people left in London during the summer are rakehells and dissolutes who would find themselves totally bored if removed to the country. Such men,' he added hardly, 'would see you as nothing more than an innocent tasty morsel to be quickly devoured and as speedily discarded!'

Jane's breasts quickly rose and fell. 'Do you speak from experience, Your Grace?' There was challenge in her tone.

Hawk eyed her with chilling derision. 'If I did, Jane, then you can be assured you would not now be sitting across this carriage from me with your innocence still intact!'

'You are arrogant, sir!'

'I am honest, Jane,' he came back tersely, having no doubt whatsoever that Jane would not last a day in London without some well-practised reprobate—his brothers Sebastian and Lucian, for example!—trying to seduce her into his bed.

Jane dearly wanted to deny the Duke's accusations. But how could she do so when she was aware of the way she still inwardly trembled from the effect of his kisses and the feel of his caressing hands against her breasts…?

That arrogant mouth twisted knowingly. 'Nothing to add to that particular argument, Jane?' he taunted. 'In that case,' he continued grimly, 'before we reach Mulberry Hall I would have your promise that you will not make any attempt to go to London until I am free to accompany you there.'

Her eyes widened incredulously. 'It is your intention to accompany me to London, Your Grace?'

'It is,' he confirmed impatiently. 'I have several estate matters that require my attention for the next few days, but after that I should be available to take you to London. In other words, Jane, I will not hear of you even *thinking* of continuing your journey alone!'

Jane frowned. Had the Duke guessed? Could she have somehow given away thoughts of that being her intent?

'I will have your promise, Jane!' The Duke reached out to firmly grasp her wrist between strong fingers, his narrowed gaze intent upon her face.

Jane's thoughts raced. If she made such a promise then she would have to keep to it. Had she not just assured him that she was not a liar? But it had never been her intention to remain in London, and the Duke of Stourbridge, albeit unknowingly, was now bringing her within a carriage ride of her real destination…

Would it still be lying to make him such a promise when London had never been her ultimate goal?

Possibly.

But not actually.

Pure semantics, Jane knew. But the Duke was really leaving her little choice in the matter.

Because it was not her intention for the Duke of Stourbridge to accompany her *anywhere*!

Her business in Somerset, her need to talk to Bessie, was completely personal to herself and certainly not in need of any witnesses. Least of all the aloofly superior Duke of Stourbridge!

She gave a cool inclination of her head. 'I give you my promise, Your Grace.'

His gaze narrowed. 'What do you promise, Jane?'

She gave a humourless smile at his obvious suspicion concerning her easy acquiescence. 'I promise that I will not attempt to travel to London until you are able to accompany me there.'

Hawk's gaze narrowed as he looked across at her searchingly. There was something about Jane's promise that did not quite ring true.

He just had no idea what it was.

Yet.

Chapter Six

‘Before introducing me to Lady Arabella as her new companion, you might have first taken the trouble to confide that fact to me, Your Grace!’

Hawk couldn't help but wonder why he was surprised at the interruption as he looked across to where the door to his library had been thrown back on its hinges. Jane Smith entered and strode imperiously across the room to stand before the wide desk behind which he sat.

Hawk had believed, when he'd excused himself from the ladies' company a short time ago, leaving the two of them to enjoy their afternoon tea together, that it would allow the two women time in which to become better acquainted with each other. And at the same time, now that the introductions were over, allow him the opportunity of escaping to the relative sanctuary of his library!

Its walls lined with leather-bound volumes, two comfortable armchairs placed on either side of the fireplace, along with a decanter of brandy within his easy reach, the room was normally beneficial in that it afforded him a few hours' solitude when he might deal with estate business.

Obviously no one had told Jane Smith that the Duke was never to be disturbed when ensconced in the library. Or, as was more likely to be the case, Jane had been given that information but had chosen to ignore it!

'Do you have nothing to say in your defence, Your Grace?' she demanded accusingly now, the colour high in her cheeks.

Hawk had plenty of things he might like to say on that subject and several others—but he doubted that any of them were suitable for Jane's delicate ears!

'It might interest you to know, Jane—' Hawk's tone was deceptively mild as he sat back in his chair to look at her from beneath narrowed lids '—that you are the only person of my acquaintance who actually dares to speak to me in this disrespectful manner.' His voice hardened glacially over the last few words.

'Really, Your Grace?' The increased flush to Jane's cheeks indicated that she was not as unchastened as her tone would have Hawk believe. 'You surprise me!'

'Do I?' Hawk rose languidly to his feet to move lightly around the desk, a hard smile of satisfaction curving his lips as Jane instinctively took two steps back. 'I think that once again you are choosing to deceive yourself, Jane,' he drawled mockingly.

Was she? Jane wondered, slightly breathlessly.

Perhaps so. But she had found herself completely over-whelmed a short time ago, when the carriage had entered through imposing iron gates that had preceded a fifteen-minute carriage ride to where Mulberry Hall itself reposed. Deer and cattle had grazed undisturbed amongst rolling parkland as the carriage had proceeded on its leisurely way along a driveway edged with hundreds of yew trees, before reaching a wide courtyard that had revealed Mulberry Hall bathed in late-after-noon sunshine.

Jane had gazed up as if hypnotised at the Hall's mag-nificence. As the Duke had helped her alight from the coach. The house was built of mellow sandstone, with seemingly a hundred windows on its frontage, and a wide balcony over huge oak doors.

One of those doors had opened wide the moment the Duke had put one of his highly polished boots upon the first stone step leading up to the entrance, an elderly butler greeting his employer with solicitous warmth as he enquired as to the comfort of his journey. Jane had continued to gaze wide-eyed at her surround-ings, sure that the whole of Markham Park would have nestled snugly into the cavernous entry hall of Mulberry Hall!

The bedroom she had been allocated had been yet another pleasant surprise after the almost cupboard-like space she had occupied at Markham Park for the last twelve years, with its highly polished floor, sunnily bright yellow walls, a four-poster bed draped with the same gold-coloured damask that adorned the two windows which, she discovered, looked out over the rolling parkland.

Jane had been happily enchanted with her new surroundings when she had returned downstairs and a footman had shown her into the drawing room where the Duke and his sister were about to take tea.

Only to have the Duke spoil it all by making the announcement to his sister that, as Lady Hammond had been indisposed since their sojourn in London— whoever Lady Hammond was—Jane was now here to act as her new companion. A companion that the Lady Arabella, once the Duke had excused himself and left the two women alone, had immediately informed Jane she had absolutely no need of!

It had been obvious from the first that Lady Arabella and the Duke of Stourbridge were closely related. That lady was several inches taller than Jane, and the aristocratic features that were so hard and unyielding on the Duke were softened to a striking beauty in the much younger Arabella. Her eyes were a dark brown, and she had hair of gold shot through with streaks of deeper honey, where the Duke's was dark with those golden streaks.

A single minute alone in Lady Arabella's company had shown Jane that that young lady had also inherited her brother's arrogantly imperious manner!

Jane's mouth tightened as she recalled the awkwardness of their conversation. She addressed the Duke once more. 'I am very sorry if you take offence at my tone, Your Grace—'

'Oh, I do, Jane. I do,' he assured her softly. 'And must I point out—yet again—that we are not in the company of others…?'

He might point out that fact as often as the occasion arose, but since arriving at the Duke's ancestral home, and seeing the deference with which his household staff treated him, Jane had become even more aware of the differences in their social stations.

In a very different way she was also aware of being alone with him now, here in the privacy of his study… Even more so since he had risen to his feet and moved to stand in front of the huge mahogany desk.

Because once he had stood up it had become obvious that the Duke had not expected to be interrupted. For he had removed the royal blue coat and waistcoat that Jane had so admired earlier, and loosened his neckcloth. Following so closely on that incident in the carriage, Jane found his less than impeccable appearance more than a little disturbing!

Hawk narrowed his gaze as he saw the flush that suddenly brightened Jane's cheeks. 'Is something troubling you, Jane…?'

'Something other than your not informing me that I was to be your sister's companion?' Her tone was waspish.

Deliberately so, Hawk surmised knowingly, allowing a mocking smile to curve his lips as he crossed his arms over his chest. He had the satisfaction of seeing Jane quickly avert her gaze. 'As I recall, Jane, our earlier conversation concerning what was to be your place here at Mulberry Hall was…interrupted…'

He was rewarded by a deepening of that blush. 'That is all very well, Your Grace,' Jane dismissed briskly. 'But my purported role here is obviously as much of a surprise to Lady Arabella as it has been to me!'

Hawk's smile immediately faded. 'My sister has said something to upset you?'

Jane looked up frowningly as she heard the sharpness that had entered his tone, inwardly relieved that she could now see only the Duke of Stourbridge in the angular handsomeness of his face, rather than the more disturbing Hawk St Claire.

But as the Duke, she had come to realise, he expected his simplest instruction to be carried out without question…

Jane chose her next words carefully. 'Lady Arabella is quite rightly displeased at having a person she is totally unacquainted with suddenly thrust upon her in this high-handed way—'

'How displeased?'

Jane blinked at what she knew—from the cold glitter that had entered his eyes and the sudden hardness to the set of his jaw—to be the Duke's deceptively mild tone. Both of which boded ill for someone. In this case Lady Arabella.

'Come, Jane,' he encouraged in that softly disconcerting tone. 'In what way exactly has my sister expressed her displeasure to you?'

Now that she was actually here in the Duke's presence—in his disturbing presence!—Jane found herself loath to pursue the subject. In truth, she dearly wished that she had waited until her own temper had cooled before even broaching this subject with him.

But it was too late for such caution now. The Duke was waiting, compelling her to answer, those dark brows raised in deceptively lazy expectation.

Her chin rose challengingly. 'I do not believe I said that Lady Arabella had given voice to her displeasure. It is merely that I believe—although Lady Arabella did not actually say so—that your sister sees me more in the role of—well, of spy for you, Your Grace,' she finished lamely.

Hawk drew himself up to his full considerable height and looked down his nose at her. 'A spy, Jane?' he repeated hardly. 'And why would my sister suppose that I would want to set a spy on her? Unless—' He broke off, his expression darkening as he glanced towards the open door. 'Damn it, what has that girl been up to now?'

'Your Grace…?'

Hawk glared, his hands clenching into fists at his sides before he turned sharply on his heel to move and stare sightlessly out of the window. 'You will leave me now, Jane. Return to the drawing room and tell Lady Arabella that I wish to see her. Now. Immediately. Did you hear me, Jane?' He turned to scowl at her darkly when he heard no movement to show she was about to do his bidding.

'I— For what purpose, Your Grace?'

Hawk became very still as he looked at the pointed angle of Jane's chin, at the stubborn set of her mouth and the challenging sparkle that now lit those deep green eyes as she steadily met his gaze.

He had doubted the wisdom of his visit to Norfolk even before his arrival there. The ill-bred behaviour of his hostess and her obvious matchmaking attempts between himself and her daughter had only confirmed those doubts, so hastening his desire to leave Markham Park at the earliest opportunity.

In the normal course of events that would have been the end of the matter, enabling Hawk to put the whole unpleasant experience behind him. Unfortunately the main irritation of his stay—and the main amusement, he inwardly admitted—was now standing before him!

With open challenge in her sparkling green gaze…

It really was a novel experience for him, Hawk acknowledged ruefully. He had become even more aware since his return to Mulberry Hall, where even his slightest need seemed to be fulfilled before he had expressed it, of how unusual it was for anyone to oppose him in the way Jane constantly did.

As a novel experience it had caused him amusement on several occasions, but it was surely not to be tolerated when it came to his dealings with his young sister!

He arched dark, arrogant brows. 'The purpose of my summons is none of your concern, Jane.'

'It is if it is something I have said that has instigated that summons!' Jane refuted impatiently. 'I cannot in all conscience—' she gave a firm shake of her head '—give Lady Arabella such an instruction if, when she arrives, you intend to inflict some sort of unjustified rebuke or cruelty upon her—' She broke off abruptly, alarmed by the way in which the Duke's face had darkened ominously.

Her breath actually halted in her throat as he strode back to the dark and rested his clenched fists on its top, to lean so far forward that his face was now only inches from her own, his eyes glittering dangerously, nostrils flared, his mouth thinned to an uncompromising line.

'I have no idea, Jane—no idea at all,' he repeated in an icily soft voice, 'what I could possibly have done in our so far brief acquaintance to give you the belief, even the idea, that I might—what was it you called it exactly?—Ah, yes, that I might intend inflicting "unjustified rebuke or cruelty" upon my sister. They were your exact words, were they not—'

'Stop it, Your Grace!' Jane cried her agitation as he once again spoke to her in that deceptively mild tone.

Because there was nothing in the least mild about the Duke's emotions at that moment. In fact, he appeared so full of suppressed fury that it might cause him to explode at any moment!

'If you wish to shout at me, Your Grace, then I would much rather you did so and got it over with. But do not, for goodness' sake, play with me like a cat tormenting a mouse—' She broke off, frowning, as the Duke gave a hard bark of laughter. 'Did I say something to amuse you, Your Grace?' she prompted, slightly indignantly.

Hawk gave an incredulous shake of his head. Anyone less like a mouse than Jane Smith he could not imagine!

This young woman challenged him, reviled him, defied him—and yet still something stopped him from telling her to go to the devil, to absent herself from his company and never show her face to him ever again.

The proudness of her carriage, perhaps? The sharpness of her spirit? The creamy turn of her cheek? The unfathomable depths of those enticing green eyes? Or maybe the fullness of her lips? Those lips that could be curved with amusement one moment and then turned down with such disapproval the next…

As they had been twisted with disapproval constantly since entering Mulberry Park an hour ago!

'Leave me, Jane,' Hawk instructed wearily, as he straightened before resuming his seat behind the desk. 'Just go now—before I cease to be amused by anything about you!'

Jane hesitated, continuing to look at him uncertainly even though she knew herself to be well and truly dismissed.

She had meant to soothe Lady Arabella's obviously ruffled feathers by talking to the Duke about the wisdom of his announcement, but instead she seemed only to have succeeded in annoying the Duke even further.

'Still here, Jane?' His tone was bitingly dismissive as he looked up at her coldly.

Jane caught her bottom lip between her teeth and turned slowly to walk to the door, dearly wishing there was something she could do or say that might somehow soften a situation that she was aware was partly of her own making—although she was not naïve enough to believe that the self-possessed Lady Arabella would have kept her opinions on the subject of Jane's presence in the house to herself the next time she saw her brother!

Nevertheless, Jane was conscious of the fact that she

had been the first to broach the subject, so causing the Duke to be more angry with his sister than he might otherwise have been.

'Your Grace…?' She hesitated in the doorway, looking back at him. His head was bent, his hands at his temples, fingers threaded through the dark thickness of his hair.

He gave a weary sigh as he slowly looked up at her. 'Yes, Jane?'

Her throat moved convulsively as she swallowed. 'Perhaps—perhaps if you were to assure Lady Arabella that I will not be staying long…?'

His mouth firmed. 'But we have no idea *how* long you will be staying, do we, Jane? I have your promise concerning your future travel arrangements, remember?'

Yes, the Duke had her promise, Jane acknowledged with a slow nod of her head, before leaving the room to close the door behind her much more quietly than she had opened it.

But the promise she had made him only applied in regard to her attempting to travel to *London*…

'Please sit down, Arabella,' Hawk invited, with an abrupt gesture towards the chair in front of his desk as his sister swept into the room some ten minutes later.

Long enough, Hawk guessed, to show him in what contempt she held his summons. An opinion supported by the fact that, instead of sitting in the chair he had indicated, his sister chose to make herself comfortable in one of the armchairs beside the empty fireplace.

What had he ever done, Hawk wondered impatiently

as he stood up to join her, to deserve two such stubborn women in his life at the same time? One openly rebellious, the other less obviously so but nevertheless just as determined to go her own way?

Arabella regarded him with cool brown eyes as he sat in the chair opposite hers. 'I cannot help but question your reasons for bringing Miss Smith here, Hawk.'

He had been expecting his sister's attack—if not actually prepared for the subject of it!—having already taken warning at the rebellion darkening the beauty of Arabella's eyes.

Arabella had grown so quickly from child to young woman, it seemed now to Hawk as he looked at her, that for once he was not quite sure how to proceed with the interview. He was certainly in no mood for cajolery, but to openly forbid a continuation of what he saw as Arabella's wilfulness might only result in her doing something totally reckless.

He quirked dark brows as he decided to ignore—for the moment—the slight she had cast upon Jane's character. And his own... 'You do not like Miss Smith?'

Arabella met his gaze unblinkingly. 'I did not say that. I merely wondered as to the propriety—'

'I advise you not to proceed any further along this line of conversation, Arabella!' Hawk cut in with harsh warning. 'Suffice to say that Jane's presence here is one of complete innocence.'

Arabella's eyes—those brown eyes that could look at a man and melt his very soul—yes, even those of her three elder brothers!—met his own with hardened scorn.

'I am supposed to believe that Miss Smith is here for my amusement only?'

His mouth tightened. 'Those are the facts, yes!'

'They are…?'

The turn this conversation had taken was highly insulting to Jane—as well as echoing Jane's own concerns of earlier—and yet even so a part of Hawk could not help but appreciate, even secretly admire, his young sister's refusal to be cowed by him.

Although that admiration in no way deflected Hawk's own determination not to be dictated to by a girl of only eight and ten. 'I did not ask you here to talk about Jane Smith, Arabella,' he said quietly.

'I very much doubt that you *asked* at all!' Arabella's tone was sharply resentful. 'Despite Miss Smith's attempt to make it seem as if you did,' she added tauntingly.

Hawk shook his head. 'We will return to the subject of Jane later. For the moment I wish only to talk about you, Arabella. You have been on your own since your return to Mulberry Hall almost two weeks ago. I wonder how you have managed to fill your time during those two weeks?'

'You forget that Lucian remained for several days after accompanying us here,' Arabella dismissed. 'Talking of Lucian—'

'Which we were not,' Hawk cut in hardly.

'Then perhaps we should have been,' his sister came back tartly. 'Have you seen or spoken to Lucian recently…?'

Hawk frowned. 'Not for several weeks, no. Why?'

Arabella sighed. 'He seems—changed. Hardened. Even cynical.'

'War does that to people, Arabella,' Hawk dismissed impatiently. 'I am sure that is only a temporary—aberration. We were talking of you, Arabella…' he reminded her firmly.

Arabella met his gaze coolly for several long seconds before turning away with a dismissive shrug. 'I have been forced to fall back upon reading and embroidery for my amusement.'

He nodded. 'And I understand from Jenkins that you have also been out riding on the estate every day, have you not? Without your groom?'

'What of it?' Arabella challenged sharply.

She loved and admired all her older brothers. Loved Sebastian perhaps the most, as he was nearest to her in age. Lucian, more taciturn and private now following his years in the army, had always been her steadfast protector—the one who had always been there to pick her up if she should fall. But Hawk—so tall and broad-shouldered, always so busy about the St Claire estates and so toplofty when it came to his rare and infrequent appearances in Society—was the brother whose approval Arabella had always sought, the brother she most wanted to please.

And she knew that she had not pleased him during the weeks of her first Season…

But Hawk was the Duke of Stourbridge, a man looked up to and respected wherever he went, and Arabella was well aware that it was because of who her brother was, because of his title, that she had received at least half the marriage proposals that had been forthcoming during those weeks in London. The other suitors perhaps had genuinely believed themselves to be in love with her, but Arabella, determined to marry a man she admired and loved as much as her brothers, had felt unable to return the feelings of any of those men.

For the first time in her young life Arabella knew she had genuinely displeased her eldest brother. It was something that she had felt, still felt, dearly. But she had hoped to talk to Hawk once he returned to Mulberry Hall—to perhaps explain the reason for her refusals. And now, instead of being alone at Mulberry Hall with her eldest brother, Arabella found him accompanied by a single woman of quite breathtaking beauty!

Miss Jane Smith.

What was she, Arabella, supposed to make of such a strange occurrence? What was she supposed to make of Miss Jane Smith?

To Arabella's way of thinking, Hawk had only added insult to injury by announcing that he had brought the other woman here to act as her companion!

Her brother raised a languid hand. 'I am merely attempting to make conversation with you, Arabella—' He broke off to look at her frowningly as she gave a hard laugh. 'Have I said something to amuse you…?'

The hard glitter in his eyes told Arabella that he, at least, was not in the least amused!

She stood up impatiently. 'I am sure that you recog-

nise scorn when you hear it, Hawk. We are both aware
that you never merely "make conversation"!' She began
to pace the hearth. 'Whatever it is you wish to say to me,
Hawk, please say it and stop prevaricating in this
tortuous way!'

Hawk watched her from behind guarded lids, appreciating how much like their mother she looked at that
moment, with the colour flaring in her cheeks and that
sparkle in her eyes. The pale lemon-yellow gown she
wore—not that garish yellow so unsuitable for Jane!—
with its touches of cream lace, suited Arabella's golden
colouring perfectly, its becoming style proof once again,
if he should need it, that Arabella was no longer a little
girl to be cossetted and spoilt.

'Very well, Arabella,' he drawled hardly. 'What I
really want to know is did you arrange to meet anyone
while you were out?'

'Arrange to meet anyone?' She frowned her puzzlement. 'What—? Ah.' A knowing smile curved her lips.
'What you are really asking is if I happened to meet any
single gentlemen whilst out alone and unchaperoned?'

Hawk pursed his lips consideringly. 'It is a possibility
that has occurred to me.'

'Hawk, if you suspect me of having taken a lover then
why do you not just say so?'

He could hear the slight trembling in his sister's voice
even as she issued the challenge, realising as he did so
that he had pushed Arabella almost to the point of tears.
He did not have to look far for the perpetrator of this
new sensitivity within him to a woman's emotions—

Jane Smith had stormed his male defences in just this way too. More than once.

He sighed. 'I am not making any such accusation, Arabella—'

'Are you not?'

Hawk's mouth firmed at her scornful tone. Damn it, he was the Duke of Stourbridge, with all the power and influence that went along with that title, and as such he would not suffer this lack of respect a moment longer!

'No, Arabella, I am not,' he bit out forcefully, standing up to look down at her censoriously. 'However, I do forbid you to go out riding on your own again.'

'You *forbid* me, Hawk?' she echoed incredulously.

'I forbid you,' he repeated tersely. 'In future, if you wish to go out riding without the protection of a groom, perhaps Miss Smith might accompany you—'

'To the devil with your Miss Smith!' Arabella stamped her slipper-clad foot in temper.

'She is not *my* Miss Smith, Arabella,' Hawk reproved frostily.

'Well, she is certainly not mine—nor ever will be!'

Hawk drew in a deeply controlling breath before speaking again. 'It is my wish that you will be kind to Miss Smith, Arabella—'

'You may wish all you like, Hawk—but unfortunately wishes are not always granted, are they?'

Hawk frowned at the acerbic comment. His mouth tightened. 'I advise you to put your own feelings aside in this matter, Arabella, and do all that you can to ensure Miss Smith is made to feel a welcome guest during her stay here with us.'

Arabella raised mocking brows. 'I thought you said she was to be an employee…?'

Hawk eyed her coldly. 'She is to be your companion, yes. But she is first and formost a guest of the Duke of Stourbridge!'

His sister looked as if she might have liked to say more on that subject—and had thought better of it when she saw the warning in his icily glittering gaze. 'Very well, Hawk.' She gave a cool inclination of her head. 'Oh, I almost forgot…' She paused in the doorway, much as Jane had done such a short time ago.

'Yes?' As then, Hawk did not think he was going to like what Arabella was about to say to him!

Arabella's smile was almost triumphant. 'I have arranged a small dinner party for three days hence, to be followed by dancing in the small ballroom.'

The 'small' ballroom would hold thirty people comfortably, at least…

Hawk grimaced. 'How small is this dinner party to be, Arabella?'

Arabella's smile widened. 'About twenty-five people, I believe—no, twenty-seven now that you and Miss Smith have arrived.' She turned to leave and then suddenly paused once again. 'Oh…and Lady Pamela Croft sent word this morning that her brother has arrived for a visit. So that will make us twenty-eight.'

Hawk had stiffened at the mention of their nearest

neighbour's brother. 'Can you possibly be referring to the Earl of Whitney?'

'I believe Lady Pamela has only the one brother.' Arabella nodded with a questioning raise of her brows.

Hawk knew that she had. And he also remembered that the last time he and the Earl of Whitney had had occasion to meet had been shortly after Hawk had usurped the other man's place in the Countess of More-field's bedchamber! A fact both men, never the easiest of acquaintances, were both very much aware of.

Was Arabella, like Sebastian, and possibly Lucian too, also aware of it...? Her almost triumphant air seemed to imply that it was a distinct possibility!

'There is just one more thing, Hawk—'

'For God's sake, Arabella,' he cut in icily, 'either leave or stay. But most certainly cease dithering about in the doorway in that unbecoming manner!'

'I take it you are not interested, then, in the fact that while we were talking I chanced to see Miss Smith passing by the library window? Ah, perhaps you *are* interested, after all?' his sister mused tauntingly as Hawk stood up abruptly to turn and look searchingly out of the window. 'Perhaps, after all, it is I who should act as chaperon to Miss Smith...?'

Hawk shoulders stiffened as he exerted every effort of his considerable will over his own temper in order to prevent himself from responding to Arabella's deliber-ately provocative taunt.

Knowing that he was responsible for leaving himself open to such comments in having brought Jane here at all in no way lessened the impatient anger he was feeling.

Why had Jane left the house?

Where could she have been going?

As far as he was aware, Jane was completely unfamiliar with her surroundings—so why would she have gone outside at all so soon after her arrival?

Chapter Seven

J ane arched mocking brows as she stared down the length of the dining table at her host. 'Do I take it that your interview with Lady Arabella did not go well this afternoon, Your Grace?' There had been no opportunity for Jane to speak to him since his conversation with his sister, although she had seen him in conversation with the butler earlier, when she'd returned from her walk outside.

Still, her observation concerning his sister was a fairly accurate one to have made, considering the two of them were seated alone at the table in what Jenkins had informed Jane was 'the family dining room'. Lady Arabella, and the Duke's aunt, Lady Hammond, had both sent down their apologies.

That Jane and the Duke were seated at either end of a table that could have seated twelve only added to the feeling of distance that had been stretching further and further between the two of them since their arrival at Mulberry Hall earlier today.

The Duke looked as immaculate as ever tonight, in black evening clothes and snowy white linen, but the impeccable formality of his dress only made Jane more aware of the inadequacy of the muslin gown she had worn on the day she'd left Markham Park, which was all she had to change into for dinner.

'My conversation with Arabella, as you so rightly guess, Jane, did not go well,' the Duke confirmed impatiently. 'Were you ever such a contrary miss, Jane?' he added with languid weariness.

Jane was very aware, even if the Duke was not, of the presence of the stiffly unreadable demeanour of Jenkins, as he quietly attended them by removing their empty fish plates from the table. She was also aware that this was definitely not one of those occasions when they were 'not in the presence of others'—which meant that the Duke was being far too familiar with a woman he had supposedly engaged as companion to his young sister. Especially as that sister had not even had the good manners to join them!

'Such behaviour would have been seen as self-indulgence, Your Grace,' she answered him, somewhat distantly.

'I suppose that it would,' Hawk acknowledged ruefully, and he realised how ridiculous had been his question after the way in which Jane had been treated by her guardians. At the same time he could see, from Jane's awkward glance in Jenkins' direction, that she was not happy conducting this conversation in front of his butler.

'That will be all, thank you, Jenkins.' He dismissed

the elderly man once the roast beef and vegetables had been served to them. 'I will ring for you when we are in need of you again.'

If the butler saw anything unusual about this turn of events he did not show it by so much as a flicker of an eyebrow as he bowed formally before leaving the room.

Hawk sighed. 'The unfortunate situation developing between Arabella and myself has shown me how little experience I have in dealing with the capriciousness of young ladies, Jane.'

'You surprise me, Your Grace.'

Hawk could not fail to notice the mocking glint in her eyes. 'Young ladies that are related to me, Jane!'

'Of course, Your Grace.' She nodded coolly. 'But if that truly is the case, perhaps the answer might be to forget that Lady Arabella is related to you…?'

Hawk had far from forgotten Jane's disappearance outside earlier this evening. Or the fact that she had returned to the house while he was in the process of questioning Jenkins as to whether or not he knew of her whereabouts—which he had not. No, Hawk certainly had not forgotten. He was simply awaiting the appropriate moment in which to introduce the subject…

He shook his head now. 'I am not sure that I understand you, Jane. Arabella may not like me very much at this moment, but there is no doubting the fact that she is my sister!'

'Assuredly not, Your Grace,' Jane answered dryly.

He raised dark brows. 'Now, why do I sense some sort of rebuke in that remark, Jane…?'

'I have no idea, Your Grace,' she came back innocently. 'But from what I have observed of Lady Arabella I believe that at the age of eighteen she wishes to be treated as an adult rather than as a child. As a child in need of a companion, for instance…'

Hawk's mouth tightened at the rebuke. 'Arabella *is* still a child, Jane, and at the moment she is behaving like a spoilt, wilful one.'

'Was it a child who received several marriage proposals only weeks ago? Was it for a child that you would have approved of her accepting one of those marriage proposals?'

'You insult me if you think I would have been happy for her to accept a proposal of marriage just for the sake of it, Jane,' Hawk defended coldly.

'The nature of any marriage proposal and the suitability of the man involved are both irrelevant to this conversation, Your Grace,' Jane reasoned softly. 'What is pertinant is that you cannot expect Lady Arabella to receive proposals of marriage one day and be treated like a child again the next. Moreover, a child who is to be told what she may or may not do, and when she may do it.'

Hawk drew in a sharp breath as he bit back his icy retort. A part of him knew that he had invited Jane's criticism by confiding in her in this way, and another part of him was surprised that he had done so…

In the years since he had assumed his role as head of the St Claire family, Hawk had expected his siblings to respect his wishes. That he did not appear to have achieved this as well as he might have wanted had been brought home to him not once but twice in recent weeks. First in Sebastian's absolute refusal to contemplate the idea of any marriage—let alone one suggested by Hawk—and yet again today by Arabella's stubbornness when it came to acceding to any of his demands.

He did not, however, appreciate having Jane, of all people, point out these failings to him! He looked down his nose at her. 'I refuse to believe I have ever been guilty of such arrogance with any of my siblings, Jane.'

'Really?' She gave an acknowledging inclination of her head. 'Then I must assume it is only where "nuisances who disrupt your peaceful existence" are concerned…?'

Hawk picked up his glass of claret and took a much-needed drink, his gaze narrowing as he looked down the length of the highly polished table at the woman who had disrupted his peaceful existence from the moment they had first met.

Jane was looking particularly lovely this evening. Her gleaming red hair was arranged in an abundance of ringlets upon her crown, with several enticing tendrils brushing her nape and brow, her creamy throat was once again bare of any adornment—possibly because Jane had no jewellery with which to adorn it?—and the simple cut of her gown succeeding only in emphasising the curvaceous perfection of her body.

A warmly seductive body that Hawk could not deny he was totally aware of. 'I believe you malign me in saying I have ever told you what you may do, Jane.' His voice was harsh.

Her mouth thinned. 'Only what I may not do, sir!'

'You are referring, I presume, to the fact that I refused to allow you to run off to London in a reckless manner?'

'I am referring, Your Grace, to the fact that at two and twenty I am perfectly old enough to make my own decisions!' Her eyes glittered warningly.

It was a warning Hawk had no intention of heeding. 'Even if those decisions are wrong?'

'Even then!'

He eyed her consideringly. 'Tell me, Jane, did you accompany the Sulbys when they came to London for the Season?'

'I did…yes,' she answered, almost warily.

'And did you meet someone whilst you were there? A young man, perhaps?' He frowned. 'Maybe that is why you are so set on returning there? In order that you might seek him out…?'

Jane gave him a pitying look. 'I met no one whilst in London, Your Grace. My only excursions during that time were to the shops, and then simply so that I might carry Olivia's purchases for her!'

Once again Hawk was reminded that Jane had been more servant than ward in the Sulby household. Her presence at the Sulbys' dining table two nights ago had been the exception rather than the rule.

He sipped his wine. 'Where did you go earlier this evening, Jane, when you decided to go outside?'

Jane stiffened. 'I trust I am at liberty to walk in the grounds, at least, Your Grace?'

She was being overly defensive, Jane knew. Probably because she had *not* simply gone for a walk in the grounds of Mulberry Hall earlier, but had in fact made her way deliberately to the stables, with the intention of enquiring of one of the grooms exactly how far it was— and how long it would take—to get to her true destination of Somerset!

Which she had done—and in such a way, Jane hoped, that she had not aroused the groom's suspicions as to the true purpose of her enquiries.

Although that might not be the case if the Duke of Stourbridge were to question the other man!

'Did I say otherwise?' the Duke prompted softly now.

'You implied it!' she snapped agitatedly.

Hawk looked at her wordlessly for several long seconds as the anger inside him grew. This situation, with both a wilfully defiant Arabella and a stubbornly determined Jane, was not only trying his impatience in the extreme, it was becoming unendurable!

'Do you find my concern for you so unacceptable, then, Jane?' The icy softness of his tone was in no way indicative of his inner frustration at this situation.

'Yes!'

Hawk drew in a sharp breath before rising to his feet. 'Then I must give you leave to put yourself in the path of danger at any time you so choose! Just so long as you accept that I will no longer be in a position to save you from your own reckless folly!' He picked up the decanter of brandy and a glass from the dresser before turning sharply on his heel to stride forcefully towards the door, very much aware that if he did not leave now he would resort to either kissing her or spanking her!

'Hawk…?'

He would not—could not—allow himself to be deterred from his resolve, his immediate need to get as far away from Jane as was possible. Neither by the uncertainty to be heard in her tone nor the fact that she had at last once again called him by his first name. He was very aware that if he did not leave this room now—right now!—he was definitely going to do something Jane would find even more unacceptable than the arrogance she complained of so bitterly.

He paused only long enough in the doorway to turn and inform her, 'I have forgotten to tell you of the dinner party my sister has arranged for three evenings hence, Jane.' His mouth twisted derisively as he added, 'The same sister with whom, according to you, I have the seemingly annoying habit of saying what she may do and when she may do it!'

Jane swallowed convulsively, never having seen the Duke in quite such a towering rage as this, and knowing, although Arabella had obviously caused him some irritation earlier, that it was *she* who had provoked this chilling anger.

She moistened dry lips. 'I—'

'I will inform that same sister,' the Duke continued icily, 'that you are in need of a new gown for the evening. And I implore you, Jane, do not say another word to contradict me!' The fierceness of his warning came through gritted teeth.

'But—'

'Will you not, just for once in our acquaintance,

accept that I am doing this for your comfort rather than my own?' His mouth had thinned ominously.

Her chin rose determinedly. 'That is the argument of all dictators, I believe.'

Hawk's gaze flared, and then glittered coldly. 'One day, Jane—one day you will go too far!' he finally managed to grind out. 'And I give you fair warning that on that day you will discover exactly what I am capable of!'

He turned and left the room before he could no longer control the urge he had to commence teaching Jane that lesson forthwith.

Leaving Jane with the uncomfortable knowledge that her plans to make her way to Somerset at the first opportunity, would probably arrive rather sooner than the Duke could ever have imagined...

'Is it the horses you are so fond of visiting, Jane, or do you have some other reason for haunting my stables in this way...?'

Jane gave a guilty start at the sound of the Duke's voice behind her, turning so sharply to face him that her slippered foot lost its purchase on the thick layer of straw that covered the floor, causing her to lose her balance completely.

She barely had time to register how handsome the Duke looked in his work clothes—a tight-fitting brown jacket and thigh-hugging breeches above highly polished brown boots—before the world tilted on its axis and she toppled over backwards.

Luckily the stall she was in had been cleaned earlier

that morning and laid with fresh straw, and this sweet-smelling mattress cushioned Jane's fall. She lay sprawled on her back, slightly winded, as she stared up at the dumbfounded Duke of Stourbridge.

He did not stay dumb for long, however. 'Are you making me an invitation, Jane? Or is it that you suddenly felt a need to lie down?' He moved farther into the confines of the stall to look down at her, heavy lids lowered to shield the expression in his eyes.

So giving Jane no idea whether the Duke was just being his normally mocking self, or if he actually meant her to take his first question seriously...

Considering the impatient manner in which he had deserted the dinner table the previous evening, Jane decided that he was being his normal mocking self!

Her own eyes glittered with impatience as she sat up. 'I would not have lost my balance at all if you had not crept up behind me in that sly fashion!' she said waspishly.

'Please do not get up, Jane,' Hawk drawled derisively as she began to do so. 'After the dampness of the dune which we once shared, the stables are a much cosier place for us to converse,' he assured her dryly, before dropping down onto the clean straw at her side.

Hawk grimaced inwardly, knowing that if any of his grooms had seen him do so they would probably seriously question the Duke of Stourbridge's state of mind. And quite rightly so!

'Converse, Your Grace?' Jane echoed guardedly, as she made a show of picking stalks of straw from the sleeve of her gown.

Several more tufts had attached themselves endearingly in the brightness of her hair, but Hawk decided that now was perhaps not the right time to point them out to her. Nor, indeed, to attempt to remove them himself...

He was aware that, apart from the slight movement and snorting of a horse in one of the other stalls, the stables were very private and quiet at this time of day, his grooms having moved on to other chores about the estate after completing the exercising of the horses and the cleaning of the stalls earlier this morning.

Meaning that he and Jane were completely alone here, with little chance of interruption.

He felt a reawakening of the same desire to take Jane in his arms and kiss her that he had known the previous evening. A desire Hawk had resisted yesterday evening by leaving her so abruptly but which he was not sure he would be able to a second time...!

Perhaps, in the circumstances, it had been unwise on his part to suggest they remain here.

He would not have sought her out at all had Jenkins not informed him that, 'Miss Smith left the house half an hour since and walked in the direction of the stables.' It transpired from his groom that she had already done so yesterday, instantly arousing Hawk's curiosity as to why it was she had felt the need to visit his stables twice in as many days.

Unfortunately, as he looked now at a slightly dishevelled Jane, her face flushed, the soft pout of her lips slightly parted, Hawk knew that it was no longer just his curiosity that was aroused.

'Your Grace…?'

He frowned down at her darkly. 'Jane…?'

She looked at him quizzically. 'You said you wished to talk to me.'

'Did I?' Hawk blinked, but the movement did absolutely nothing to dispel the tempting vision of Jane's moistly parted lips.

Jane felt a frisson of alarm course through her as she saw the direction of the Duke's gaze, quickly followed by a wave of heated awareness as that gaze moved down to the creamy swell of her breasts above her simply styled muslin gown.

She could hear him breathing now, feel the softness of that breath move over her skin as he suddenly seemed much nearer. Had he moved? She had not been aware that he had, and yet he was definitely much closer than he had been a moment ago.

Jane stared up at him in mesmerised fascination, held in thrall by the deepening gold of his eyes as he moved even closer, her lids dropping, lips parting, as he raised one of his hands to cup her cheek. The soft pad of his thumb caressed those parted lips with an eroticism that made her gasp as she raised her lids to look up at him with darkened green eyes.

He stared long and hard into those emerald depths before he groaned achingly, 'Dear God, Jane…!' His mouth claimed hers, his arms moving about her as he drew her close against the hard strength of his body.

His gloriously male body that only days ago Jane so clearly remembered viewing in all its almost naked glory.

Inexperienced as she was, she had still been able to appreciate the broadness of his shoulders and chest, the stomach muscles clearly defined, his hips lean and powerful…!

And those firm lips—lips that could so often be thinned in disapproval or quirked in mocking humour—now moved against hers searchingly, devouring, causing Jane's pulse to leap wildly and heat to course wantonly throughout her whole body as she arched closer against him in urgent need.

He should never have been tempted into kissing her, Hawk admonished himself impatiently, even as he began to press Jane back onto the warm cushion of straw. But the warmth of her body, her own enticing perfume, both acted as a heady temptation it was impossible for him to resist.

He lay half across her as he deepened the kiss, knowing by the way Jane's body arched against his, by the fact of her hands now beneath his jacket as she restlessly caressed the length of his back through the thin material of his shirt, that Jane was as aroused as he was—even if her inexperience gave her no idea how to deal with that arousal.

Neither did Hawk know quite where this was taking them. He was aware only of the need he had to touch her, to taste her. His lips left hers to travel the length of the arched column of her throat, down to the creamy swell of her breasts, his fingers dealing deftly, quickly, with the buttons of her gown as he lowered the material to reveal pouting breasts covered only by the thin material of her chemise.

His fascinated gaze fastened on the rosy hardness of her nipples, clearly visible through that material, and lightly caressing fingers moved across those aroused tips, causing Jane to gasp before arching her back in breathless supplication.

It was too much. Jane was too much temptation for Hawk to be able to deny her. His glittering gaze briefly held hers before he lowered his head to draw one of those rosy tips into the heated cavern of his mouth, his tongue rasping across the already aroused nipple as he suckled her deeper into his moist warmth—harder, fiercer. He heard her groans of pleasure and felt her fingers curl convulsively into the hardness of his back, nails scraping as she held him tightly against her.

Hawk's hand moved to cup her other breast, and he felt it swell beneath his touch, her nipple a tight bud as he ran the pad of his thumb across it in the same rhythm with which he suckled its twin.

His thighs were rigid with arousal, with the need to claim her fully, to slide into the heat that awaited him inside her before giving them both the release they craved.

He should stop now—should pull away from her before that need overwhelmed them both. But he was powerless to resist as he felt Jane's hands unfastening the buttons of his waistcoat and shirt to push the material aside. She sought to touch his naked flesh, her hands echoing his own caress, and his groan was one of aching defeat as her tiny fingers touched his own hardened nubs.

No woman had ever touched Hawk so innocently, so erotically before. Jane's lack of experience in physical intimacy gave her no boundaries, no set of rules to follow, and her fingers touched, caressed, her nails gently raking his hardness, causing his thighs to pulse wildly as he grew more swollen still, his arousal almost painful.

He wanted her. Now. Here amongst the sweet-smelling straw. He was filled with such an urgent need for posession, that his senses were fully awakened by the pleasure-ache of her caresses, the sweet, drugging sensation of her womanly perfume.

Jane had known herself lost to reason, to caution, at Hawk's first touch, and she was totally unable to deny him now, as she felt his hand move from her breast to push the material of her gown up to her waist. He caressed the length of her leg from her knee to the aching heat that had pooled between her thighs. Her hips arched invitingly against him as he placed that hand against her most intimate place, cupping, pressing, those caressing fingers igniting a pleasure that Jane could never have imagined even in the nightly dreams she had of this man.

She gasped, falling back weakly against the straw, as Hawk's lips, mouth and tongue continued to minister to her aching breast and his fingers began to stroke against her. Her head moved restlessly from side to side as she felt the pressure building inside her, her legs parting in heady expectation as the heat between her thighs became hot and urgent.

'I told him that, no, I hadn't seen the Duke out and about at all this morning. How about you, Tom? Have you seen him anywhere on the estate?'

Reality, like the icy shock of a bucket of cold water,

penetrated Hawk's desire-befuddled brain the moment he heard the voice of his head groom talking of 'the Duke'. He raised his head sharply. The look of dazed shock on Jane's face as she stared up at him told him that she was also aware they were no longer alone.

Hawk's gaze darkened as he stared down at her—as he acknowledged the rumpled dishevelment of her gown, its skirt pushed up almost to her thighs, its bodice unbuttoned. Her chemise was clinging damply to her breasts, their nipples still hard and aroused from the ministrations of his lips, tongue and hands.

He gave a low groan of self-disgust as he fell back onto the straw beside her to stare up at the wooden ceiling above.

Dear God! Seconds ago, before this timely interruption, he knew his intention had been to make love to Jane fully. To take her here in the stables as if she were some willing serving wench, enjoying a tumble with her wealthy patron. As if he were some untried youth unable to keep his arousal in his breeches.

Forget his employees questioning his state of mind— Hawk now questioned it himself!

'Hawk—'

'Silence, Jane!' he hissed fiercely, even as he moved to place his fingers against her lips. His head tilted as he listened intently and waited to see if his head groom and Tom, one of the grooms Hawk had brought with him from London, would venture farther into the stables in their search for him.

'Nah. We'd see 'im if he was in 'ere,' Tom dismissed.

'Better go an' tell Mr Jenkins that we don't know where 'e is neither.'

The sound of their boots retreating could clearly be heard before the stable door closed noisily behind them.

Hawk's breath left him in a shaky sigh of relief as he heard their departure. But nevertheless he continued to keep his hand gently over Jane's lips for several more seconds, just in case either Jack or Tom should change their minds and decide to give the stables a more thorough search for him.

At the same time he was aware that his precaution was not being taken entirely so that Jane should not do or say anything that would reveal their whereabouts. No, the fierce accusation in those green eyes as she stared up at him from behind that restraining hand was enough to warn Hawk that when Jane *did* next speak it was likely to blister his eardrums!

Deservedly so.

Damn it—not only was Jane a young lady without experience of physical intimacy, but the reason she was here at Mulberry Park at all was in order that he might protect her from such unwanted attentions.

He slowly removed his hand before standing up and moving as far away from her as was possible in the confines of the stall. 'This was a mistake, Jane. A regrettable mistake.' He ran an agitated hand through the dark thickness of his hair. 'I should not—'

'No, you most certainly should not!' Jane acknowledged breathlessly as she scrambled hastily to her feet, her gaping gown clutched in front of her.

She stared across at him for several seconds before turning suddenly on her heel and running from the stables.

And him…

Chapter Eight

'You look wonderful, Jane!' Arabella's face was flushed with excitement two evenings later, as she looked with pleasure at Jane's transformed appearance in the new gown she was to wear for the dinner party this evening.

To Jane's heartfelt relief she had not seen much of the Duke of Stourbridge in the days that had followed that embarrassing incident in the stables, his time having been occupied with estate business.

Everything about that time together was an embarassment to Jane. The wantonness of her response. The evidence of that response when she had seen that she had actually ripped off one of the buttons on the Duke's fine linen shirt in her desperation to touch his flesh. Even worse had been the moment when she had looked down and seen her own state of undress, and realised just how intimately she had allowed the Duke to touch her.

Jane had been so stricken by that realisation, so mortified by what she had encouraged to happen between them, that at that moment she had only been capable of gathering together her dishevelled clothing before fleeing the stables as if the devil himself pursued her.

Not the Duke. *He* was not the devil who pursued her. It was the evidence of her own wanton behaviour that did that.

That the Duke was just as shocked by what had occurred between them had become equally apparent when he had avoided even taking his meals with the ladies of the house over the next two days.

Jane had caught the occasional glimpse of him from her bedroom window as he walked the parkland with seemingly tireless energy, checking the livestock, or the crops in the ploughed fields with his estate manager, with little apparent concern for the state of his clothes and boots. Or for Dolton's tearful state when he saw them. This was an occurrence Jane had had occasion to witness for herself one evening, when Dolton had trailed unhappily from the Duke's apartments with dirt-spattered clothes and boots in his hands.

Fortunately Lady Arabella, realising from the Duke's lengthy absences from the house that Jane was no more in his confidence than she was herself, had first grudgingly and then more readily begun to spend time in Jane's company. The only negative aspect of this was that Jane, filled with a new urgency to escape Markham Park, now had very little opportunity in which to find a way to further her travel arrangements to Somerset.

It had occurred to her to wonder at one point whether

Lady Arabella was deliberately preventing her from having time alone in which to achieve that goal—possibly at her brother's instigation, following the suspicions he had voiced concerning Jane's visits to his stables. But as Arabella's demeanour became distinctly frosty whenever the Duke's name was so much as mentioned, Jane decided that was not the case.

Arabella had, however, thrown herself wholeheartedly upon her brother's instruction that Jane would need a new gown for the dinner party—resulting in the two women having taken a carriage ride into the nearest town, and then making a second journey on the following morning so that the gown might be fitted and have last-minute alterations made.

Obviously there were some advantages to being the sister of a Duke. Her gown had been made to fit perfectly in just twenty-four hours!

'Did I not tell you that the pale cream silk with the slightly paler lace would be perfect on you?' Arabella prompted now with satisfaction.

Yes, Arabella had assured her of that. And as Jane's experience of choosing material and style for a new gown was non-existent, she had been only too happy to allow the other woman to take charge.

One glance in the mirror showed Jane that she looked transformed. High-waisted and styled off-the-shoulder, with tiny puffed sleeves and a low neckline, the cream silk dress seemed to drape round her shapely curves rather than cling to them, and her hair had been styled into fashionable curls and escaping ringlets this evening by Arabella's own maid.

It was difficult to imagine, as Jane looked at this pleasing image, that she was the same young lady who had been forced to wear that unbecoming yellow gown only days ago.

'I wonder what Hawk will make of your appearance?' Arabella mused gleefully.

Jane had been wondering the same thing—although probably not for the same reason!

Tonight she looked elegant—pretty, even—the gown giving her poise and style, and a maturity she had hitherto lacked. Completely unlike that yellow gown, which she believed had made her look like a huge piece of unbecoming fruit!

Jane could not deny, however, that her pleasure in her changed appearance was marred a little by the fact that, much against her protests, the Duke was to receive the bill for her new gown.

But how could it be otherwise when Jane had so very little money of her own? Sir Barnaby had given her a small allowance, and Jane had managed to save some of it, but she was not even sure it would be enough to pay for her passage to Somerset, let alone purchase a new gown and gloves.

Arabella's assurances that the Duke would not even notice one new gown amongst her own costly purchases had done very little to allay Jane's feelings of discomfort at having to accept such largesse from a man who could have nothing but the worst opinion of her.

'Oh, what could I possibly have said to bring that frown to your brow?' Arabella clasped Jane's hands in her own as she looked down at her searchingly. 'Does the mere mention of my autocratic brother make you unhappy, Jane?'

'In all probability, the answer to that is yes, Arabella.' The Duke spoke abruptly from behind them before Jane could make any reply, causing both women to turn— Arabella with some surprise, Jane with reluctance. 'Well, well, well,' he drawled as he stood languidly in the doorway. 'I am not sure Mulberry Hall or its guests this evening will be able to accommodate two such lovely ladies.'

Jane felt the blush that warmed her cheeks and heated her body as that unfathomable golden gaze moved over her with slow deliberation. She was relieved that Arabella forestalled the need for her to respond to the Duke's mockery as she moved to her brother's side and smiled up at him triumphantly.

'Have I not done well, Hawk?' She beamed. 'Does Jane not look beautiful?'

'You have done very well, Arabella,' Hawk confirmed dryly.

In truth, he was more than a little stunned by how ravishingly beautiful Jane looked in her new finery. The cream gown with its delicate lace adornment adding a lustre to the smooth perfection of her skin, her eyes were a clear, translucent green in her heart-shaped face, and a cream ribbon threaded amongst her red curls added to their fiery depth of colour.

He was aware that Jane had avoided being in his company at all these last two days, quietly leaving the room if he should enter it, her gaze averted as she did so.

Not that he did not deserve to be treated with such coldness after almost making love to her—in such a way, and in such a place, that she could not help but be insulted by it.

Oh, yes, Hawk knew he completely deserved Jane's newly felt aversion to him. Knew it, and aided that aversion by retreating to his library when he was not working about the estate.

Unfortunately for him Jane looked every inch a beautiful and confident young lady tonight. So much so that Hawk was having trouble keeping his gaze from her.

'I came to bring Jane these,' he bit out abruptly, and he held up the pearl necklace and earbobs he had brought with him in the hopes of them becoming a possible truce-offering between them.

It seemed that Arabella had been far too busy these last days, organising her dinner party and ministering to Jane's need for a new gown, to notice the coldness that now existed between himself and Jane. But Hawk did not doubt that once this evening was over his sister would not be able to help but become aware of the strain between them.

His mouth twisted ruefully. 'But I cannot help but wonder, now that I have seen how lovely she looks already, if it would not be gilding the lily…?'

'Oh, no, Hawk. I think the pearls are a perfect choice!' His sister beamed her approval, herself a vision of loveliness in a glowing-pink gown. 'Do you not agree, Jane?' she prompted warmly.

Jane could only stand and stare at the necklace and earbobs that looked so delicately lovely in the Duke's large but elegant hands, totally stunned, after days of silence, by his making such a gesture.

She wondered where the pearl jewellery could have come from. Surely the Duke had not purposely purchased them for her…? If so, then no matter how enchanted Jane might be at the idea of his having done such a thing on her behalf, it would be the height of impropriety for her to accept.

'Of all Mother's jewels, these will certainly suit Jane the best,' Arabella approved delightedly.

Jane's startled gaze rose from the pearls to the Duke's now unreadable expression. The necklace and earbobs had belonged to his mother? The former Duchess of Stourbridge?

Somehow that knowledge made his offer that Jane should wear them this evening an even more intimate gesture than if the Duke *had* gone out and purchased them for her.

She gave a firm shake of her head. 'I am sure your offer is a kind one, Your Grace, but I really could not even think of wearing something of such a—a personal nature to your family.'

Hawk looked at her searchingly. Those green eyes were now huge in the otherwise paleness of Jane's face. Was Jane refusing to wear the jewellery because it had belonged to another woman? Or because it was he who suggested she should do so? Was Jane so angry with him, so disgusted with him, that she would not even accept this gesture of apology on his part?

Despite Jane's avoidance of his company since the episode in the stables, Hawk had been pleased to note the two young women were much together, and he was grateful to Jane for taking such an interest in his young sister. Remembering that Jane had no jewellery of her own to wear tonight, he had impulsively decided to bring her the pearls.

But one glance at Jane's slightly stricken expression and he knew he had once again acted in error. Could he do nothing right where this young woman was concerned…?

'Come now, Jane—they are only on loan to you,' he assured her irritably as he stepped farther into a bedroom that, apart from the gown she had recently taken off, which now lay draped over a chair, showed little sign of Jane's occupation. But then, from the little luggage she had brought away with her from Markham Park, Jane did not *have* many personal possessions with which to adorn it. 'Turn around, Jane, so that I might put the necklace on,' he instructed with impatient briskness, his inner anger directed at his own behaviour towards Jane as much as at the guardians who had treated Jane with such neglect.

Hawk did not doubt that Jane had been warm, clothed and fed during the years she had lived at Markham Park, but when those things had been so grudgingly given he felt that Jane might have been better served going to people less wealthy who might have loved her. Now that he knew Jane better—perhaps too well…?—Hawk was sure that the Sulbys' emotional dereliction had been more cruel to someone of Jane's temperament than any deprivation of food or warmth could ever have been.

He had followed Jane to the stables that day with the intention of telling her of his plans to make enquiries on her behalf concerning other, more kindly relatives that she might have. He had failed to do so, and her frosty manner since he had made love to her had certainly not invited confidences of any nature.

Hawk had not yet received any word back from his enquiries, but the moment he did he knew he would no longer be able to delay discussing Jane's future with her. And whether Jane believed him or not—and no doubt she would not!—he had acted only out of concern for her.

But those enquiries had become all the more urgent, he acknowledged grimly, since making love to her!

Jane looked up at the Duke guardedly, where he stood before her expectantly, not knowing quite how to respond to his instruction. If she refused absolutely to wear the pearl jewellery then she knew she would upset Arabella as much as the Duke. She had come to value the other girl's friendship these last few days, and did not doubt that to refuse to wear the jewellery of Arabella's dead mother would put that intimacy in jeopardy.

It was a dilemma the Duke made no allowances for as he took Jane firmly by the bareness of her shoulders to turn her so that her back was towards him.

Jane tensed expectantly. She knew that in a few

seconds the Duke's fingers would once again brush against her nape as he secured the clasp of the necklace.

Her breath caught as his arms moved about her, so that he might drape the necklace about her throat. The slightest touch of those long, elegant fingers seemed to sear the bareness of Jane's flesh, causing her to quiver involuntarily, quickly followed by an uncontrollable trembling as he smoothed the ringlets from her nape.

If the two of them had been alone then Jane would have lost no time in turning to confront him, to firmly assure him that she was perfectly capable of securing the necklace herself. But they were not alone. Arabella was standing as silent witness to any exchange between them.

Jane could only hope that the Duke did not intend to attach the earbobs himself…

No matter that it was two days since the Duke had kissed her, nor that they had rarely exchanged a word since then, Jane knew that her insides would melt entirely if the Duke did not soon stop touching her so intimately.

How could it be that his slightest touch made her feel this way? The touch of a man who, when he was not making love to her, provoked her to such feelings of antagonism at his arrogance that she argued with him constantly?

Jane did not have the worldly experience to answer these questions herself. Neither did she have someone to whom she could voice these questions—no one in whom she could confide. She certainly could not tell Arabella of the unimaginable longings that surged up inside her whenever the Duke—Arabella's own brother—touched her!

It did not help that he seemed to be taking an age—or possibly it just seemed that way to her sensitised flesh?—to secure the clasp. Jane was starting to feel slightly light-headed, and she found it difficult to breathe…

This had not been one of his better ideas, Hawk acknowledged with self-disgust as the gentle arch of Jane's nape, the soft perfume of her hair, her very closeness, all seemed to cause him more physical discomfort than he would have wished.

'There,' he rasped dismissively, as the catch finally caught and he could step back from Jane's disturbing proximity.

'Oh, they really are perfect on you, Jane!' Arabella moved forward to clasp Jane's hands in her own as she looked at her admiringly. 'You have exquisite taste, Hawk,' his sister added, with what Hawk realised was the first genuine smile she had directed at him in some time.

Even so, it was a smile that Hawk had no chance to respond to, because Jane turned to face him and all of his attention became transfixed on her.

The delicate cream-coloured pearls nestled softly against the swell of her breasts, visible above the low neckline of her new gown. Breasts which gently rose and fell as she breathed, causing Hawk's jaw to clench and his mouth to tighten. He could not seem to take his gaze from her rounded softness.

The Duke looked so grim, Jane noted regretfully, as she moved one of her hands to touch the pearls at her throat. 'Perhaps…' she began, her voice husky. 'Perhaps now that you have seen the pearls again, Your Grace, you would prefer it if I was not to wear them?'

They were his mother's pearls, after all, and had once adorned the no doubt delicate throat of the Duchess of Stourbridge. As such it must surely seem like something of an insult to her memory for them now to be worn by a young woman whose irritating presence had been forced upon him.

A young woman who, although the Duke was not aware of it, did not even know the identity of her real father…

'I hope you realise, Jane, just how insulting it is to even suggest that might be either Arabella's feeling or my own!' he rasped impatiently. 'As Arabella has already assured you, the pearls complement your gown perfectly,' he added with haughty dismissal, before turning away. 'Come, Arabella.' He held out his arm to his sister. 'It is time we went downstairs to await the arrival of your guests.'

Even as Jane inwardly acknowledged how well brother and sister looked together, both so tall and elegant, she could not help but feel disappointed—contrarily so!—that the Duke had made no particular comment on her own appearance. His only compliment had been upon how beautiful the new gown was, and how well the pearls looked with that gown. A gown that he himself had instructed to be chosen and which, in time, he would also pay for.

Despite Jane's inner turmoil of emotion over the last

few days, whenever she had recalled the way the Duke had kissed and caressed her, she had found Arabella's excitement about her dinner party infectious. Had even found herself looking forward to the occasion almost as much as the young hostess.

But now Jane had been reminded of the fact that the gown she wore was not really hers—that the pearl jewellery was only on loan to her for the evening. She was, in effect, merely a cuckoo in borrowed plumage.

She bowed her head. 'I will join you both downstairs shortly. I—I have the earbobs to put on yet,' she excused lightly, when she saw that Arabella was about to protest her need for delay. 'I assure you that I will not be long, Arabella,' she said warmly.

'See that you are not, Jane.' The Duke was the one to answer her stiffly as he escorted his sister to the door.

Jane waited until the two had left her bedchamber before moving to sit down in front of the mirrored dressing table.

The pearls *did* look well with the gown and Jane's newly styled hair, but as she looked at her reflection she could find no pleasure in them. Could only look at herself and berate herself for a fool.

For she had made a great discovery about herself when the Duke had touched her and the warmth of his breath had softly caressed her nape. Had realised in the last few minutes, when her main emotion when she'd turned to face him had been deep hurt as he had looked and spoken to her with such coldness, that she was falling in love with the Duke of Stourbridge.

A man even more unsuitable for Jane to fall in love with—if that was possible!—than Jane's real and married father had been for her mother…

Chapter Nine

Hawk was aware of Jane—as were several other pairs of male eyes—from the moment she stood, slightly hesitant, at the top of the sweeping staircase to stare down at the guests who had already arrived and were now milling about the entrance hall, chatting and laughing with friends they had not seen for several weeks or months.

For a few seconds Jane looked slightly overwhelmed by the prospect of meeting so many people, and then Hawk saw her bare shoulders straighten and her chin rise determinedly, before she held her head regally high and began her slow descent of the staircase.

She really did look magnificent this evening. The simplicity and colour of her gown gave her skin the creamy texture of velvet, and the deep red of her hair made her stand out from the other women in the room like a beautiful, exotic butterfly amidst less colourful moths.

Hawk was not even aware of making excuses to his

guests as he began to cross the room to Jane's side, barely acknowledging the remarks addressed to him as he did so, the intensity of his gaze fixed firmly on Jane as she reached the bottom of the staircase.

But his gaze narrowed, his mouth thinning disapprovingly, when he realised, despite his own promptness, that another man had already stepped forward to take Jane's hand in his own and raise it to his lips.

Justin Long, Earl of Whitney. The very last man Hawk would wish anywhere near a young woman under his protection!

A man who, the last time the two men had met, had made known his displeasure at being asked to relinquish his place in the Countess of Morefield's bedchamber to Hawk.

It was so typical of Whitney that he had seen and at once sought out the only young lady present not already known to him! A young lady who surely could not help but be drawn to and flattered by the attentions of a man such as the rakishly handsome Earl of Whitney.

Would Jane be flattered and attracted…?

The older man certainly had much to recommend him—and not only to the matchmaking mamas of Society. Oh, the Whitney estates were very wealthy ones, but it was Justin Long himself that the women of the ton seemed to find so fascinating. His blond good looks and rakish exploits seemed to challenge the interest of both old and young women alike.

Whitney had been a widower since his wife and young son had died of influenza twenty years ago, and since that time had displayed absolutely no inclination to repeat the marital experience. Neither did the man show the slightest hesitation when it came to taking advantage of his boyish good looks, his ruthlessness where women were concerned was legendary.

And Jane did look very desirable this evening…

Hawk's mouth tightened grimly as he moved forward to join them. 'Whitney.' His greeting was deliberately cool.

Whitney turned to look at him with amused blue eyes. 'Stourbridge.'

Hawk bristled at his amusement. 'The Countess has not accompanied you this evening?' he challenged hardly, immediately knowing from the light of challenge that entered the other man's gaze that he should not have done so. It had been extremely indiscreet on his part to so much as mention in front of Jane the woman who had been mistress to both men.

That he had done so Hawk knew was due solely to the fact that he was disturbed enough by Whitney's interest in Jane to feel goaded into the challenge.

'I believe that is now *your* privilege…?' the Earl taunted.

Hawk eyed the older man coldly. 'I have not seen the Countess for several months. I was not aware that you had been introduced to my ward, Miss Jane Smith…' he added tersely.

'Your ward?' The older man raised his brows in surprise before returning his speculative blue gaze to Jane. 'In that case perhaps you would care to make the introductions now, Stourbridge?' he prompted dryly, as he continued to look at Jane.

Far too familiar for Hawk's liking. But in his role of host this evening he had little choice but to comply. 'Jane—may I present Justin Long, Earl of Whitney?' he bit out harshly. 'Whitney—my ward, Miss Jane Smith.'

'My Lord.' Jane inclined her head politely. 'What a pity that your Countess was unable to accompany you this evening,' she added lightly.

The Earl's eyes glinted wickedly. 'You misunderstood, my dear,' he drawled. 'It was not *my* Countess to whom Stourbridge alluded.'

'Oh…' Jane looked even more confused.

As well she might, Hawk acknowledged, as his narrowed gaze dared the older man to explain exactly whose Countess she was—or indeed had been!

Whitney ignored the challenge and instead bestowed his most charming smile on Jane. 'I hope you will forgive any offence I may have caused earlier by speaking to you so impulsively, Miss Smith? I had thought this to be an evening spent amongst old friends and acquaintances, with none of the stuffy formality that invariably makes an evening with the ton so incredibly tedious.'

In truth, Jane had been slightly surprised, but not in the least offended, when this handsomely distinguished man had approached and spoken to her. In view of the nervousness she had felt as she descended the stairs, Jane's principal emotion had been relief at having someone speak to her at all!

But she knew from just one glance at the Duke, as he looked so contemptuously down his arrogant nose at the older man, that he, at least, did not like or approve of at least one of his sister's guests this evening.

And who exactly *was* the Countess the two men referred to so challengingly…?

'I have taken no offence, My Lord,' she assured the older man coolly, as she gently but firmly released the fingers he still held in his own. 'And, never having spent an evening with the ton, I have no idea if their company be tedious or otherwise.'

'No?' The Earl's eyes widened. 'Where can you have been hiding Miss Smith until now, Stourbridge?' he taunted the other man softly.

The Duke stiffened. 'Miss Smith resided with relatives in the country until very recently.'

'Really?' The Earl still mocked the younger man. 'And which part of the country would that have been, Miss Smith?' His narrowed blue gaze returned to Jane.

'It is surely of little consequence where Miss Smith once resided, Whitney, when it must be obvious she now resides here in Gloucestershire with my family,' the Duke cut in harshly.

Jane was finding the intensity of the Earl's gaze upon her more than a little disconcerting. The shrewdness in those blue eyes was a complete contradiction to the lazily mocking drawl he affected when speaking.

'Of course,' the Earl answered the other man dryly. 'I was merely showing polite curiosity, that is all.' He shrugged dismissively.

Despite the fact that the other man's estates seemed to prosper, and his business interests to thrive, Hawk had always considered Whitney something of a wastrel—a man who spent his time in London, when not at the gambling tables, occupying the bed of one bored wife or another of his fellow peers.

He was certainly not a man Hawk could ever approve showing an interest in an innocent such as Jane!

Hawk reached out to lift Jane's hand and place it firmly upon his arm. 'I believe it is time for us to go in to dinner.' He nodded his cool dismissal of the other man before turning away, the firmness of his hand over Jane's leaving her no choice but to accompany him.

'You will stay away from the Earl of Whitney for the remainder of the evening, Jane,' he rasped grimly, once they had moved out of the Earl's hearing. 'Besides being far too old for you, the man is an obvious rake who is only interested in bedding a woman rather than wedding her!'

Jane gasped—both at the Duke's arrogance in once again telling her what she should do, and at the indelicacy of his warning about the Earl. He almost made it sound as if she had deliberately set out to engage the other man's interest.

Well, she might be inexperienced in the ways of men, but that did not mean Jane did not recognise a consummate flirt when she met one. Although, strangely, the Earl's behaviour had not been in the least flirtatious with her until the Duke had appeared at her side...? But after days of not knowing exactly how she should behave towards the Duke since he had made love to her, she now found herself consumed with anger at the return of his high-handedness.

She also recognised that the apparent intensity of her conversation with the Duke was now attracting attention from Arabella's other guests...

'Surely you are mistaken, Your Grace?' she said evenly, her expression deliberately serene in acknowledgement of those curious glances. 'I thought it was the case that *all* titled gentlemen needed to marry and produce an heir?'

The Duke turned to scowl down the sharp blade of his arrogant nose at her. 'It may have escaped your notice, Jane, but *I* have not yet chosen to do so.'

'I am sure that is only because you have so far been too busy.'

'My estates—'

'I was not referring to work on your estates, Your Grace.'

His dark brows rose. 'Then to what were you referring, Jane...?'

Her lips curved into a smile even as her eyes glowed with challenge. 'I had assumed that the reason you are still unmarried at the age of...thirty...?'

'One and thirty,' Hawk supplied cautiously, sensing from Jane's too-innocent demeanour that he was about to receive another one of her infamous setdowns.

'Exactly.' Jane nodded coolly. 'I had assumed that the reason you are still unmarried at such an advanced age must be because you are far too busy interfering in other people's lives to have time to attend to your own...'

For what had to be the second time in Jane's company—or possibly the third?—Hawk found himself unable to repress the hard bark of laughter provoked by this woman's wicked sense of humour.

At his own expense this time!

The unexpected laughter also served to dispel the tension he had been feeling since he first saw her in Whitney's company.

'Touché, Jane,' he drawled dryly.

'You are more than welcome, Your Grace,' she returned pertly.

'I never doubted for a moment that would be the case.' He nodded, still smiling, relieved that after days of awkwardness Jane at last seemed to be showing signs of returning to her more forthright self. 'Perhaps you will now allow me the honour of escorting you in to dinner, Jane?'

Her brows rose. 'Is there not some other, worthier lady present this evening, who is eagerly awaiting the Duke of Stourbridge's attentions?'

Yes, Hawk knew that Lady Pamela Croft, the most highly raved lady in the room, and Whitney's older sister, would be expecting him to escort her into dinner.

But, unlike that evening at Markham Park almost a week ago, when Hawk's offer to take Jane in to dinner had been thwarted by Jane herself, Hawk felt no more inclined to bow to Society's dictates than Whitney. At an evening 'spent amongst old friends' he could ignore rules of etiquette for once.

'Perhaps,' he dismissed arrogantly. 'But none that I

would rather have on my arm,' he added distractedly, as his attention was drawn to the fact that a blushingly pretty Arabella had accepted being escorted into the dining room by a smugly triumphant-looking Earl of Whitney.

Damn the man.

First Jane. Now Arabella.

Surely he would not have to spend the entire evening fending off the other man's attentions from one or the other?

'If you are sure, Your Grace?' Jane answered him huskily.

'I am very sure, Jane,' Hawk confirmed tersely, and he turned his gaze reluctantly away from Arabella and Whitney.

Jane's hand trembled slightly as it rested on the Duke's arm, and her face felt flushed as the other guests turned to watch the formidably arrogant Duke of Stour-bridge escorting her, a young woman with whom none of them were as yet acquainted, through to the formal dining room.

Neither could she help but notice the narrowed blue gaze of the Earl of Whitney as he too turned to watch the two of them. It was an intense blue gaze that was fixed firmly on Jane. And, unless she was mistaken, not in the least rakishly.

She was aware of his shrewd gaze several times during dinner, but deliberately ignored it. The Earl even smiled at her in a frankly conspiratorial manner on one occasion, as if encouraging her to share with him the joke of such pompous formality. Jane did not so much as acknowledge the smile as she turned her attention to Lord Croft, where he sat to the left of her at the table.

The Duke presided over the head of the table, of course, with Arabella, as his hostess, seated at the other end. Arabella had placed Jane between Lord Croft and his son Jeremy. Both men were charming and affable as they easily put her at her ease. The younger man was especially attentive after learning that Jane had spent her early years in Somerset, proceeding to talk knowledgeably about the area from memories of his own visits there as a child.

But still Jane could not help but be aware of the intensity of the Earl of Whitney's interest as he sat across the table from her, listening intently to her conversation rather than taking any part in it…

Hawk found his attention wandering constantly from the dry wit of Lady Pamela's conversation. Instead he watched Jane with a brooding intensity. The fact that several other men were looking at her as intently, the Earl of Whitney and Jeremy Croft but two of them, caused his brows to draw together darkly.

'Miss Jane Smith has become quite the darling of the evening, has she not?' Lady Pamela commented dryly.

'What?' Hawk turned to bark tersely.

His friend and neighbour arched teasing brows at his obvious irritation. 'I was commenting on the fact that Miss Smith seems to hold my husband entranced, my son beguiled, my brother amused and the Duke of Stourbridge mesmerised,' Lady Pamela drawled.

Hawk frowned at her. 'You are imagining things, Pamela.'

'I do not think so.' She shook her head slowly. 'Can it be possible that the elusive Duke of Stourbridge has at last settled on his choice of bride…?'

Bride?

Could Pamela possibly be referring to Jane…?

'Do not be ridiculous, Pamela.' He snapped his impatience at the absurdity of her suggestion that he could seriously be contemplating making Jane his Duchess. 'Jane Smith is my ward, not my future bride.'

'Really?' Pamela drawled derisively. 'In that case, Hawk, and unless you wish others to make the same assumption I did, I would advise you not to spend quite so much of your time staring at her in that hungrily devouring way.'

'Now you are being deliberately provoking, Pamela,' Hawk bit out harshly, before emptying his wine glass and motioning for it to be refilled.

'And you are drinking far more wine than usual this evening, too, Hawk.' As a friend of his mother, and his closest neighbour these last thirty years, Lady Pamela felt no hesitation in speaking her mind to him whenever she chose.

Hawk bared his teeth in a humourless smile. 'When I wish for your advice, Pamela, be assured I will ask for it!'

She gave a softly indulgent laugh. 'Be assured, Hawk, you will receive it whether it is asked for or not!'

Hawk gave a rueful shake of his head, knowing that there was no point in arguing with Pamela—that since the death of his own mother Pamela had chosen to take on that role for herself.

Could there possibly be some basis for her observation concerning the way in which he had been watching Jane? *Had* his gaze been 'mesmerised' and 'hungrily devouring'…?

Surely not?

Admittedly, he had not liked Whitney's attentions to her earlier, and nor did he particularly care for the way that Pamela's own son was paying Jane such marked attention, but surely that was no reason for Pamela to imply that his own interest was any more personal than any guardian for his charge?

No, of course it was not, he assured himself determinedly. He was merely concerned for Jane, that was all. Because she was young and innocent, and could have no idea of the danger a man with Whitney's reputation represented to that innocence.

It was an ignorance Hawk had every intention of correcting as he made his way immediatately to Jane's side once dinner was over, when she and all the other guests were making their way to the small ballroom where dancing was due to commence.

Unfortunately for Jane, an hour of watching as both Jeremy Croft and the Earl of Whitney seemed to become more and more captivated by her every word had not diminished the force of Hawk's temper in the slightest.

'I think it might be as well, Jane, if for the remainder of the evening you were to refrain from flirting with every man in the room under the age of sixty!' Hawk bit out harshly as he glared down at her.

Jane gave a gasp, her face paling at the unexpectedness of the Duke's attack. In fact she had been quietly congratulating herself on having successfully negotiated the intricacies of social behaviour, and now the Duke was accusing her of doing the opposite.

She returned his glare unblinkingly. 'I have not yet had the opportunity to flirt with *you*, Your Grace!'

'Neither will you, if you know what is good for you!' Those gold eyes glittered warningly.

Jane looked up at him challengingly. 'Could you possibly be threatening me, Your Grace?'

His jaw was clamped tightly together. 'I am trying to assist you, Jane—'

'By insulting me?'

'By advising you.'

'I was mistaken, then, Your Grace. For your advice sounded distinctly like an insult to me!' Jane breathed indignantly.

Hawk's nostrils flared angrily. 'You—'

'Sorry to interrupt your little *tête-à-tête* with your ward, Stourbridge, but perhaps I might have your permission to invite Miss Smith to dance?' the Earl of Whitney interrupted smoothly.

Hawk turned a quelling glance on the older man, having every intention of telling Whitney that he most certainly did not have his permission to dance with Jane. Or indeed to do anything else with her!

'I do not need the Duke's permission to dance, My Lord.'

Jane was the one to answer before Hawk had a chance to do so, not sparing Hawk so much as a second glance as she took the other man's arm and allowed herself to be taken onto the dance floor.

Leaving Hawk no choice but to stand impotently by and watch as the rakish Earl of Whitney took a hold of Jane's hand and led her confidently into the dance.

An unpleasant image that was reflected back at Hawk many times over from the mirrors that adorned the walls of the small ballroom at Mulberry Mall.

'I am so pleased to see that Jane is enjoying herself.' Arabella spoke softly beside Hawk.

Hawk turned to scowl at his young sister—who, as hostess, should have been on the dance floor herself. 'Whitney is hardly a suitable companion for her to be enjoying herself with!'

Arabella looked up at him steadily for several seconds, before allowing a knowing smile to curve her lips. 'So, Lady Pamela was right in her assertion that you are far too interested in your young ward,' she murmured with satisfaction.

'I—'

'I must admit I was a little taken aback when Lady Pamela described Jane as such,' Arabella continued lightly. 'I had not realised. Exactly *when* did Jane become your ward, Hawk?' She arched blonde brows.

'You are being deliberately obtuse, Arabella,' he snapped dismissively.

'I do not think so.' Arabella shook her head.

Hawk gave an impatiently snort. 'Obviously I made that distinction for Jane's sake. It simply would not do for our friends and neighbours—for the ton—to realise that an unmarried young lady with no family connection to us is staying here at Mulberry Mall under the protection of the Duke of Stourbridge.'

'Perhaps you should have given some thought to that possibility before bringing Jane here…?'

'Given a choice, I would not have brought Jane here—' Hawk broke off as he realised he had been provoked into being indiscreet for the second time this evening. Something that, as the haughty Duke of Stourbridge, he never was. Or at least he never had been before Jane came crashing into his life.

'If you had been "given a choice", Hawk?' Arabella echoed curiously. 'You never have fully explained to me how you came to be acquainted with Jane, or your reasons for bringing her here. Perhaps—'

'I do not think now is the right time for us to discuss this, Arabella.'

'Will there ever be a right time?'

Hawk's mouth thinned. 'No.'

'I did not think so.' Arabella shrugged. 'But you must admit that captivating the Earl of Whitney would be a marvellous feather in Jane's social cap…'

'I admit nothing of the sort!'

Arabella turned towards the dancing couples. 'They do look very well together, do they not…?'

Hawk turned to follow the direction of his sister's

gaze, his own eyes narrowing ominously as once again he found himself looking at Jane as she danced assuredly with the Earl of Whitney.

Arabella was quite right in her assertion: Jane and Whitney did look well together. The two were of a similar height, one so blond while the other a fiery redhead, and their movements were both light and graceful. And when the dance allowed, their conversation was softly exclusive.

Hawk frowned darkly as he wondered what subject two such mismatched people could possibly have found to talk about so earnestly…

Chapter Ten

'Have you been Stourbridge's…ward for very long, Miss Smith?'

Jane had been lost in the enchantment of the 'small' ballroom, as Arabella called it. Dozens of candles illuminated the room, and the dancing couples were reflected in the ornate mirrors that covered the walls. A warm breeze came in through the open doors that led out into the garden beyond.

Now she looked up frowningly at the Earl. 'Why do you ask, My Lord?'

He raised mocking blond brows. 'Possibly because Lady Arabella describes you as her companion, and the Duke as his ward. I wondered which of them spoke in error…?'

Jane stumbled slightly in the dance—a slip the Earl deftly masked as he matched his steps to her own. 'Perhaps neither of them, My Lord,' she finally dismissed smoothly. 'There is surely no reason why I cannot be both ward to the Duke and companion to Arabella?'

'None at all,' the Earl conceded. 'But neither description tells me who you really are.' All humour had now left that handsome face, and he stared down at her with that same intentness of purpose that Jane had found so disconcerting during dinner.

Jane withstood the intensity of that gaze as she gave a rueful smile. 'I am nobody, My Lord. Absolutely nobody.'

'One thing Lady Arabella and the Duke do seem in agreement on is your name…Jane Smith…?'

For all that the Duke had warned her the Earl was reputed to be a charmer and a seducer, Jane was finding his persistence in asking her personal questions irritating in the extreme.

The Earl shook his head. 'I am sorry to disagree, Jane, but I really cannot accept any loving mother with the surname of Smith baptising her child Jane.'

'Then perhaps she did not love me!' Jane snapped, still trying to come to terms with her emotions towards her mother after discovering that Janette had married a man who was not the father of her baby. 'She died on the day I was born,' Jane explained flatly, as the Earl continued to look down at her speculatively.

His expression instantly changed to one of frowning regret. 'Please forgive me if I have caused offence, Jane.' He sighed. 'My own wife and child died many years ago, too,' he added, with a grimace.

It was an explanation that at once touched Jane's tender heart, and perhaps explained many things about this man's rakish reputation… 'You did not cause any offence, My Lord,' she assured him huskily.

'You may call me Justin, Jane,' he drawled.

'I would rather not, My Lord,' she came back firmly.

The Earl gave a rueful shake of his head. 'You do not seem to be part of the artifice that makes up the world of the ton, Jane…?'

Perhaps that was because Jane did not belong to this world. She was merely an intruder, there on sufferance only because the Duke of Stourbridge had decided it should be so!

She gave him a sharp look. 'That is the second time this evening that you have spoken so disparagingly of your peers, My Lord.'

He gave a humourless smile. 'Perhaps because for the main part that is how I choose to think of them…'

'Why?'

The Earl shrugged his broad shoulders. 'I doubt you would understand the reason for my cynicism, Jane.'

'Perhaps if you were to explain your reasons to me…?'

His gaze became quizzical at the earnestness of her expression. 'Talking about one's past does not make it any less painful, Jane. Nor does it make it possible for the ton to forgive those past indiscretions,' he added harshly.

'Not even if one is genuinely repentant?'

'Ah, but there lies the problem, Jane. For, you see, I remain totally unrepentant.'

'Then you cannot expect forgiveness.'

The Earl gave a rueful shake of his head. 'Have things always been so black and white to you, Jane?'

She nodded. 'My father—a parson—brought me up to be honest, I hope.'

'He did indeed.' The Earl gave a hard smile of acknowledgment.

'But a lack of artifice and guile is unusual in any woman, I have found, Jane, let alone one so young as you,' he added.

'Indeed, My Lord?' she said dryly.

'Oh, yes.' His smile became derisive. 'But perhaps your own honesty is due in part to the fact that you have no interest in becoming my Countess…'

Her eyes widened. 'I certainly do not, sir!'

The Earl gave an appreciative chuckle. 'And so you intrigue me even further, Jane!'

'I can assure you it was not my intention to do so,' Jane told him primly.

'Perhaps it is for that very reason I find you so interesting, Jane,' he murmured tauntingly.

Jane moved back slightly to look up at him. 'Are you flirting with me, My Lord?'

'As it happens…no, Jane. I am not,' he assured her hardly. 'Strangely, you bring out a protective element in me that I have not felt since—' He broke off abruptly, his frown dark. 'Why is that, do you think, Jane?'

'I have no idea, My Lord.' Jane was tired of this enigmatic conversation, but she was even more annoyed with the way the Duke stood at the side of the room, glaring at her so disapprovingly. As if he feared that at any moment she might do or say something to embarrass him or one of his guests. She curtseyed to the Earl as the dance ended. 'If you will excuse me, My Lord? I believe I would like go outside for some air.' She turned in the direction of the open French doors.

'An excellent suggestion.' He fell into step beside her.

Jane turned to frown at him. 'My suggestion was not an invitation for you to join me, My Lord.'

'I am well aware of that, Jane,' he acknowledged unconcernedly.

She gave a tight smile. 'But you choose to accompany me anyway?'

'I do, indeed.' He gave an inclination of his head as he took a light hold of her arm. 'I am not yet ready to relinquish my… interest, you see, Jane.'

'But I am not trying to interest you, My Lord!'

'Now you are starting to repeat yourself, Jane, and I really would prefer that you not become as boringly predictable as all the other ladies of my acquaintance.' He grimaced.

It was much cooler outside on the terrace, the sun having set, leaving the surrounding gardens dappled in the half-light between night and day.

But Jane wasted no time on appreciating the beauty of her surroundings as she turned to face the Earl, her chin determinedly high. 'I do not care, one way or the other, My Lord, in whether you find my company boring or intriguing.'

He shrugged stiffly. 'I have not conversed for this length of time with a lady so young as you for a very long time, or so frankly,' he repeated frowningly. 'Where do you come from, Jane? Who are your family?'

'I have already told you that I am nobody—'

'But I do not believe you, Jane. There are Smiths in the Lakes, Kent and Bedfordshire. Can you be related to any of them…? I warn you, Jane,' he added softly, 'you will only deepen my interest further by your determination to remain a mystery…'

Jane frowned her consternation; having yet another person curious about her was the very last thing that she wanted or needed. 'Release me, sir.' She was breathing heavily in her agitation.

The Earl's narrowed gaze studied her face searchingly for several long seconds, before his handsome features relaxed into a wolfish smile. 'I have already told you, I am not ready to do that, Jane.'

Her eyes widened as his fingers tightened about her arm, that single movement enough to make her aware of how alone they were out here on the deserted terrace.

She had been foolish in allowing the Earl to accompany her outside, Jane realised belatedly. Not that he had really given her any choice in the matter, but even so…

'Do not look so concerned, Jane,' he taunted softly. 'You really are far too young for me to be genuinely enamoured of you. But perhaps it is you who explected a light dalliance in the moonlight—'

'Whether that is Jane's wish or not, it most certainly is not mine!' An icily furious voice—the Duke of Stourbridge's icily furious voice!—cut in at the same instant Jane felt herself being pulled from the Earl's grasp and back against the hard strength of the Duke's chest.

The Earl's pale gaze glittered challengingly in the

moonlight. 'Is it your intention to spoil *all* Jane's fun this evening, Stourbridge?' he taunted mockingly.

Fun? Until Hawk's appearance, this man's conversation had been far from light or flirtatious!

Did the Duke believe otherwise?

One glance over her shoulder at the chilling expression on Hawk's face and Jane knew that was exactly what he believed!

Hawk drew in a harsh breath as he glared coldly at the older man. 'I have not given you leave to call her by her first name!'

'Perhaps the lady herself has allowed me that liberty?' the Earl taunted derisively.

Hawk's mouth tightened. 'As was explained to you earlier, Miss Smith is unfamiliar with the ways of the ton. She is especially naïve, Whitney, when it comes to men like you,' he added insultingly.

Jane felt as light as thistledown as Hawk held her firmly against him, as slender as a nymph, with the softness of her bright curls brushing against his chin. But as Hawk's most recent memory of that slenderness was of Jane standing far too close to the Earl of Whitney, he found he was in no mood at this moment to appreciate any of her womanly charms.

'A man like me?' the Earl repeated softly. 'I will have you know, Stourbridge, that I have called men out for lesser insults!'

Hawk was well aware of the other man's reputation for duelling, even though it was no longer approved of—either by the ton or the Crown.

Hawk, a master swordsman an an excellent shot, had never been involved in such idiocy himself, but he would be willing to make an exception where the Earl of Whitney was concerned!

'Yes?' he challenged hardly, even as he put Jane firmly out of harm's way.

The Earl thrust his face close to Hawk's, his eyes glittering coldly. 'If you would care to name a time and a place I will have my seconds call upon yours—'

'Now, really!' An indignant Jane interrupted impatiently. 'You cannot seriously intend to challenge each other to a duel over such a trifling matter?' She looked incredulous.

Having been sure that Whitney was about to take Jane into his arms, no doubt with the intention of kissing her, was no 'trifling matter' as far as Hawk was concerned. In fact, it had made him feel more than a little murderous.

'And how else would you suggest we settle this, Jane?' Hawk demanded scathingly, even as his gaze remained unwavering on the older man.

'Settle what?' she gasped incredulously. 'You are both behaving like children rather than two titled gentlemen who should know better!'

'My dear Jane, this is exactly how two titled gentlemen settle their differences,' the Earl told her dryly.

'I have warned you against calling her by her first name!' Hawk reminded him chillingly.

The Earl quirked mocking brows. 'You reserve that privilege, for yourself, eh, Stourbridge?'

Hawk's hand clenched into fists at his sides. 'Explain that remark, if you please!'

'Do not explain that remark—or indeed any other!' Jane instructed impatiently, and she put out her hands and rested one on either man's chest, her face flushed with anger, green eyes glittering warningly as she glared at them both. 'Really, I have never encountered such nonsense in my life,' she continued fiercely, keeping her hands on the men's chests in order to hold them at bay. 'You will *not* name a time and a place,' she told the Duke disgustedly. 'And you, My Lord—' she turned impatiently to Whitney '—you will not challenge the Duke to a duel for mentioning a reputation that I have absolutely no doubt you took great delight in acquiring and which you have long enjoyed!'

Whitney gave an appreciative grin. 'How well you have come to know me in such a short time, dear Jane. But nevertheless…' He sobered as the Duke gave a warning snort of impatience '—it simply is not done for a gentleman to cast aspersions upon another's reputation—'

'I do not believe they can be called aspersions when they are the truth,' Jane cut in disgustedly.

'From a lady they might be considered the truth,' the Earl conceded. 'From another gentleman they are an insult,' he assured her. 'In Stourbridge's case deliberately so, I am sure.' He looked at Hawk from between narrowed lids.

'Nevertheless,' Jane said determinedly, 'I absolutely forbid either of you to continue with this foolishness.'

Hawk looked down at her as she stood between

himself and Whitney, a hand still on each of their chests. A completely ineffective gesture when both men were inches taller than she, with powerfully muscled chests and arms that could easily have put her tiny form to one side before they continued with their argument.

That neither man chose to do so was due in part, Hawk knew, to the fact that Jane looked so magnificent in her outrage. The red vibrancy of her hair seemed almost to crackle like flame, her eyes glittered like emeralds, her normally full lips were thinned to a disapproving line, and those creamy breasts were quickly rising and falling in her agitation.

A glance across at Whitney showed the indulgent laughter lurking in the other man's eyes, as he too looked at the spitting little vixen Jane resembled in her outrage.

She really did think that she was stopping the two men from fighting with a paltry hand on their chests. And she 'absolutely' forbade them from duelling.

It was too much to endure. For either man.

Jane looked at the two men incredulously as first the Duke and then the Earl burst into deep-throated laughter.

Laughing? After the last few fraught minutes the two men were now actually *laughing* together?

Seconds ago she had been literally terrified—either that the Duke was going to be killed or else put in prison for killing the Earl of Whitney. Both prospects had filled her with dread.

And now, instead of duelling the two men were laughing together. Her own indignant expression seemed only to increase their humour. The Earl was actually bent double, his hands braced on his knees, as he laughed so long and heartily he could barely catch his breath. The Duke fared little better, almost seeming to have tears in his eyes as he openly guffawed.

Jane stood, hands on hips, bristling with indignation at this unwarranted humour. 'Perhaps when you two gentlemen have ceased this hysteria, one or both of you might care to tell me the source of your amusement?'

'I am afraid you are, dear Jane.' The Earl was the first to regain some sort of decorum as he straightened to take a handkerchief from his pocket and dab the moisture from his eyes. 'Just now, as you stood so bravely between the two of us, you gave every appearance of a bantam hen rebuking her chicks!' He gave a rueful shake of his head.

'You were laughing at *me*?' Jane breathed disbelievingly, her eyes wide as she glared first at the Duke and then the Earl.

'Unforgivable, I know, Jane. But nonetheless true,' the Earl confirmed, a smile still curving his lips.

Not a good move, as Hawk could have warned the other man—but he chose not to, and two bright spots of temper appeared in Jane's cheeks.

'You were laughing at *me*?' she repeated softly. 'Do you have any idea how ridiculous the two of *you* looked a few minutes ago? How absolutely—'

'That is enough, Jane,' Hawk cut in sternly.

'After your most recent—your absolutely childish behaviour just now, you will not even attempt to tell me what to do, Your Grace!' She turned on him fierily.

'She is priceless, Stourbridge,' Whitney remarked admiringly. 'Absolutely delicious!'

Hawk's humour had faded as suddenly as it had occurred, but he sobered completely as he realised he did not care for the other man's last comment. 'Now, listen here, Whitney—'

'Not again!' Jane burst out exasperatedly, her tiny hands now clenched into fists at her sides. 'I wish I had let the two of you duel. I wish you had pierced each other through the heart with your swords. I wish— Oh, never mind what I wish!' she concluded disgustedly. 'If you two gentlemen will excuse me?' She turned sharply on her heel—not in the direction of the ballroom, but towards the steps leading down into the moon-shadowed garden.

Hawk's hand snaked out to grasp her wrist. 'Where do you think you are going?'

'I do not *think* I am going anywhere—I *am* going into the garden!' Her eyes glittered up at him in challenge.

Hawk refused to release her arm. 'I cannot stand by and let you walk off into the darkness, Jane—'

'I do not advise you to try and stop me, Your Grace!'

Green eyes battled with gold for several seconds, before Jane lifted her slippered foot and brought the heel down forcefully on top of Hawk's instep. The unexpectedness of the attack caused him to move sharply backwards and so loosen his grip on her wrist. A lapse in concentration that Jane took full advantage of as, with one last sweeping look of disgust, she turned and marched away.

In the direction of the garden—as she had said she would!

'Magnificent!' the Earl murmured wonderingly as he stared after her. 'Truly magnificent.'

Despite—or because of—the pain in his foot, Hawk bristled angrily. 'You will stay away from her, Whitney!'

The other man turned to look at him with amused eyes. 'Will I?'

'Yes, you damn well will—'

'Surely that is for the lady to decide?' Whitney taunted. 'Unless, as I suggested earlier, you have a prior claim…?'

Hawk drew in a sharp breath. 'Jane is my ward—'

'So you have said.' The other man nodded. 'But from what I have just witnessed I would say the young lady has a definite mind of her own.'

Hawk could not deny that. Nor could he deny that, if anything, he admired that trait in Jane even more than Whitney did.

He *knew* her to be priceless. And delicious. And magnificent…!

'Yes, she does,' he confirmed tightly. 'But I can assure you that she is also one hundred per cent of sound mind!'

The Earl quirked blond brows. 'I trust, Stroubridge, that you are not implying that she would have to be *out* of her mind to be attracted to me?'

'And if I were?'

The older man shrugged. 'I have already told you I will be more than happy to meet you at a time and place of your choosing…'

Yes, he had. But Hawk knew, despite what Jane had

said minutes ago, that she would never forgive him if he should enter into a duel with the Earl of Whitney with her at the centre of it.

That he was even thinking of doing so told Hawk just how ludicrous this situation had become.

He was the Duke of Stourbridge. The formidably correct Duke of Stourbridge. A man with a deliberately spotless reputation. A man he had heard his peers hold up to their children as an example of one of the finest members of the aristocracy, for them to emulate.

And yet here he was, on the terrace of his own family seat, contemplating challenging another man to a duel over a young woman who had already told him how much she deplored such behaviour.

'I do not believe Jane would approve,' he said flatly.

The Earl arched mocking brows. 'And that concerns you?'

'That surprises you?' Hawk grated.

Whitney gave a derisive smile. 'You know, Hawk, I still remember you when you were the disreputable Marquis of Mulberry. Before you became every inch the superior Duke of Stourbridge.'

Hawk stiffened. 'Meaning?'

The older man shrugged. 'Meaning you might do well to remember it too sometimes.'

Hawk shook his head. 'I have no idea what you are talking about.'

But he did know.

Life had been much simpler ten years ago. Hawk had been a different person then. As Marquis of Mulberry he had only been *heir* to the Dukedom, and as such able to be as riotously devil-may-care as he knew Sebastian now was.

But that had been in a different life. And he a different man. He was the Duke of Stourbridge now, with all the responsibility that title implied. He could no longer do what he wanted without thought to the consequences.

'In my opinion, your Jane Smith is unique, Stourbridge.' The Earl nodded towards the direction Jane had taken when she had left them so abruptly.

'A young woman to be priced above— I believe Jane is wearing pearls this evening, Stourbridge? Your mother's pearls, are they not…?' he taunted softly.

Hawk stiffened. 'What if they are?'

'Idle curiosity on my part. That is all.' The Earl shrugged uninterestedly. 'But be assured, Hawk, that if you do not care to claim Jane for your own, then some other lucky man soon will.'

Hawk's jaw clenched. 'Not you!'

The Earl gave a humourless smile. 'No, not me,' he conceded wryly. 'Although I am sure that not even the estimable Jane would dismiss the idea of becoming the Countess of Whitney.'

Hawk eyed the other man scornfully. 'And we all know how devoted you were to your last Countess!'

'Have a care, Stourbridge,' Whitney grated harshly, all humour gone as his eyes glittered dangerously in the darkness. 'Just because I did not love my wife, it does not mean that I am incapable of understanding the emotion—'

'Understanding it, perhaps,' Hawk conceded derisively. 'But feeling it? Somehow I do not think so.'

'I have loved, Stourbridge,' the other man bit out coldly. 'Too much to ever feel the emotion for another woman! I—'

'Ah, there you are, Hawk,' Arabella greeted him brightly as she came out onto the terrace. 'And the Earl of Whitney, too,' she recognised happily. 'The absence of two such eligible gentlemen has left some of the ladies in desperate need of dancing partners for the next set,' she added, with a playful tap of her fan on the Earl's arm.

The last thing Hawk felt like doing at the moment was playing the polite host to Arabella guests—male or female. In fact, he had never felt less polite in his life!

'As long as you will promise to be my partner, I will indeed return to the ballroom, Lady Arabella,' the Earl drawled in reply to her rebuke.

'Hawk…?'

'Oh, I believe your brother has…some urgent business about the estate he has to take care of before he is free to rejoin us,' the Earl dismissed lightly as he drew Arabella's hand into the crook of his arm. 'Is that not so, Stourbridge?' he added, with a challenging glance in Hawk's direction.

Hawk met the other man's gaze in a silent battle of wills, knowing Jane to be the 'urgent business' Whitney referred to.

'Hawk…?' Arabella said uncertainly as the silence stretched between the two men. 'Surely whatever it is it can wait until morning…?'

'Doubtful, hmm, Stourbridge?' the Earl drawled mockingly.

Hawk gave the other man one last narrow-eyed glance before turning to his sister. 'I will rejoin you as soon as I am free to do so, Arabella.' He could not, after all, simply return to the ballroom when he knew Jane was alone somewhere out in the garden.

'Oh, very well,' his sister accepted, with an impatient flick of her fan.

'Our dance, I believe, Lady Arabella?' the Earl prompted smilingly, as the sound of the quartet of musicians hired for the evening could be heard once more.

Hawk waited until his sister and the Earl had returned to the ballroom before turning his narrowed gaze in the direction of the garden. But he could detect no sign of movement either on the lawns or along the hedges to indicate Jane's presence.

Where could Jane have disappeared to so completely? The stables once again? Or somewhere else?

Chapter Eleven

Jane sensed rather than heard the Duke's presence behind her in the darkness of the summerhouse to which she had fled so angrily such a short time ago.

Angrily? She had been more than angry; she had been incensed.

'Have you come to once again laugh at my fears?' she demanded, without turning.

'Fears, Jane…?' he echoed softly.

Jane had not lit the lamps when she entered the summerhouse, preferring to hide her blushing cheeks in the darkness as she acknowledged how close she had come to revealing her feelings for the Duke—both to Hawk himself and to cynical the Earl of Whitney.

She turned now, her chin stubbornly high as she stared across the distance that separated her from the Duke as he stood silhouetted in the doorway.

Arabella had shown Jane the summerhouse yesterday afternoon, and the two women had lingered to enjoy a glass of lemonade on the veranda surrounding it in the heat of the afternoon.

But the single room that had seemed so bright and airy during the day was full of shadows this evening, and the Duke appeared very tall and imposing in the darkness, the haughty arrogance of his face all sharply etched angles.

Jane made a brief movement of her shoulders. 'I would not like to see you imprisoned, or more likely hanged, for killing another man.'

His teeth glinted white in the gloom as he drawled. 'That is always supposing, Jane, that it was not I who was killed.'

That had been her real fear, of course. The fear Jane had almost revealed, and along with it her newly discovered love for this man. The same fear she dared not reveal now, for that very same reason.

'Was that ever a possibility?'

He shrugged. 'Whitney has something of a reputation as a swordsman.'

Jane repressed the shiver than ran through her. 'Then you were doubly foolish to have challenged him in that way.' She snapped her impatience with his recklessness.

'Was I, Jane?' He moved farther into the summerhouse to close the door softly behind him.

Jane resisted the impulse to take a step backwards, determined that she would not reveal how much being alone here with him like this disturbed her. Even if it did. Very much so. 'Very foolish, indeed, Your Grace.' She nodded abruptly.

'Are you not cold in here, Jane?' he prompted huskily, instead of responding to her rebuke.

'Perhaps a little,' she acknowledged frowningly. 'But it was not my intention to remain here for long…' Her voice dwindled off as the Duke went down on his haunches by the fireplace and put a flame to the kindling already laid there. The yellow-orange flames that instantly flared into life illuminated his sharply etched profile.

'There.' He rose slowly back to his feet before turning to look at her. 'Is that not better, Jane?'

It was certainly warmer. Cosier. More intimate. None of which was in the least 'better' after what had happened the last time she and the Duke had been so alone together.

'Jane?' he prompted huskily, those gold-coloured eyes warmly searching on her upraised face.

The warm flames now crackling in the hearth were as nothing compared to the flames leaping inside Jane as she stared up at the Duke. Her pulse was beating erratically. Her heart thumping so loudly she thought he must hear it. Her palms were slightly damp. Her breathing shallow.

She nodded abruptly. 'Much better, Your Grace.'

Hawk watched the movement of her tiny pink tongue as it moved moistly across her lips, her throat moving convulsively as she swallowed, and the soft swell of her breasts slowly rising and falling as she breathed softly.

It had taken him several long, anxious minutes to locate Jane here in the darkness of the summerhouse, but now that he had found her he questioned the wisdom of being alone with her like this.

The summerhouse was situated in a copse of trees at the far end of the spacious gardens that surrounded Mulberry Hall, well away from the main house, and was the place that he and his siblings had disappeared to as children, when they had wanted to escape the restraining company of adults.

As he and Jane had now escaped the restraining company of other adults…

A move, he now realised, not without its own dangers.

'Did it not excite you earlier, Jane, to have two men challenging each other to a duel over you?' he prompted huskily.

She arched auburn brows. 'Over me, Your Grace?'

Hawk frowned darkly. 'Who else, Jane?'

She gave a derisive shake of her head. 'Perhaps some other lady of your mutual acquaintance? This Countess, for example?'

Hawk's eyes widened at the directness of her attack. Although he should perhaps have expected nothing less from a young woman who was never less than forthright.

She gave a knowing smile. 'Ah, I note by your scowling silence that my surmise is possibly the correct one. The Countess was your mistress as well as the Earl's?'

Hawk stiffened. 'I do not believe this to be a suitable subject for discussion between us, Jane—'

'Why?' Her eyes were curiously wide. 'Or is it that the Countess is a married lady?'

He frowned darkly. 'She is widowed.'

Jane frowned her puzzlement. 'The Earl has informed me he is also widowed. And you are a single gentleman.' She shrugged. 'I do not see where the problem lies…?'

Hawk looked at her in exasperation. 'The problem lies, Jane, with the fact that a single young lady such as yourself does not discuss a man's mistress—ex-mistress!—with him.'

'Why not?'

'Because it simply is not *done*, Jane!'

She gave a derisive smile. 'Perhaps in the polite company that you keep, Your Grace, for which the Earl voices such contempt.' She nodded. 'But, young as I was, for lack of anyone else in whom to confide my father occasionally discussed such matters with me when it involved one of his parishioners.'

'I am not one of your father's parishioners, Jane!' Hawk muttered irritably.

Inwardly, he was wishing that he had never met the Countess of Morefield—let alone so briefly and, as it had transpired, so unsatisfactorily shared her bed!

He had no doubt that it was because of that brief dalliance that Whitney was behaving so provokingly this evening, in monopolising the company of both Jane and Arabella. The other man had made it obvious at the time that he had taken exception to Hawk's interest in the Countess, which had resulted in her changing from sharing her bed with an Earl to a Duke.

'No, you are not,' Jane acknowledged ruefully, staring into the flames of the fire as she wondered what her father would have made of a man such as Hawk St Claire, the forceful Duke of Stourbridge.

Her father—her adopted father—had not been a man of the world, but a simple country parson. Nevertheless, in the boundaries of his parish there had existed avarice, jealousy, incest, adultery and even murder. Perhaps not, as the Duke had said, subjects for a young girl's ears, but in the absence of a wife to share his worries Jane's father had sometimes talked to her about such matters.

'What manner of man was your father, Jane?'

She looked up sharply at the softly spoken query. 'He was a good man,' she stated defensively. 'A good, kind and loving man.'

The Duke's mouth twisted derisively. 'All things I am sure you believe me not to be!'

'Untrue, Your Grace!' Jane gasped.

He looked grim. 'Was it a kind man who refused to let you continue on your journey as you wished and instead brought you here, Jane? Was it a kind or loving man who only days ago took advantage of your lack of a protector?' He shook his head self-disgustedly. 'In the six days of our acquaintance, Jane, it seems to me I have shown you I am not any of the things you so admired in your father!'

They were two very different men, yes. But these last three days, as Jane had watched the Duke work so tirelessly about his estate, he had shown himself to be just as good a master to the people who lived on his estate as her father had been minister to his parishioners.

Besides, her feelings towards the Duke—the wild,

soaring love she felt just looking into that aristocratically handsome face—bore absolutely no resemblance to the sweet, uncomplicated love she'd had for her adopted father!

She shook her head. 'I do not think of you in that way, Your Grace.'

Hawk looked down at her searchingly. 'Then how *do* you think of me, Jane…?'

That pink tongue ran once more over the softness of her parted lips. 'I—I see you as a man. A strong, arrogant, forceful man who expects—demands—to be obeyed without question.'

Hawk smiled ruefully at her description. '*You* do not obey me, Jane.'

She gave the ghost of a smile. 'Perhaps that is why you are here with me rather than with the Countess…?'

Hawk found his breath catching in his throat. That was exactly the reason he was here with Jane rather than any other woman. Jane challenged him. Thwarted him. Disobeyed him. Aroused him.

As he gazed into the beauty of Jane's face, as he looked at her softly parted lips and into the unfathomable depths of her eyes, as he felt the fierce desire that ripped through him, he knew that it had been a mistake to follow her here. That being alone here with Jane like this, desiring her as he did, was the last thing he should have allowed to happen.

'Jane…' He was not aware of having made a step towards her, or of her making one towards him, but knew that he—that she—must have done so. His arms moved about her and he drew her fiercely against him as his mouth claimed hers.

She was all softness and the sweet perfume that was uniquely Jane, her lips parting willingly beneath his as Hawk deepened the kiss, feeling his desire raging hotly out of control as her slender fingers threaded into his hair and her ample breasts and slender hips curved invitingly against his own chest and thighs.

Hawk had never known such fierce desire. The need to possess. To own. His thighs pulsed with that need, and the hardness of his arousal moved restlessly against her as he strained to draw Jane even closer.

There were too many clothes between them. Too many layers of fabric between Jane's body and his own. Between the feel, the sensation, of her silken nakedness pressed against his.

Hawk groaned low in his throat as her own actions seemed to echo his need, her hands trailing down his throat to splay against his chest as her fingers dealt deftly, quickly, with the buttons of his waistcoat and shirt before she touched his burning flesh and those fingers became entangled in the silky hair beneath.

Her touch was too much. Jane was too much. Hawk deepened the kiss hungrily, devouringly, drinking in her sweetness as his tongue plunged hotly, ravenously, into the heat of her mouth.

Seeking. Capturing. Claiming her for his own.

For Jane was his.

His.

She belonged to this man, Jane acknowledged

feverishly, clinging to his shoulders. Hawk was continuing to kiss her even as he swung her up into his arms to carry her across to a chaise, laying her gently down upon it before quickly joining her there, the hard length of his body pressing her down amongst the cushions as his lips and tongue continued to plunder her own.

At that moment Jane cared for nothing else—needed nothing else but Hawk's lips and hands upon her. She arched her back as he reached to release the fastening of her gown and slide it down the length of her body. She was wearing only her stockings and chemise now, and closed her eyes in ecstasy as she felt the caress of his tongue across her silk-covered breast before he suckled her deep inside his mouth, drawing on her greedily, hungrily, even as his tongue continued that wild caress across the hardened tip.

But she wanted—needed—to touch him too, and slid the jacket from his shoulders, the waistcoat quickly following, then his shirt, until Jane knew the sheer pleasure of touching his naked flesh. Her fingers were caressing as they glided over the hardness of his muscled chest, tangling in the silky hair that covered him, before she touched him, her nails scraping accidentally against one of the hardened nubs that nestled there.

His sharply indrawn breath was enough to tell Jane that the caress gave Hawk pleasure too, making her bolder still as she touched him deliberately now, and felt him quiver, shudder in uncontrollable response.

Before Hawk, she had never caressed a man's naked body before, but now, as she began to experiment with what gave Hawk pleasure, Jane felt a sense of her own power over the flesh that hardened and quivered at her slightest touch.

Hawk fell back with a gasp as he felt Jane's hands upon him, his groan one of aching longing as he lay on his back and felt the lap of her tongue against him. Her hands were running the length of his chest now, his muscles quivering, tensing at her slightest touch. A touch that was all the more arousing because of her lack of experience or artifice.

Hawk looked down at her in the firelight, at the play of flames against her hair as it fell free of its confining pins onto his bared chest. His hand shook slightly as he raised it to touch that brightness, his fingers tangling convulsively in its silkiness as her kisses followed the line of hair that moved from his chest down to his navel.

He sucked in a sharp breath as he felt the experimental dip of her tongue into that sensitised well, that shy plundering sending him very close to losing complete control.

Jane raised her head to look at him, eyes dark with her own arousal. 'Did I hurt you…?'

His short bark of laughter was self-derisive as he moved so that she now lay beneath him. 'Jane, if you "hurt" me any more in that particular way I am not sure I will be answerable for the consequences!'

She looked up at him quizzically. 'You liked my touching you so intimately…?'

Hawk grimaced. 'I liked it too much, Jane, to let you continue.'

'I do not understand…?'

How could she? How could Jane know that just to look at her as she lay there, with her long hair spread on the cushion beneath her, her lips swollen from his kisses, wearing only her stockings and chemise, her nipples hard and pouting beneath the silky material, her curving hips and thighs turned invitingly towards him, was more than enough temptation without the added arousal of her lips and hands upon his own body?

'Let me show you, Jane,' he groaned throatily, as he slipped the slender straps of her chemise from her shoulders to bare her breasts completely and gaze down hungrily at those rosy aureoles of pleasure. 'How do you feel when I do this, Jane?' He bent his head to run his tongue lightly across the sensitised nipple, instantly feeling her quivering response. 'And this?' He bestowed the same caress upon its twin, and again felt Jane tremble. 'And perhaps this…?' He moved his hand to push up her chemise and bare her thighs to his slow caress, as first touching the silken curls there before moving lower.

Her lids closed at Hawk's first touch of her silken folds, her flesh already swollen and moist with arousal as her thighs parted to his caressing fingers.

Hawk stroked her slowly, purposefully, circling the hardened nub but never quite touching as he allowed her to become accustomed to the intimacy of his touch, waiting until Jane arched instinctively against his hand before deepening the caress. The soft pad of his thumb then sought and found the swollen centre of her arousal before moving rhythmically against her.

Jane, having been lost in a wondrous sea of pleasure only seconds earlier, now opened wide, incredulous eyes to look up into Hawk's fiercely concentrating face as her pleasure intensified to fever pitch—burning, scorching, flooding her.

She could feel her own slickness as Hawk probed gently against her with one experimental finger, felt as it entered her slowly, questioningly, before he withdrew. Only to repeat the caress, again and again, the pad of his thumb a constant caress against her, fiercely and then more gently.

Fierce and gentle. Fierce and gentle.

Each time Jane imagined she was about to discover that there was more—much more!—as Hawk gentled his caress and withdrew, and the ache between her thighs, at the tips of her breasts, became unbearable.

'Please...' she finally groaned achingly, wildly. 'Please, Hawk!' She sat up slightly against the cushions, offering her breasts in silent plea. 'I want—I need—'

'I know exactly what you need, Jane!' he growled triumphantly, before his head swooped and his mouth claimed one aching nipple, drawing it deeply into his mouth as he suckled, tongue stroking, teeth biting. The caress of his hand was no longer in the least gentle as he thrust rhythmically inside her and felt the first of her pleasurable convulsions.

'Hawk...' Jane gasped mindlessly as pleasure both burned and filled her. 'Hawk...!' She fell back, her hands clenching on the chaise, as wave after wave of pleasure claimed her, beginning as a fire that raged between her thighs and spreading like an ever-increasing flame to her every extremity—licking, throbbing, consuming all in its path.

'Yes, Jane. Yes!' he groaned fiercely, before transferring his attentions to her other breast, drawing it deep into the hot cavern of his mouth as he continued to stroke her swollen flesh until Jane had experienced every last moment of wondrous pleasure.

Incredible. Amazing. Miraculous pleasure.

Jane fell back weakly against the cushions, never having known that such pleasure existed. Never having known that this was what happened between a man and a woman. Never guessing at the shared intimacy that resulted in such ecstasy.

Was it always this way between a man and a woman? Had it been this way between her mother and her lover? If so, Jane could perhaps at last understand how Janette had succumbed to his seduction. As Jane had just succumbed to Hawk's…!

Did that make her the things Lady Sulby had accused her of being? Was she indeed a harlot and a whore?

'What is it, Jane?' Hawk demanded as he saw the shadows racing across her face—a face that seconds ago had been lit from within as she reached the climax of her pleasure. But now it was shadowed with—with what? With embarrassment at her own lack of control? Or with regret for what had transpired…?

Neither of which was acceptable to Hawk.

His hands moved to cradle each of her cheeks as he tilted her face towards him. 'Look at me, Jane,' he ordered firmly, when she kept her lids determinedly closed. 'Jane!' he rasped impatiently as she did not immediately comply.

Jane bit down painfully on the trembling of her bottom lip as she resolutely kept her lids closed. 'I think it would be best if you left me now, Your Grace—'

'How dare you attempt to put a distance between us by addressing me in that cold, distant way?' he cut in fiercely. 'Jane, you *will* look at me now!' His hands moved to her shoulders, digging into the softness of her flesh as he shook her.

How could she possibly look at him ever again? How could she bear to look into his face—the hard, arrogant face that she loved—and see the disappointment, the disgust that must be written there as he recalled her wanton writhings as she pleaded with him to pleasure her?

'Look at me, Jane!' Hawk demanded again harshly, as he sensed that inwardly she was withdrawing even further away from him.

Minutes ago he would have sworn that Jane had wanted his attentions, his caresses, but now he doubted that certainty. Jane could not even bear look at him— as if the very sight of him repulsed her.

Had Jane merely acquiesced to his kisses, the intimacy of his caresses, because she had not been strong enough to deny him? Or, worse, because she felt beholden to him for aiding her escape when she could no longer tolerate Lady Sulby's cruelty?

The thought that that might be the case filled Hawk himself with revulsion.

He released her abruptly to sit up on the chaise, his face turned away as he stared sightlessly into the flames of the fire which minutes ago had bathed Jane's nakedness so seductively.

Had he forced his attentions on Jane? Had Jane surrendered to the Duke of Stourbridge because she'd felt she had to, rather than to Hawk the man because she desired him as fiercely as he desired her?

Oh, yes, Jane challenged, thwarted and disobeyed him when it suited her, but had she felt unable to do so just now? The very force of his desire having alarmed her into submission?

He was sure that had to be the case when he recalled how distantly she had addressed him as 'Your Grace', immediately after his caressing hands had brought her to a climax it must now shock and revolt her to recall.

His expression was grim as he stood up abruptly to pull on his rumpled shirt, his back towards Jane as he refastened the buttons with fingers that were not quite steady. 'I believe it best if I leave you, after all, Jane,' he rasped harshly.

Jane had taken advantage of Hawk's distraction to pull her chemise back into some sort of order, wincing slightly as the material brushed against breasts that were still achingly sensitised from his ministrations, between her thighs was even more so.

She stared up at the rigid implacability of Hawk's back, at the silkiness of his dark, gold-shot hair brushing the collar of his shirt in unaccustomed disarray—a fact he seemed aware of too, as he pushed impatient fingers through the mahogany darkness before pulling on his waistcoat and jacket and turning to face her.

Jane almost recoiled from the fierceness of his expression. His mouth was a thin, uncompromising line above his clenched jaw, and those golden eyes glittered coldly as he looked down his long, arrogant nose at her. Every trace of the indulgently attentive lover had now disappeared from his harshly etched features.

But she refused to allow herself to show weakness. Her nature was such that she refused to be cowed by anyone—least of all the arrogant Duke of Stourbridge. 'By all means return to your sister's guests, Your Grace,' she told him lightly as she swung her legs to the floor and sat up on the chaise. 'But I trust you will understand if I do not join you?' She quirked mocking brows.

She knew she should pick up her gown—her beautiful gown of cream silk which had been thrown aside so uncaringly only minutes ago!—and cover her semi-nakedness, but the stubbornly proud part of her nature refused to let her do so. Minutes ago Hawk had seen her in all her naked glory, making it far too late for her to act like an innocent miss now.

Even if that was what she was.

Or had been…

Jane was sure she would never be completely innocent ever again now that Hawk had introduced her to such a world of physical intimacy and pleasure.

She forced herself to meet his imperiously haughty gaze. 'Would you please tell Arabella that I have retired to my room with a headache?' Her voice was husky, the headache she had just mentioned actually becoming a reality as Hawk's face darkened ominously at her words. 'I think it better if we do not return to the house together after such a long absence,' she added.

Hawk knew that the gossips present tonight would be sure to make much of the fact that although Jane had left the ballroom earlier in the company of the Earl of Whitney it was on the arm of the Duke of Stourbridge that she returned some time later. And he had already caused Jane enough distress for one evening without adding the ruination of her reputation in Society to his list of crimes. As it was, his return and Jane's absence were sure to be noted.

He nodded abruptly. 'I will make your excuses to Arabella. But do not remain out here alone for too long, Jane,' he continued harshly. 'I was not the only man attracted by your beauty this evening,' he added, with a disapproval he had no control over.

Her eyes widened briefly before her gaze became mocking. 'I do believe that one lover in an evening is more than enough for any woman!'

His mouth tightened at the mere thought of Jane ever sharing of her lush beauty with any man but himself. It was unacceptable. Insupportable. Unbearable.

She belonged to *him*, damn it!

His jaw clenched. 'If it really is your wish to avoid being seen again this evening, then I suggest that you go to your room by way of the back stairs.'

Like one of the servants, Jane acknowledged dully. But was that not what she was? Here on sufferance only? As a temporary companion to Lady Arabella?

And as occasional lover of the powerful Duke of Stourbridge…?

Her chin rose proudly. 'I think not, Hawk.' Her tone was coldly dismissive as she deliberately used his given name. 'I have no intention of behaving in the manner of a serving girl returning to her room after an illicit tryst with the master of the house!' she added, as he frowned darkly.

His face darkened ominously. 'I do not think of you as a servant, Jane—'

'Then do not suggest that I behave like one!'

As was usual for them, Hawk acknowledged grimly, they were arguing now they were not caught in the throes of physical desire. But for Jane to even suggest that he thought of her in the same terms as one of the maids at Mulberry Hall was utterly ridiculous. Utterly provoking!

His mouth twisted grimly. 'I believe you were the one to suggest that as your given role, Jane. Not I.'

Her eyes sparked with temper. 'You implied it, Your Grace,' she snapped.

'No, Jane, I did not,' he sighed. 'But who am I to argue with a woman when she has made her mind up to something?' he added grimly.

Her eyes glittered. 'You are the arrogant Duke of Stourbridge!'

'Undoubtedly,' he drawled, with an acknowledging inclination of his head, absolutely positive that Jane was trying to provoke an argument with him. Another argument with him… 'I believe, Jane, that we will resume this conversation when you are feeling less argumentative.'

'And I believe we will not!' Jane snapped, as she stood up to begin pulling on her gown.

Hawk's breath caught in his throat as he watched, stood transfixed at her agitated movements.

Jane could have no idea how beautiful she looked, with her red hair falling in loose curls almost to her waist, that silky chemise barely covering the fullness of her breasts and the alluring curve of her thighs before she pulled her gown over that nakedness. But Hawk was very aware of it as his body once more ached, throbbed with the return of his desire, leaving him in no doubt that he would find little rest tonight in the loneliness of his ducal bed.

It had been this way since he had first met Jane, he acknowledged ruefully. At Markham Park she had been a constant source of disruption, as he had been at first irritated by her and then amused by her. She had become more than an irritation on his journey to Mulberry Hall, and even the work that had kept him so busy about the estate the last few days had not been enough to dispel thoughts of Jane once he retired to his suite for the night. The added memory of their time together in the stables was enough to totally chase away any idea of rest.

But tonight, with the taste and feel of Jane still upon his lips and hands, he knew that he would find sleep impossible!

'As is your wish, Jane,' he bit out tersely. 'But that has been the usual way of things in our acquaintance to date, has it not?' he added hardly.

Did he really believe that? Jane wondered frowningly. Did he really believe that, given a choice, she would leave his side ever again?

She loved this man. Loved him as Hawk St Claire. Loved the Duke of Stourbridge.

And there lay the real problem.

As Hawk St Claire there might have been some hope, albeit a slim one, of him one day returning her love. But as the Duke of Stourbridge—a man destined to marry well in order to provide the ducal heir, to take as his wife a woman of a status and breeding suitable to be the mother of that heir—there was absolutely no hope of Jane, a woman who did not even know who her real father was, being able to measure up to his exacting standard.

She forced a deliberately mocking smile. 'As you say.' She gave a derisive nod. 'Please do not let me delay you a moment longer from returning to your sister's guests.'

His eyes glittered dangerously. 'You will not dismiss me in that contemptuous tone, Jane!'

Jane's soft laugh was deliberately taunting. 'I am so sorry, Your Grace.' She made him an exaggerated curtsey. 'Please forgive me, Your Grace.' She eyed him tauntingly as she straightened. 'For one very brief moment I actually believed you when you said you did not believe I was subservient to you!'

Hawk wanted to shake her. Wanted to put her over his knee and spank her.

But more than either of those things he wanted to take her in his arms once again and make love to her! Completely this time. Wanted to bury himself deep inside her silken sheath before losing himself in the inferno of her inner heat.

But as he dared not trust himself to do either of those first two things, knowing either would immediately lead to the third, he took the only other course open to him— he turned sharply on his heel and strode forcefully, de- terminedly, away from her and from the privacy the summerhouse offered to his real needs and desires.

Jane waited only long enough to ensure that the Duke had really gone before falling down onto the chaise in a devastation of grief-stricken tears so heated they seemed to burn as they cascaded unchecked down her cheeks, knowing she had alienated Hawk for ever with the wantonness of her behaviour.

Chapter Twelve

'Come in, Jane, and close the door behind you.'

Jane had been sitting alone in the parlour eating a late breakfast, Arabella being still upstairs in her rooms, following the dinner party the previous evening, when one of the maids had come to inform her that the Duke wished to see her at once in the library. Jane had lingered—delayed—at the breakfast table long enough to finish her cup of tea as she contemplated the reason for Hawk wanting to speak to her again so soon after they had parted so angrily the evening before.

Perhaps to tell her she would have to leave his household?

Immediately?

If so it was the same conclusion Jane herself had come to during her long hours of sleeplessness.

The tone of his voice now—undoubtedly the Duke of Stourbridge's voice, cold and imperious—was more than enough to compel her into stepping softly into the library and carefully closing the door behind her before once more turning to face him.

The tall, imposing, imperious man who stood so broodingly silhouetted in front of the window—dark clothing expertly tailored, hair brushed neatly back from that arrogant brow, hands linked behind his rigidly straight back—bore very little resemblance to the piratical lover of the previous evening, with his clothes in disarray and the darkness of his hair curling onto his broy.

As she, Jane hoped, bore no resemblance to the tumble-haired, half-naked woman he had aroused to such unimagined pleasure!

She quirked one auburn brow as those gold-coloured eyes continued to look at her so chillingly. 'I have entered, sir, and I have also closed the door behind me…'

Hawk drew in a sharp breath at her barely concealed derision. 'I warn you, Jane, do not even attempt to annoy me this morning!'

Her eyes widened with beguiling innocence. 'By doing as you bade me to do…?'

Hawk's mouth thinned at Jane's display of innocent subservience, very aware that she was the least subservient woman he knew! 'This is not a time for humour, Jane,' he assured her harshly.

'No?' Her brows rose even higher before she walked gracefully across the room to sit in one of the armchairs that flanked the empty fireplace, smoothing her gown neatly into place and folding her hands demurely on her knees before lifting her head to look at him. 'Then what *is* it a time for, Your Grace?'

Hawk's hands clenched behind his back in a supreme effort to prevent himself from marching across the room and lifting Jane to her feet before shaking her unmercifully.

As he had known it would be, his night had been a disturbed rather than a restful one, as images of Jane, with her loosely curling red hair reaching to her slender waist, her breasts bared and pert, her thighs parted invitingly, had tortured and tormented him until morning light.

At which time he had finally given up all hope of sleeping and instead dressed before going down to the stables to saddle his stallion Gabriel and riding across the surrounding hillside for several hours. The brisk morning air had cleared his senses—if not his mind—of those tantalising memories of Jane in her half-naked abandon.

Not so now, as he looked at her sitting there so primly, her disapproving expression much like his old nanny's had been when she'd wished to rebuke him for some childish misdemeanour. On Jane a totally ineffective expression—because memories of her sensual beauty the previous evening crowded his already tormented mind.

His mouth thinned, nostrils flaring, as he refused to let those memories deter him from the reason he had summoned her here this morning. 'I have decided that it is time—past time—for us to discuss exactly why it was you decided to leave the home of your guardian so abruptly.'

Jane was so stunned by the Duke's topic of conversation that for a moment she could think of no reply. She had thought—believed—he had asked her to come here so they might talk about the events of the previous evening. Had prepared herself for that as she had lingered in the breakfast parlour drinking her cup of tea—had even thought of several replies she might make on the subject.

She could not think of a single response to the question he had just asked her! Instead she answered with a question of her own. 'Why, Your Grace...?'

'Why.' He nodded abruptly, his golden gaze totally unreadable as he looked down the long length of his nose at her.

Jane frowned. 'But you know why, Your Grace.'

'No, Jane, I do not,' he rasped harshly. 'As I recall, your only explanation at the time was that you no longer felt you could reside under the same roof as Lady Sulby.'

And that was true, as far as it went. But there was more, so much more, to Jane's flight from Markham Park. Reasons she could not share with this stranger who looked at her so coldly. For at this moment he was every inch the haughtily superior Duke of Stourbridge.

'I stated the truth,' she confirmed tightly.

'But what caused you to feel that way, Jane?' He took two long steps so that he towered over her.

She blinked at the intensity of that golden gaze as it seemed to bore down into hers. 'My reasons are entirely personal to me—'

'Not when you now reside in my home!'

'That can easily be remedied, sir!' Jane stood up abruptly, too restless to remain seated any longer—although she had not been completely prepared for how close the Duke was now standing to her. Her arm brushed against his as she attempted to step past him, instantly sending a tingling thrill of awareness down to her fingers and up to her breasts.

The Duke reached out and curled steely fingers about one of her wrists, preventing her from moving away from him. 'We will discuss the subject of your departure from Mulberry Hall later, Jane,' he rasped coldly. 'First I would like—I demand—a full explanation as to your reasons for leaving Markham Park.'

First? Hawk intended for her to go soon, then? Might even have made arrangements for her immediate departure once she had answered his questions…?

Because of what had occurred between them the previous evening? Or because of something else…?

Jane looked up searchingly into that hard, implacable face. Hawk's gaze was coldly compelling as it met hers, his expression unreadable. 'What has occurred, sir, to suddenly bring about the need for this conversation?' she ventured cautiously.

Hawk had never for a moment during their acquaintance underestimated Jane's intelligence. He did not underestimate it now. 'This morning I received word of your guardians' reaction to your disappearance.'

'I did not disappear!' Her cheeks were flushed with indignation. 'I simply left a place where I had never been made welcome!'

'Indeed, Jane?'

'Indeed, Your Grace,' she echoed impatiently. 'I—Would you release my arm please? You are hurting me.'

She frowned up at him, and his fingers tightened briefly before he gave a disgusted snort of frustration and released her.

Hawk turned away, knowing that if he did not he might do a lot more to hurt Jane than merely grasp her wrist and hold her against her will.

He was furious. Livid. Wanted to hit out and hurt someone. Anyone. Even Jane. Especially Jane—for putting him in the untenable position he now found himself in.

He kept his back firmly turned towards her as he bit out, 'No matter how unwelcoming, the Sulbys are nevertheless your guardians. Uncaring ones, perhaps—'

'Perhaps?' Jane scorned incredulously.

Hawk nodded abruptly. 'You were fed and clothed within their home, Jane. Which is more than many other penniless orphans can boast.'

'And I am to be *grateful* for that?' she challenged contemptuously. 'I am to bow and scrape and feel grateful for every morsel of food I have allowed to pass my lips these past twelve years?'

'Yes!' The Duke reached out once again to grasp her arm, his expression one of stingingly cold fury. 'Admittedly, I too have found Lady Sulby to be a contemptible woman. I have no doubt that you felt wronged by her, but that cannot be offered as an excuse for your own actions!'

Jane blinked up at him, more than a little alarmed by the fierceness of his expression. She had seen the Duke's anger before—had been the reason for that anger more times than she cared to remember!—but it had never been like this. Had never been underlined by this steely edge of absolute coldness.

'My own actions…?' she repeated slowly. 'What did I do that was so wrong?' She gave a puzzled shake of her head. 'Exactly what have you learned of my guardians' reaction to my sudden departure from their home, Your Grace? And from whom?'

His mouth tightened. 'It does not matter from whom—'

'It matters, Your Grace!' Jane cried emotionally. 'Your tone is accusing, and I believe it is unfair of you to talk to me in this way without first telling me the name of my accuser.'

He looked down at her wordlessly for several long, searching seconds before abruptly releasing her arm to turn sharply away and stride over to stand in front of the window once again, his back to the room. And to Jane.

'When we returned here four days ago I sent word to Andrew Windham, my man of business in London, asking him to make enquiries—to ascertain, if he could, your guardians' actions following your disappearance. I felt—justifiably, I believe—that it was wrong of me to harbour you within my household without at least some effort being made on my part to discover if in fact the Sulbys were scouring the countryside looking for you.'

'I assure you they were not!' Jane scorned knowingly. 'And you had no right to make such enquiries—'

'I had every right!' the Duke grated harshly as he swung fiercely back to face her. 'Damn it, woman, the Sulbys could have been dragging neighbouring ponds and searching the woods for miles around for your dead body!'

Jane frowned at his vehemence. 'And were they?' she finally ventured, with a return of her earlier caution.

He flexed his tensed shoulder muscles. 'The report I received this morning claims that Lady Sulby has suffered a complete collapse of the nerves following your disappearance, and has had to be removed to her brother's home in Great Yarmouth in order to take advantage of the bracing air to be found there.' His tone was grim.

Jane's frown became scathing. 'Are you saying that I am the cause of Lady Sulby's supposed collapse?'

Hawk's mouth was a thin, uncompromising line. 'You doubt the information acquired by my man of business?'

'Not at all.' Jane gave a weary shake of her head, sure that anyone the Duke employed was certain to be impeccably meticulous in his duties. 'What I doubt is that Lady Sulby would feel anything but jubilation at having finally rid herself of my unwanted presence in her household!'

The Duke did not speak for several long, tense seconds. 'Perhaps,' he finally rasped icily. 'But I am given to understand that it was not only your own departure that caused that lady's collapse, but the loss of her jewellery.'

Jane stared at him blankly. Lady Sulby's jewellery? Could Hawk possibly be referring to the only jewels that Lady Sulby possessed of any value? The Sulby diamond earrings and necklace given to her by Sir Barnaby on the event of their marriage twenty-five years ago?

But what relevance did they have to Jane?

'Several of Lady Sulby's jewels disappeared on the same day you did, Jane,' the Duke continued flatly.

Her eyes widened incredulously, her face paling. Was Hawk saying—? Could he possibly be accusing her of—?

'I know absolutely nothing of their disappearance!' Jane burst out incredulously, her expression anxious. 'Hawk, you do not seriously believe that I—'

'What I do or do not believe about this matter does not signify, Jane.' His mouth was set grimly.

Her hands clenched at her sides. 'It matters to me!'

He shook his head. 'The fact is that on the day you left the Sulby household Lady Sulby's jewels also disappeared. The matter has been reported to the appropriate authorities and an order issued for their recovery. And for your arrest. Do you understand what that means, Jane?' he prompted impatiently.

Jane understood exactly what it meant. But the fact that the authorities were actively looking for her, that they would arrest her for the theft of Lady Sulby's jewels when they found her, paled into insignificance when compared to the fact that Hawk obviously did not believe her when she told him she had no knowledge of the disappearance of Lady Sulby's jewels…

Hawk's frustrated anger with the situation increased as he looked upon Jane's bewildered countenance. If she thought for one moment that he was enjoying this conversation…

'I know how upset you were that day, Jane.' His tone

gentled slightly. 'I appreciate that Lady Sulby had deeply wounded you in some way—'

'How dare you?' Jane cut in furiously, angry colour having returned to her cheeks now, and the green of her eyes glittering with that same anger. 'How dare you stand there as my accuser and my judge on the word of a woman who on the last occasion we met expressed nothing but hatred towards me?'

The last thing Hawk wanted to do was judge Jane, or condemn her. He wished only to help her. But he could not do that if Jane would not tell him why she had left the Sulbys' that day.

'It is not only Lady Sulby's word, Jane,' he told her softly.

'Who else accuses me?' she demanded angrily.

'Miss Olivia Sulby—'

He was interrupted by Jane's dismissive snort. 'She is of the same mould as her mother, and her opinion does not count.'

'In that you are wrong,' Hawk told her impatiently. 'I can assure you that Olivia Sulby's testament against you is as valid as any other. And Olivia Sulby claims that on the day prior to your sudden flight she remembers accompanying her mother to her bedchamber, and that both of them chanced upon you there, in possession of Lady Sulby's jewellery box.'

Jane thought back to that day a week ago. It was the day the guests had been arriving for Lady Sulby's house party. The day Hawk himself had arrived…

She remembered going upstairs to collect Lady

Sulby's shawl and noticing the jewellery box had been left out on the dressing table before being totally distracted by the arrival of the magnificent black coach bearing the Duke of Stourbridge.

Then there had been that momentous first meeting with the Duke on the stairs, followed by Lady Sulby's scathing comment that Jane had brought her the wrong shawl and she was to return to her bedchamber at once and collect the correct one—and Jane's own embarrassment when she had returned up the stairs and realised that the Duke had stood on the gallery above as silent witness to the whole exchange.

Jane also remembered Lady Sulby's reaction when she had burst into the bedroom a short time later, Olivia behind her, and found Jane loitering in the room, the jewellery box still sitting on the dressing table.

Jane recalled how bewildered she had felt—how Olivia had looked at her with such triumphant satisfaction when the older woman had questioned Jane accusingly as to whether or not she had looked at the contents of her jewellery box.

But the following day Jane had learnt the reason for Lady Sulby's sharpness when the other woman had acknowledged that she had hidden there the letters Jane's mother had written to her married lover…

And now Hawk—the man who had made love to Jane so intimately the evening before—chose to believe the word of the two vindictive Sulby women over her own…

'Jane, I cannot even attempt to help you if you will not be honest with me,' he reasoned frustratedly.

Jane drew herself up proudly, determined not to show how hurt she was by his lack of faith in her complete innocence in this matter. 'I do not remember asking for your help, Your Grace.'

'You prefer to be arrested and imprisoned?' Hawk could barely contain the anger he felt at her stubborn refusal to confide in him.

Her mouth twisted scathingly. 'For something I did not do?'

Hawk was a local magistrate. He knew far better than Jane how the law worked. And with two such credible witnesses against her as Lady Sulby and her daughter, coupled with her own sudden flight from Markham Park, Jane would be found guilty before the case was even presented in a court of law.

He stepped forward to grasp her shoulders impatiently and shake her into looking up at him. 'Can you not see, Jane, that it will not matter whether or not you are guilty of the crime?'

'Of course it will matter!' she assured him fiercely, the glitter in her eyes not just from anger now, but also unshed tears. 'I know nothing of the theft of Lady Sulby's jewellery. *Nothing!*' she repeated vehemently. 'I do know that Lady Sulby hates me, as she hated my mother before me—'

'Your mother, Jane?' Hawk probed softly, when she broke off abruptly. 'Did you not tell me that your mother died when you were born?'

'She did. But—' Jane broke off again as she realised she had been about to tell more than she wanted him to know. Bad enough that he believed her to be a thief and a liar, without adding illegitimacy to that list of sins. 'Lady Sulby was acquainted with my mother.' Jane chose her words carefully. 'She told me she did not like her—that she did not approve at all when Sir Barnaby accepted guardianship of Janette's daughter.' Jane paled as a sudden thought—truth?—hit her with the force of a blow.

Her mother's letters to her lover confirmed Lady Sulby's claim that he had been a married man.

Twenty-three years ago Sir Barnaby had already been married to Lady Sulby for two years. Lady Sulby hated and despised Jane, she had told her, as she had hated and despised her mother before her.

Could it be that it was *Sir Barnaby* who had been Janette's lover twenty-three years ago? That Jane was *his* illegitimate daughter?

It would explain so many things if that were the case—most of all Jane being left to the guardianship of a man she had never even heard her adopted father mention, let alone one whom Jane had actually met before he and Lady Sulby had come to collect her from Somerset on that desolate day twelve years ago.

Could it be that Jane's mad flight to find her real father had been completely unnecessary? That she had been living under his guardianship all along…?

It was difficult to imagine the rotund Sir Barnaby as the dashingly handsome lover who had swept her mother off her feet all those years ago, whom her mother had so described in her letters when she had expressed the hope that her unborn child would resemble him.

But Sir Barnaby could have—must have—looked far different twenty-three years ago…

'Jane…?'

She blinked dazedly as she focused on Hawk. On the condemning Duke of Stourbridge. 'I will leave Mulberry Hall immediately.'

'No, Jane, you will not!' Hawk cut in forcefully, having been angered seconds ago at Jane's sudden distraction of thought. What could possibly be more urgent for her to contemplate than the dire situation she found herself in?

And, no matter how Jane might choose to dismiss the whole incident, it *was* dire. An accusation of theft had been made against her, her arrest ordered, and mere claims of innocence on Jane's part would not suffice to cancel that order.

But as the powerful Duke of Stourbridge Hawk did have some influence. 'I am willing to help you, Jane—'

'As I said before, I do not remember asking for your help, Your Grace,' she cut in coldly.

Hawk looked down at her searchingly. Did Jane really not see how precarious her position was?

'Neither do I ask for it now, Your Grace,' she continued haughtily as she attempted to shake off his hold on her shoulders. 'Release me, sir,' she ordered coldly when she was unsuccessful in that attempt.

He shook his head impatiently. 'Jane, if you leave Mulberry Hall without my protection you will be exposed to immediate arrest and imprisonment.'

She gave him a pitying look. 'I am willing to take my chances.'

Even the thought of Jane exposed to the harshness of a prison cell, to the cold and the rats and the untender mercies of the turnkey, was enough to make Hawk shudder.

She would rather suffer all that than accept his help…?

His hands dropped from her shoulders before he stepped back. 'Then you are a fool, Jane!' he assured her harshly.

Her eyes glittered challengingly. 'I would rather be thought a fool than live any longer under the protection of the Duke of Stourbridge!'

Hawk flinched as if Jane had physically struck him. Was that really how she felt? Did Jane despise him— hate him so much after what had occurred between them yesterday evening that she was willing to suffer imprisonment rather than accept his help?

The defiant expression on her face, the scorn directed towards him that she made no effort to hide, was answer enough…

He drew in a ragged breath before speaking again. 'Jane, I advise you to put aside your feelings of enmity towards me and instead concentrate on the matter at hand.' His expression was grim. 'I can intercede for you with Sir Barnaby. I have found him to be a kind and reasonable man, and I am sure—'

'No!' Jane cut forcefully across the Duke's reasoning speech. 'I will speak to Sir Barnaby myself, when I return to Markham Park.'

'You mean to go back there?' The Duke looked incredulous.

Yes, Jane intended going back to Markham Park.

She had thought to find answers to her past in Somerset, but now it seemed that Sir Barnaby might be the person who had those answers. That he might be her real father…

Whether he was or he was not, Jane knew she needed to return to Markham Park in order to clear her name as a thief. To expose Lady Sulby for the liar that she was.

For Jane became more and more convinced by the second that Lady Sulby's jewels were not missing at all—that Lady Sulby herself had hidden the jewels away somewhere, and merely taken advantage of Jane's flight in order to blacken her name even further.

She refocused on the Duke, her lips curving into a humourless smile at the disbelief in his expression. 'Yes, of course I mean to go back there.'

'Jane, you cannot—'

'I must go,' she assured him firmly, implacably.

And, whether she planned to return to Markham Park or not, Jane knew that she could not remain under the Duke's roof for a moment longer. He could not be further from the truth when he said Jane had feelings of enmity towards him. How could she possibly have feelings of ill-will towards the man she loved with all her heart?

The man who minutes ago had broken that heart when he refused to believe in her innocence…

Hawk looked down at Jane searchingly, knowing by the stubborn expression on her face that he would not be able to change her mind either by argument or cajolery. 'If you insist on this foolhardy course of action—'

'I do!'

'Then I will come with you.'

'No, you will not!' she refused with a vehement shake of her head. 'I am grateful for the help you have given me thus far, but whatever happens next I must deal with myself. Do you not understand, Hawk, that I do not want you to come anywhere with me?' she continued impatiently, as he would have once again protested. 'As you have mentioned on more than one occasion—' a slight, self-derisive smile curved her lips now '—you were forced into the role of my protector by my own impetuous actions. It is an obligation I now release you from.'

He gave a weary shake of his head. 'Have I not just explained that it is not as simple as that, Jane?'

'I assure you, Your Grace, our conversation has made several things clear to me,' she said enigmatically.

Hawk grimaced his impatience at her stubborn refusal to listen to him. 'Perhaps you are right, Jane, and we should talk of this again later. When you have had more time to think the matter through?'

'Perhaps,' she responded unhelpfully, giving a slight inclination of her head before turning to leave.

Hawk's expression was one of brooding frustration as he watched her cross the study to the door, her movements elegantly graceful, her head angled proudly.

But how long would Jane maintain that elegance and grace, let alone her pride, if Lady Sulby had her way and Jane was imprisoned for theft…?

Chapter Thirteen

'Jane…?'

Jane did her best to ignore the curricle—and its driver—as it drew alongside her, and walked determinedly along the lane that would take her to the road to London.

'Is it you beneath that bonnet, Jane?' The query was repeated impatiently.

She turned her face to the curricle, her smile rueful as she looked into the frowningly handsome face of Justin Long, Earl of Whitney, where he sat atop his curricle in complete control of a pair of lively-looking greys. 'It is indeed I, sir,' she confirmed dryly as she continued to walk.

'What the deuce are you doing wandering around the countryside unchaperoned?' he demanded disapprovingly.

Jane raised mocking brows. 'Our conversation yesterday evening led me to believe that you are the last person to be concerned with the proprieties, sir.'

He looked irritated by the jibe. 'Some of those proprieties are unavoidable, Jane. The unsuitability of a single young lady roaming the countryside unchaperoned is one of them,' he added with a frown. 'You—Jane, will you stop marching along in that military style and tell me what the devil you think you are doing?'

'Partaking of the air?' she returned tauntingly as she continued to 'march'.

Blond brows met over censorious blue eyes. 'I do not believe my question was an invitation to facetiousness, Jane.'

No, Jane was sure that it was not. It was only that if she didn't answer him in this offhand manner she knew that she would in all probability burst into the tears that had been threatening since she had packed her small bag and departed from Mulberry Hall an hour ago.

And she didn't want to cry—was sure that once she started she would not be able to stop.

'Jane, have I not instructed you to cease this infernal marching?' the Earl reminded her sternly.

Jane came to an abrupt halt in the lane and turned to glare up at him, an angry flush to her cheeks. 'I no more take orders from you, sir, than I do the Duke of Stourbridge!'

'Ah.'

Jane bristled at his knowing expression. 'And exactly what is meant by *that*, My Lord?' she demanded resentfully.

His expression was mockingly derisive. 'Argued with the young Duke, have you?'

'And what business is it of yours if I have?' Jane eyed him challengingly.

The Earl gave a rueful smile. 'Only that I would dearly have liked to witness that unusual occurrence!'

'Because you are still annoyed at his conquest of your Countess?'

The Earl gave an appreciative shout of laughter. 'Please tell me that you and the Duke did not argue over dear Margaret?'

'We did not,' Jane snapped, deeply irritated by his amusement at their expense. 'Now, if you will excuse me, My Lord, I must be on my way— What are you doing?' She frowned as he secured his reins before leaping agilely down from the curricle to stand at her side, looking as rakishly handsome as ever, in a tailored blue jacket that matched the colour of his eyes, breeches so tight in fit it was obvious that he owed none of his physique to padding, and a pair of highly polished Hessians.

'My dear Jane,' the Earl drawled, 'you do not seriously think that even the Earl of Whitney, having been made aware of your lonely state here on a public byway, would simply continue his journey back to London as if nothing untoward had happened?'

That was exactly what Jane had been hoping. Although the Earl's mention of his destination changed her thoughts somewhat…

She forced a smile. 'If you really wish to be of help to me, sir, then you will offer me a seat in your curricle to London.'

The frown returned to his brow as he eyed her speculatively. 'And what happens then, Jane? Does your guardian challenge me to another duel? Or will you settle for those damned matriarchs of Society demanding that as I have compromised you I must now marry you?'

Jane gasped. 'I wish for neither of those things, My Lord! I care nothing for the demands of the matriarchs of Society. The Duke and I have—parted ways. It is my belief that he is no longer concerned with what becomes of me.'

No doubt Hawk, once he got over his anger at Jane for having disobeyed him once again, would actually be relieved at having her disruptive presence removed from his household. Especially as she was now accused of being a thief!

'Then, my dear Jane, it is *my* belief that you do not know the Duke of Stourbridge as well as he might wish.' The Earl eyed her pityingly. 'The man is enthralled by you, you little goose!' he added impatiently at Jane's blank expression.

She could not deny that the Duke found her physically appealing—that would be impossible after the events of yesterday evening!—but he most certainly was not 'enthralled' by her. If Hawk had felt any affection for her at all then surely he would have believed her earlier this morning, when she had assured him of her innocence concerning the disappearance of Lady Sulby's jewels?

'I assure you that you are mistaken, My Lord,' she said flatly.

He smiled. 'And I assure *you* that I am not,' he drawled, staring at her wordlessly for several long minutes before giving an impatient inclination of his head. 'Very well, Jane,' he murmured slowly. 'For you I will break the rule of a lifetime and allow a woman up into my curricle with me.'

Her face lit up with pleasure. 'Oh, thank you, My Lord! You will not regret your decision, I promise you,' she vowed, as she plucked up her skirts in order that he might help her climb into the elegance of his open carriage.

'Believe me, Jane, I already do!' the Earl muttered, his expression grim as he moved to climb in beside her and take up the reins once more.

Jane smiled happily as the greys moved forward, completely unconcerned by the Earl's sarcasm now that he had agreed to take her to London with him. Although she did seem to be making rather a habit of accepting lifts in the carriages of unmarried gentlemen, she acknowledged ruefully. Rakishly handsome unmarried gentlemen.

'I may rethink my decision if you do not cease looking so smugly self-satisfied, Jane!' the Earl warned her with a scowl.

Jane at once lowered her head to look at him demurely from beneath her bonnet.

The Earl raised scathing brows. 'If anything, that is worse!'

She gave a relaxed laugh. 'You are very difficult to please, My Lord.'

'Am I…?' He easily maintained control of the greys as he continued to look at her frowningly.

'Yes…' Jane found herself disconcerted by that look. None of the consummate flirt of the evening before was now evident in the seriousness of the Earl's expression. Her smile faded. 'Why do you look at me so intently, My Lord?'

He turned sharply away. 'It is of no matter, Jane.'

Jane continued to look at him for several long seconds. 'It is my belief, sir, that you are not quite as others see you…' she finally murmured slowly.

His gaze was puzzled as he glanced at her. 'What can you mean, Jane?'

She shook her head. 'You would have people believe there is no more to the Earl of Whitney that the flirtatious rogue.'

His mouth twisted. 'But Jane Smith does not believe that to be so?'

'I know it is not so, My Lord.' She nodded. 'There is a kindness in you—the same kindness as coming to my rescue just now—that you do not like others to see.'

His mouth twisted into a grimace. 'You are far too astute for a young lady of such tender years, Jane Smith.'

'So I have already been informed, My Lord.'

'By Stourbridge, no doubt.' He nodded knowingly. 'Poor devil.' He gave a rueful shake of his head. 'You seem to have succeeded in shaking him from his pedestal of untarnished superiority.'

She shook her head. 'Not so untarnished, My Lord, considering that the two of you appear to have recently shared a mistress!'

The Earl gave a shout of appreciative laughter. 'Far too forthright, Jane!'

She shrugged. 'I am merely stating the facts. It is you

and the Duke who must take credit for the contents of that truth.'

The Earl's attention was drawn to the greys for several minutes. 'I believe, Jane,' he said grimly, once he had the lively greys under control, 'that we will save the rest of this conversation until I can give it—and you—my full attention.'

As far as Jane was concerned they could continue the rest of their journey in silence. Her only interest was in reaching London and from there continuing on to Norfolk. Talking of Hawk only caused her pain. Discussing his most recent mistress with the man who had been the Countess's previous lover only reminded Jane of her own immodest behaviour with Hawk the previous evening.

From there it was only a short distance to remembering their conversation earlier this morning.

And the disturbing conclusion she had made during that conversation.

Could it truly be that Sir Barnaby was her real father? All the evidence—the previously unknown Sir Barnaby being appointed her guardian, Lady Sulby's hatred of her and her mother—pointed to that being the case.

In those circumstances it had perhaps been unwise of her adopted father to have made Sir Barnaby her guardian, but the fact that there had been no one else he could leave Jane's future care to had probably meant he had had no choice in the matter.

No, any mistake must lie at Sir Barnaby's door, by his even attempting to introduce his illegitimate daughter into his own household, let alone expecting her to be accepted by his wife and legitimate child…

'This is not the way to London, My Lord!' Jane realised frowningly as they passed a sign at the side of the road that indicated London was in the opposite direction from the one in which they were now travelling.

The Earl gave an abrupt inclination of his head. 'It really is most unsuitable for you, a woman alone, to go to London with me, Jane.'

She glared at him fiercely. 'It is for me to decide where I will go and who I will go with, My Lord!'

'No, Jane, it is not.' He gave a firm shake of his head.

'Where are you taking me?' Jane demanded. But she already knew the answer to that question. The countryside about the Stourbridge estate was familiar to her…

'I am sure that you believe your reasons for leaving Mulberry Hall to be valid ones—'

'They most certainly are!'

'Perhaps,' the Earl allowed grimly. 'But I somehow doubt Stourbridge would agree with you.'

'I believed you to be a man who was not frightened of the high-and-mighty Duke of Stourbridge!' Jane scorned.

'I am not, Jane,' the Earl assured her softly. 'It is you that frightens me,' he added enigmatically.

'Me?' she echoed impatiently, her desperation rising as she saw the mellow outline of Mulberry Hall in the distance.

'You.' He nodded frowningly, his mouth twisting derisively. 'Did you not fear what might happen to you once you found yourself alone and unprotected in London?'

'No, of course not.'

'That is precisely the reason you frighten me, Jane,' he said grimly. 'You are too innocent, Jane.'

'I am not such an innocent, My Lord,' she assured him dully, fully aware that yesterday evening she had all but given that innocence to Hawk St Claire, Duke of Stourbridge.

The Earl pulled his greys to a halt before turning to study Jane, and her cheeks coloured under the intensity of that experienced gaze.

'Stourbridge made love to you last night?' he finally rasped harshly.

Jane gasped. 'That is none of your concern, sir—'

'I am making it so, Jane!'

She was tired, so very tired, of the Duke of Stourbridge and now the Earl of Whitney taking such an interest in the innocence that was surely hers to give where she pleased.

'I will find some other way in which to travel to London,' she dismissed impatiently, and she turned to climb from the carriage.

The Earl moved swiftly, already on the ground at her side as she stepped down from the curricle. Steely fingers grasped her arm. 'You are not going anywhere until I have got to the bottom of this situation.'

'Can you not see that I do not require your help, My Lord?' Jane demanded impatiently, glaring up at him as he refused to release her.

His mouth twisted derisively. 'I do not believe that I asked for your permission to help you.'

Jane's brows rose disgustedly. 'Heaven preserve me from interfering, over-protective men such as you!'

He gave a humourless smile. 'And Stourbridge?'

'I neither wish to speak of nor see the Duke of Stourbridge ever again!'

The Earl shrugged. 'That is rather unfortunate.'

Jane eyed him suspiciously. 'Why?'

The Earl's gaze moved over and past her flushed face to a distance over her left shoulder. 'Because, unless I am very much mistaken, we are about to be joined by the man himself,' he drawled pointedly.

Jane turned sharply on her heel to look at a horse and rider some distance away, the colour draining from her cheeks as she recognised—as, obviously, had the Earl of Whitney!—that rider to be none other than Hawk, Duke of Stourbridge.

She found herself too surprised to move as horse and rider drew steadily nearer. In fact, as they drew near enough for her to see the grim savagery of Hawk's expression, Jane actually found herself moving a step closer to the Earl of Whitney.

'Now the fun begins,' the Earl murmured dryly, as Hawk drew the prancing black horse to a halt only feet away, before jumping lithely to the ground and striding purposefully towards them.

Fun? Jane was sure that she had never felt less like having 'fun' in her life!

Hawk had never experienced such rage. It filled him. Consumed him. Until he could see nothing but Jane, as she stood looking at him so defiantly next to the Earl of Whitney. A man Hawk was rapidly coming to view as his enemy.

When Hawk had realised Jane had once again fled—after being assured by Arabella that Jane was nowhere to be found, either in the house or about the estate, that in fact she feared Jane had left without a word to either of them—he had hurried to Jane's room to confirm her disappearance for himself.

As Arabella had claimed, the bedroom was empty except for the new cream lace gown and gloves she had worn the previous evening, which he had taken such delight in removing.

And, tauntingly, on the dressing table, lay his mother's pearl necklace and earbobs…

To then seek her, and find her in the company—pre-arranged?—of a man such as Whitney was intolerable.

'So,' he bit out between gritted teeth as he came to a halt only inches from the pair. His hands clenched at his sides as the fierceness of his gaze moved from the paleness of Jane's face to the mockingly challenging face of the Earl of Whitney.

'Indeed,' Whitney drawled derisively. 'As you can see, Stourbridge, despite protests to the contrary by the lady concerned, I have safely returned your little bird to the nest.'

A nerve pulsed in Hawk's rigidly clenched jaw. 'Before or after you have seduced her?'

'Oh, the former, of course,' the older man taunted. 'The latter, it seems, I may leave to you,' he added hardly.

Hawk's narrowed gaze met the censoriousness of that hard blue look. 'You will explain that remark!'

Whitney shrugged broad shoulders. 'Do I really need to do so?'

No, he did not. Hawk was only curious as to what could have prompted Jane to confide the events of yesterday evening to a man like Whitney.

Which in no way excused his own behaviour, Hawk acknowledged in self-disgust. He had taken advantage of a young woman he had promised to protect. A young woman who had subsequently needed to seek protection from *him*.

But could Jane not see that Whitney was the last man—the very last man—she should have run to for that protection?

'Do stop the self-flagellation, Stourbridge,' Whitney dismissed dryly. 'Just accept for once in your ordered life that you have behaved like any other man when presented with such a tasty morsel as Jane.'

Hawk's eyes glittered coldly. 'You will not talk of Jane in such a familiar manner.'

'Will I not?' the other man challenged. 'May I point out, Stourbridge, that it was Jane's intention to leave for London with me rather than remain here with you…?'

Hawk was well aware of the choice Jane had made. That she had preferred the uncertainty of Whitney's intentions towards her rather than remain at Mulberry Hall with him. That choice only made his own role in this situation more unbearable.

Jane had been momentarily stunned by Hawk's

sudden appearance following so quickly her realisation
that the Earl of Whitney had not been taking her to
London with him at all but instead returning her to
Mulberry Hall.

But, as always seemed to happen when these two
men met, the conversation had taken a ludicrous turn.
'I was not leaving *with* you, My Lord, only accepting a
ride in your curricle,' she reminded the Earl snappily.
'As for you, Your Grace.' She turned to glare at Hawk.
'I believe the events of this morning have nullified any
promises I might previously have made concerning the
need to inform you of my movements.'

'This morning as well as yesterday evening?' the
Earl scowled. 'You have been busy, Stourbridge!'

'You—'

'Gentlemen, please!' Jane's voice rose sharply as she
saw the conversation once again rapidly deteriorating
into insults.

'Anything for you, dear Jane,' the Earl drawled.

Jane looked at him censoriously. 'You will cease this
deliberate provocation, My Lord!'

'I will? Oh, very well,' he conceded dryly, as Jane
continued to glare at him fiercely.

Jane turned to the Duke. 'And *you* will cease
behaving as if you actually care what becomes of me,'
she told him scathingly.

Behaving as if he cared? Hawk frowned darkly.
Damn it, he had made love with this woman last night—
of course he cared what became of her!

The fact that the two of them had argued yet again

this morning, resulting in Jane fleeing Mulberry Hall as well as himself, did not—could not—alter the intimacy that existed between them.

His mouth set grimly. 'I wish you to return to Mulberry Hall, Jane, so that we might discuss this like two reasonable adults.'

'You *wish* it?' she repeated scornfully, shaking her head. 'It is my own wishes that are important to me now, Your Grace. And I do not feel any desire to return to Mulberry Hall with you—either now or at any time in the future.'

'Dear, dear, Stourbridge—can your powers of persuasion, both last night and this morning, really have been so clumsily inelegant?' the Earl of Whitney murmured scathingly. 'I would have thought you a more accomplished lover than that.'

Hawk really was going to be forced into resorting to physical violence if the conversation continued in its current vein!

His patience—what little he possessed—was being stretched to the limit, both by Jane's stubborn refusal to accompany him back to Mulberry Hall and the unwanted presence of Whitney at their exchange.

'Perhaps Jane was right to leave you, after all, in order to seek out a more…experienced protector,' Whitney continued tauntingly.

'Will you cease this nonsense, sir? You know as well as I that our paths crossed this morning only by accident!' Jane instructed impatiently.

'But I assure you, dear Jane, I consider it a most fortuitous accident…' the Earl drawled with a narrow-eyed look at the younger man. 'It is my belief that someone needs to make Stourbridge answerable for his behaviour!'

'You will explain that remark, sir!'

Jane felt her face pale and turned slowly to look up at Hawk, a shiver of apprehension slithering down the length of her spine when she saw the coldness of his expression as he looked at the other man with eyes of icy gold.

In that moment he was neither the haughty Duke of Stourbridge nor her lover Hawk St Claire. He was instead a man who looked capable of cold-blooded murder…

The Earl of Whitney looked just as implacable. 'I am sure we are both aware of how inappropriate your behaviour has been regarding Jane—'

Jane didn't quite see what happened next. Hawk had moved so quickly, so assuredly, that before she knew it, it seemed, the Earl of Whitney lay prostrate on his back in the lane, his rapidly reddening jaw indicating exactly where Hawk had struck him.

Chapter Fourteen

'What have you done, Hawk?' Jane murmured faintly, before moving down on her knees beside the prostrate Earl. 'Are you hurt, sir?' She touched his arm. 'Can I—?'

'I have knocked him to the ground, as he deserves!' the Duke rasped, and he reached out to grasp her arm with steely fingers.

'Unhand me!' She turned to glare at him even as she tried to shake off his hold on her arm. A useless exercise, as it happened, because his fingers refused to be dislodged. 'How dare you?' Jane rose sharply to her feet. 'How dare you treat me so abominably this morning and then proceed to attack the defenceless man who has been kind enough to assist me in escaping such injustice?'

Hawk believed he had never met a less kind or defenceless man than Whitney. As he knew only too well, besides having the tongue of a viper, the man went several rounds thrice a week with 'Gentleman' John Jackson—and won as many times as he lost!

But the bright wings of angry colour in Jane's cheeks, the accusation in her gleaming green eyes, told Hawk that he had committed a tactical error in giving Whitney the beating he deserved—that by doing so he had only helped to convince Jane he was an unprincipled savage.

Whitney added to that impression as he gave a pained groan. 'I believe you may have broken my jaw, Stourbridge!'

Hawk transferred the coldness of his gaze to the other man. 'If I had broken your jaw you would not be able to talk—which would be a blessing for us all!'

'Cold, sir, when you have rendered me almost sense-less.' Whitney gave another pained groan. 'Is he not cold and unfeeling, Jane?' he murmured weakly, as she moved to kneel beside him once more and carefully placed his head upon her lap.

'Very cold and unfeeling, sir,' Jane confirmed tautly, and turned to give Hawk another brief, censorious glare.

So totally missing the conspiratorial wink that Whitney gave Hawk over her left shoulder!

The man was feigning, damn it! Simply acting more hurt than he was in order to gain Jane's sympathy! And he was succeeding!

'I think perhaps you will have to remove me to Mulberry Hall and send for the doctor, Stourbridge,' the Earl murmured from his comfortable position cradled on Jane's lap, and only the glint of a mocking eye was visible as Jane ran a soothing hand across his brow.

It was a move guaranteed to once again fill Hawk with an unaccountable fury of emotions—the strongest one being a wish to knock Whitney to the ground for a second time!

'Perhaps you might help me into my curricle, Stour-bridge…?' the other man goaded.

'Yes—do help him, Hawk,' a distracted Jane encouraged worriedly. 'We must put a cold compress on that jaw as quickly as possible. Hawk?' she prompted impatiently.

Hawk conceded that there were the beginnings of redness appearing on Whitney's jaw, but he certainly did not feel it merited the other man leaning quite so heavily on his shoulder as Hawk helped him to his feet and over to his curricle.

'A bad tactical error on your part, Stourbridge,' Whitney murmured, so softly that Jane, having moved to climb into the other side of the curricle so that she might help from there, couldn't hear him. 'Did no one ever tell you that where a woman is concerned it is usually the case that to the loser go the spoils of war?'

Hawk's mouth tightened at the deliberate taunt. 'Jane is not a prize to be won!'

'Perhaps that has been your mistake…' The other man arched a derisive brow. 'You—'

'Did I not tell you Jane is a woman to be "priced above pearls"…?' the Earl reminded him softly.

Hawk had no opportunity to reply as the other man assumed a pained expression as he stepped into the curricle, and allowed himself to once again be given into Jane's solicitous care.

'You will have to secure your horse here, Hawk, and

take charge of the curricle,' Jane instructed sharply, as she made the Earl's head comfortable upon her shoulder.

Returning to Mulberry Hall had not been her plan, Jane acknowledged frustratedly, but in the circumstances she really had little choice.

What had possessed Hawk to attack the Earl in that way? Admittedly the Earl had been being his usual provocative self, but that really was no excuse for Hawk to resort to using fisticuffs. The Earl would be perfectly justified, after this, in issuing Hawk with yet another challenge to a duel.

At which time Jane would probably get her previous wish that the two men might kill each other!

'What on earth—?' A stunned Arabella came to an abrupt halt halfway down the stairs as the three entered the house—the Earl of Whitney being supported by Jane on one side and the Duke on the other. 'Has the Earl met with an accident…?' Arabella's face was pale with concern as she hurried down the long staircase.

'Only your eldest brother's fist, Lady Arabella,' the Earl roused himself to reply dryly, his arm draped about Jane's shoulder as he leaned heavily against her.

Arabella looked suitably shocked by this disclosure. 'Hawk…?'

'Do not fret yourself, Lady Arabella. I can assure you that dear Jane has already more than soothed my fevered brow,' the Earl said softly. 'Although a medicinal brandy would probably help speed my recovery,' he added wryly.

'Jane…?' Arabella looked bewildered now.

'Do not concern yourself, Arabella. I am sure that the Earl's injury is not serious.'

It was a conviction Jane had become more and more convinced of during their short journey in the curricle to Mulberry Hall. The Earl's jaw seemed in no danger of swelling, and only a slight discolouration to the skin had appeared, rather than the bruising she had feared.

In fact, Jane was not completely convinced that the whole thing had not been an exaggeration on the Earl's part in order that he might return her, without further argument on her part, to Mulberry Hall!

'Cruel, Jane,' he murmured now in dramatic rebuke. 'Too, too cruel!'

Jane gave Hawk a glance from beneath lowered lashes, knowing by the cold disgust in his expression as he stepped away from the other man that he was no more convinced by the Earl's incapacity than she now was.

She extricated herself from beneath the Earl's arm, having her suspicions confirmed when he remained perfectly steady on his feet without their support. 'I believe it is time—' past time! '—that I continued on my way,' she said.

'On your way where, Jane?' Arabella still looked totally bewildered by this sequence of events, although her eyes widened as she took in Jane's appearance in travelling cloak and bonnet. 'You really are leaving us?'

'I—'

'No, Jane is not going anywhere.' Hawk was the one to answer grimly.

Jane looked up at him, but the cold implacability of his expression told her none of his inner thoughts. 'Is it now your intention to hand me over to the appropriate authorities?'

'Authorities?' The Earl was the one to echo her sharply, making a very speedy recovery indeed as he straightened to his full height without assistance from anyone. 'What nonsense is this, Stourbridge?' He turned frowningly to the Duke.

Jane and Hawk's gazes were locked in a silent battle of wills as she answered the Earl. 'I believe it is the intention of His Grace, the Duke of Stourbridge, to have me arrested as a jewel thief. Is that not so, Your Grace?' she added challengingly.

'Arrested…? Jewel…?' Arabella repeated sharply. 'Hawk, what have you done?' She looked at her brother accusingly.

Why was it, Hawk wondered impatiently, that everyone, including Jane herself, believed he was capable of all manner of misdeeds—including cold-bloodedly giving Jane up to the caprices of English law?

'Surely you are mistaken, Jane?' Arabella frowned. 'I saw my mother's pearls and earbobs upon the dressing table in your room myself only an hour ago—'

'It is not those jewels I am accused of stealing,' Jane assured her wearily. 'But those of my guardian in Norfolk.'

'Guardian in Norfolk…?' Whitney looked stunned.

'I thought that you had claimed Jane as your own ward, Stourbridge?'

Hawk's mouth tightened. 'I have that dubious honour, yes.'

'I believe I relieved you of that temporary responsibility during the unpleasantness of our conversation earlier this morning!' Jane cut in firmly.

Hawk was breathing hard as he looked at her from between narrowed lids. 'And it is my belief that you deliberately chose to misunderstand me this morning, Jane.'

'Did I misunderstand when you accused me of stealing Lady Sulby's jewels? Did I misunderstand when you suggested I hand those jewels over to you, so that you might return them in an effort to persuade Sir Barnaby to drop the charges against me? Tell me, Your Grace, did I misunderstand any of that?' Her eyes glittered with challenge and unshed tears.

'Yes, damn it—' Hawk broke off his angry exclamation as Jenkins came into the hallway from the servants' quarters. 'I believe we should retire to the privacy of the drawing room if we are to continue with this conversation, Jane,' he bit out tautly.

'But we are not going to continue with it, Your Grace,' she assured him determinedly. 'You have insulted me enough—'

'You are recently come from Norfolk, Jane?' the Earl of Whitney cut in harshly.

Jane frowned at the interruption. 'I have, sir.'

Whitney shook his head frowningly. 'But when you spoke to my nephew at dinner yesterday evening I distinctly heard you talk of Somerset as having been your home…'

'My childhood home—yes, My Lord. But I have not lived there for some years now. Not since my father died twelve years ago and I was sent to live with—with acquaintances of my mother's.' Jane's face was extremely pale beneath the green of her bonnet.

'And would the name of these acquaintances be Sir Barnaby and Lady Gwendoline Sulby, Jane?' the Earl pressed forcefully.

Hawk gave the Earl a sharply questioning look. Did the other man know the Sulbys? From the look of almost distaste on Whitney's face as he spoke of them Hawk believed that he must.

Although he couldn't say he particularly cared for the intentness with which Whitney was now staring at Jane…

'Jenkins, bring a tray of tea things through to the drawing room, would you?' he instructed the hovering butler.

'Tea!' the Earl echoed disgustedly.

'Tea,' Hawk repeated firmly. 'For four,' he added dryly as he saw it was both the Earl's and Arabella's intent to accompany them.

Arabella moved to walk beside the obviously reluctant Jane, leaving Hawk to fall into step beside Whitney.

'What do you know of the Sulbys, Whitney?' Hawk prompted evenly.

Whitney seemed not to hear him for a moment, his gaze fixed intently on the rigid tension of Jane's back as she walked ahead of them. 'Who is she, Stourbridge?'

he finally managed to grind out harshly, every last trace of the flirtatious rake gone from his face and manner.

Hawk gave a shrug of his shoulders. 'I know no more about her antecedents than you.'

Blue eyes glittered fiercely as the other man turned to look at him. 'But it's true she is the ward of Sir Barnaby Sulby?'

'She is.' Hawk gave a terse inclination of his head.

'Good God…!' Whitney groaned hollowly.

Hawk looked at the other man searchingly, wondering why this information should so disturb him. To his certain knowledge, nothing and no one had been allowed to disturb the capricious Justin Long, Earl of Whitney during the last twenty years. Hawk had sensed that even Whitney's enmity towards him over the conquest of the Countess of Morefield had been more of an affectation than any genuine feelings of ill-will.

'I take it from your response that you *do* know the Sulbys?'

'I am acquainted well enough with Lady Sulby at least to know I would not even *consider* allowing her the care of one of my hounds, let alone a young lady of Jane's tender years!' the other man confirmed harshly.

Hawk's mouth thinned as he recalled that Jane herself had once made a similar comment to him concerning her guardians.

Jane…

Hawk could still remember his feeling of impotence earlier when he had discovered Jane gone, and grudgingly acknowledged that, if not for the timely interven-

tion of the Earl of Whitney, he might have been too late
to find her, allowing her to reach London and just disappear amongst the crowd of people there.

'I offer you my thanks for—for Jane's safe return to
Mulberry Hall,' he bit out hardly.

The other man eyed him derisively. 'How much did
that hurt?'

Hawk's brows rose. 'No doubt much more than the
blow I delivered to your jaw!'

Whitney grimaced. 'No doubt,' he acknowledged dryly.

Jane had no idea what the two men were discussing
so intently as they walked behind her and Arabella down
the hallway to the drawing room. Her own attention
was focused on Arabella, as the other woman questioned her concerning the accusations levelled by Jane's
real guardians.

'But it is surely just a coincidence, Jane?' Arabella
frowned. 'I have come to know you these last few days,
and I do not believe for one moment that you could have
taken Lady Sulby's jewellery.'

Arabella's absolute faith in Jane's innocence only
highlighted Hawk's total disbelief in that innocence!

She chose to position herself as far away from him
as possible once they had entered the drawing room,
standing beside the fireplace while Hawk moved to
stand before a window, his face in shadow as the sun
shone in at his back.

Not that Jane needed to see his expression to read his
mood. The stiffness of his stance—shoulders rigidly
back, spine ramrod-straight, chin angled arrogantly—

was enough to inform her that this interview was going to be no more pleasant than the one that had taken place in the library earlier that morning.

No one seemed inclined to speak at all until after Jenkins had delivered the tea tray, and Jane took advantage of this lull in the conversation to remove her cloak and bonnet, and shake her curls loose after their confinement.

'What is your connection to the Sulbys, Jane?'

Her eyes widened on the Earl of Whitney as the harshness of his tone disturbed the silence. 'I believe I have already stated, sir, that they were acquaintances of my mother.'

'Your mother who died in childbirth?'

Jane gave a humourless smile. 'I had only one mother, sir.' Two fathers, she might have added, but didn't. The Duke already had a bad enough opinion of her without regaling him with the tale of her illegitimacy. She turned to him as he stood so still and silent in front of the window. 'If, as you claim, sir, it is not your immediate intention to have me arrested—'

'It is not!' the Duke rasped harshly.

Jane gave an acknowledging inclination of her head. 'Then what are your immediate plans for me, Your Grace?'

That was a very pertinent question. And one that Hawk did not have an answer to. What he wanted to do—sweep Jane up in his arms and carry her to his bed-chamber, and once there make love to her until they were both weak and in need of sustenance other than each other—was obviously out of the question in the presence of Whitney and Arabella.

But that did not mean he couldn't at least try to correct Jane's impression that he intended consigning her to a prison cell at the first opportunity!

'I would like the two of us to talk, Jane,' he said stiffly.

'Talk?' She raised surprised brows. 'About what, Your Grace?'

Hawk drew in a ragged breath. 'Let us start, Jane, with the coldness with which you continue to address me!'

It was apparent from the way Jane's cheeks coloured so prettily that she was well aware of the reason he disclaimed the need for such formality between them.

She shrugged. 'I feel it is for the best, Your Grace.'

'Whose best?'

'Yours as well as my own!' Her eyes glittered warningly.

If only Whitney and Arabella were not present Hawk would have wasted no time in demonstrating just how much he disagreed with that claim. Yesterday evening he and Jane had shared a degree of intimacy usually reserved for the marriage bed, and as such her coldness towards him this morning was intolerable.

'Such formality between the two of us is unpalatable to me, Jane,' he assured her hardly.

'Then perhaps it is only I who feels that need, Your Grace!' Jane shot him another quelling glance.

'What is happening, Hawk…?' Arabella prompted uncertainly.

He held Jane's rebellious gaze for several more

meaningful seconds before turning to address his sister. 'I have not had an opportunity to discuss this matter with Jane yet, Arabella, and until I do I feel it would not be…wise on my part—' his mouth twisted ruefully '—to relay our news to others.'

'What news?' Jane echoed incredulously. 'That you believe me to be a thief and a liar—?' She broke off as Hawk quickly crossed the room, his expression one of savage fury as he grasped the tops of her arms and shook her. 'Hawk…!' she gasped when she managed to regain her breath. 'Hawk, you are hurting me!'

'As you are hurting me,' he ground out between gritted teeth. 'Damn it, Jane, I do not believe you to be a thief or a liar!'

'But—'

'I did not believe it this morning and I do not believe it now!'

'But—'

'My advice is to take him at his word, Jane,' the Earl of Whitney told her laconically.

'Oh, do be quiet!'

'Stay out of this, Whitney!'

Jane's eyes widened on the fierceness of Hawk's expression as they both answered the Earl at the same time, her gaze searching now as she looked into the dangerous glitter of those predatory gold eyes. 'I do not understand…' she finally murmured, with a puzzled shake of her head.

His mouth thinned in the arrogant austerity of his face. 'Perhaps it will help your understanding if I tell you it is my wish to make you my Duchess at the earliest opportunity?'

Jane felt the colour drain from her cheeks even as she stared up at him disbelievingly.

Chapter Fifteen

Hawk, the Duke of Stourbridge, wished to marry her?

And yet everything in his manner since their shared intimacy the evening before had pointed to him wishing the opposite—that he had never so much as set eyes upon her!

If that was so then what possible reason could the arrogant Duke of Stourbridge now have for making such an announcement—

The arrogant, but so impeccably honourable Duke of Stourbridge!

Could it be that despite her orphaned state, her lack of a place in Society, Hawk felt honour-bound—compelled, following their intimacy of the evening before, to make her an offer of marriage?

Jane's hope—that brief bubble of happiness that had risen so swiftly on hearing his announcement, on so fleetingly believing that Hawk might return the love she felt for him—burst painfully within her chest.

Her mouth twisted with regret. 'I cannot believe that you truly wish to take an accused thief as your wife.'

'You are not accused by me, Jane!' His face was stony.

'No?' She viewed him sadly. 'That was not my impression earlier today.'

'You misunderstood the content of my conversation earlier, Jane, and did not give me a chance to explain.'

'I will not allow you to propose the idea of a marriage between us, Your Grace.' She firmly extricated herself from the hands that no longer gripped her arms as tightly as they had. 'I could not—would not—marry you if you were the last man upon this earth!'

'Oh, cutting, Jane,' the Earl of Whitney murmured frowningly. 'Very cutting.'

Hawk ignored the other man. 'Why not, Jane?' A nerve pulsed in the tightness of his clenched jaw.

She eyed him stonily. 'Is it not enough that I have refused to even contemplate the very idea, Your Grace?'

It had never occurred to Hawk—he had not expected, never considered—that Jane might turn down his offer of marriage!

He had waited one and thirty years to make such an offer. Had evaded the avaricious clutches of young women and their marriage-minded mothers too numerous to recall. And now, when he finally felt compelled to make an offer, Jane had refused without hesitation.

Hawk had realised when he'd found Jane had fled Mulberry Hall without so much as a word of goodbye that he must find her and bring her back. Had known without a doubt, when he had found her again, that the thought of Jane leaving his life never to be seen again was unacceptable to him.

All for nought.

Because Jane did not feel the same reluctance at being parted from him.

He stepped back. 'I apologise if I have offended you by so much as mentioning the possibility of marriage between us,' he said stiffly. 'I assure you it was not my intention to cause you distress.'

Jane held her chin regally high. 'Your apology is accepted. Now, if there is nothing else you wish to say to me, I would like to be on my way.'

'Ah, but there is something else *I* would like to say to you, Jane.' It was the Earl of Whitney who addressed her this time.

Jane turned to look at him, her gaze mocking. 'Surely you are not about to make me an offer of marriage too, My Lord?'

'Hardly!' He looked horrified at the idea. 'I would, however, like to hear more about these guardians of yours…'

Jane stiffened warily. 'Why?'

He gave a shrug. 'I believe I may once have been acquainted with Lady Sulby. If her name was previously Gwendoline Simmons, that is,' he added.

Jane's wariness increased. 'I believe that was her name prior to her marriage to Sir Barnaby, yes,' she confirmed reluctantly.

She didn't want to talk of Lady Sulby or Sir Barnaby. She badly needed to leave this place—to get as far away from Hawk as she possibly could—before she broke down in front of him and begged him to love her as she loved him!

She gave a shake of her head. 'I do not believe such a conversation would serve any purpose, My Lord.' She turned away to pick up her cloak and bonnet. 'Now, if you will excuse me—'

'Jane, I have to know if— Was your mother's name Janette?'

Jane froze. Halted in mid-flight. Barely able to breathe. Her eyes deep green pools of pain as she turned slowly, oh-so-slowly, to face the Earl of Whitney. 'How is it that you know my mother's name, sir…?'

'Dear God…' the Earl groaned weakly, his face—that rakishly handsome face, that had been breaking female hearts for over thirty years—having gone deathly pale. 'You are Janette's daughter!' He reached out a hand to tightly grasp the back of a chair, his knuckles showing white. 'I thought—I was drawn to you yesterday evening because you had the look of her. The same red hair and sparkling green eyes.' He shook his head self-derisively. 'But you see, Jane, I have looked for her face in so many others over the years,' he acknowledged heavily. 'So many women. But none of them ever Janette…'

Hawk took a protective step towards Jane as she seemed to sway slightly, her eyes limpid green pools in a face now gone white with shock.

His expression darkened warningly as he looked at the other man. 'Can you not see that you are distressing her, Whitney?' he rasped frowningly.

The Earl had eyes only for Jane. 'Am I distressing you, Jane? *Am* I?' He reached out to grasp her hands tightly within his.

Jane looked up at him searchingly. 'How—when did you know my mother?'

'When, Jane?' the Earl repeated harshly. 'Would you like the exact date and hour of when I last set eyes upon her? Or will you settle for just the month and year…?'

Jane moistened lips gone stiff with shock. 'Please, My Lord, just tell me what you know of my mother!'

'Hawk, I really think that Jane should sit down,' Arabella cut in concernedly. 'She is ill…'

'No, I am not ill, Arabella,' Jane turned to reassure her huskily. 'I am merely— Please, My Lord.' She turned back to the Earl. 'Tell me all that you know of my mother.'

Hawk felt his heart clench in his chest at the wistfulness he detected in Jane's voice as she pleaded for knowledge—any knowledge—of the mother who had died giving birth to her.

He did not even begin to understand why the conversation had become so intense. He only knew that, like Arabella, he feared for Jane's health if this interminable situation continued. 'Pour the tea, Arabella,' he advised abruptly. 'Hot and strong for Jane, with plenty of sugar.'

Jane shook her head. 'I have refused sugar ever since my father explained the cruelty associated with its origins.'

'Today you will take sugar, Jane,' Hawk assured her firmly. 'Today you are in need of it.' He sent Whitney a censorious glance.

The Earl blinked, as if awakening from a dream. 'Yes, you must take tea, Jane,' he encouraged huskily, as he led her over to one of the armchairs and sat her down upon it. 'Perhaps I will join you,' he added gently, and he sat in the chair opposite, his gaze intent upon her face, her hands still held tightly within his own. 'You really are so very like her, you know,' he murmured softly.

Hawk continued to look at Jane concernedly as she released her hands from Whitney's in order to drink the tea Arabella had carried over to her. Some of the colour returned to her cheeks as she sipped the hot, sugary brew. And all the time Jane's gaze remained riveted upon the Earl's face. As if she dared not let him out of her sight. As if she feared that if she did so he might simply disappear.

That hungry need in Jane's face as she looked at the other man caused Hawk's heart to clench inside his chest like a fist.

Could it be—had Jane fallen in love with the Earl of Whitney? Could that be the reason she would not even countenance the idea of a marriage proposal from Hawk?

Jane placed her empty cup carefully upon the tea tray. 'Please tell me all that you know of my mother, My Lord,' she encouraged the Earl huskily.

'Where to start?' The Earl grimaced, his own tea ignored as it sat upon the table beside him. His gaze remained on Jane in unhidden fascination. 'I cannot believe—it is incredible, after all this time, to meet Janette's daughter. I— Forgive me, Jane. I digress.' He gave a dazed shake of his head. 'Tell me what you already know of her…'

Jane gave a rueful smile. 'From my father, I know that she was good and kind and beautiful.'

'She was, Jane.' The Earl nodded. 'Oh, yes, she was all of those things!'

Jane grimaced. 'From Lady Sulby I know that my mother was none of those things. That she was wild and sinful. That her wanton behaviour brought disgrace upon her family and friends—'

'The witch!' The Earl stood up impatiently, a dark frown upon his brow. 'You did not believe her, Jane?' He scowled his impatience.

Jane shrugged. 'I tried not to, sir—'

'But you *must* not, Jane!' The Earl protested vehemently, his hands clenched into fists at his sides. 'Gwendoline Simmons—Lady Sulby—' he grimaced with distaste '—is a spiteful, vindictive woman. She was jealous of Janette's beauty always. Of the warmth that so easily drew people to her. Of the fact that from the day I met Janette I loved her more than life itself…' he added, in voice gone husky with pain.

Jane stared up at him. Justin Long, Earl of Whitney, had once been in love with Janette…?

Hawk stared at the Earl too. Whitney was twenty years older than himself—had already been established as a rake beyond compare when Hawk had entered Society fourteen years ago. The other man's behaviour had never quite gone beyond the pale, but had certainly flirted along the edges of it. His Countess was reputed to have died of a broken heart rather than of the influenza that was claimed to have taken her life and that of her young son.

If Jane's mother had died at her birth, twenty-two years ago, then surely Whitney had to have been already a married man when he claimed to have loved Janette…?

Hawk looked searchingly at Jane, wondering what she was making of the Earl's conversation. She didn't look as surprised as he might have expected. In fact she looked almost calm at Whitney's claim to having been in love with her mother…

'Perhaps, Hawk,' Arabella put in quietly, 'it might be better if you and I were to absent ourselves from what appears to be a very personal conversation?'

Hawk scowled across at his sister for her suggestion. Jane might have turned down his marriage proposal out of hand, but that did not lessen the protectiveness he felt towards her.

'There is no need for that, Arabella,' Jane assured her warmly. 'In fact, I believe it might be informative for you both if you were to remain,' she added, with a brief glance in Hawk's direction.

A glance that contained—what? Hawk could not be sure. Apprehension, certainly. But what else…?

Whitney seemed to gather his thoughts together with an effort. 'First, Jane, I have to tell you of Gwendoline Simmons—of her obsession. With me.' He grimaced as Jane looked puzzled. 'I was twenty-four when she came to London for her first Season. I was rather full of myself, I am afraid. Engaging in discreet affairs with married ladies while flirting outrageously with all the new debutantes of the Season.' He gave a disgusted shake of his head. 'I was full of conceit, Jane.'

'You were single and eligible and only twenty-four years old, My Lord,' she excused him softly.

'That is no excuse, Jane,' he assured her hardly. 'Gwendoline Simmons took my interest to heart, you see, and fancied herself in the role of my future Countess.' He sighed. 'Of course my intentions towards her were not serious. I was merely playing with her. Honing my seduction skills. But Gwendoline's pursuit of me became—intense. Whenever I turned around, it seemed she was there—at my elbow, simpering and flirting and generally making a nuisance of herself. In the end I had to be cruel to be kind.' He frowned darkly. 'She did not take my rejection well.'

'I can imagine.' With the personal knowledge Jane had of Lady Sulby's greedy and manipulative nature, she could imagine the scenario the Earl described only too well!

The Earl's mouth tightened. 'I am sure that you can, Jane.' He grimaced. 'Unfortunately my father deplored my rakish behaviour, and demanded that I find myself a wife and settle down. That I became a more worthy heir to the Earldom.'

'And did you?' Jane prompted huskily.

'I did.' He nodded. 'I cast my eye uninterestedly over the rest of the debutants that Season and chose the one I believed would cause me the least inconvenience. Not a pretty tale, is it, Jane?' he prompted self-disgustedly.

'Not one you can be proud of—no, My Lord.'

He gave a brief, humourless laugh. 'Now I know you are truly Janette's daughter! She said exactly the same thing when I told her my reasons for having taken Beatrice as my wife,' he explained, at Jane's questioning look.

Jane nodded, already able to see where this tale was leading. Except she still wasn't completely sure of the Earl's role in Janette's life. In her own life, perhaps…

The Earl sighed. 'Gwendoline returned to Norfolk, and it was almost five years later when she made her appearance back in London Society as Lady Sulby, chaperon to her young sister-in-law.' He looked grim. 'I had been married for five years by this time, and had an infant son. I am not proud of what happened next, Jane.' He shook his head. 'But I—I took one look at Janette and knew myself well and truly lost! She was everything that was beautiful, Jane. With glorious red hair and emerald-green eyes. Her vivacity, her joy in life, was contagious. I was drawn to her in a way I had never experienced before. And, miraculously, she felt the same attraction. Oh, we tried for weeks to deny how we felt about each other, to fight our attraction, but it was impossible. Every time we met the attraction, the love, became more intense. We were like two halves of a whole suddenly come together, and to deny that connection was— We could not, Jane.' He groaned. 'The two of us became lovers—'

'Stop, My Lord!' Jane instructed breathlessly when finally she found her voice. 'Are you saying—?' She swallowed hard. 'Janette was *sister* to Sir Barnaby?'

'His young half-sister from his father's second marriage.' The Earl looked surprised by the question. 'But you must know that already, Jane? Did you not say that Sir Barnaby has been your guardian in the twelve years since your father died?'

She had said that—yes. And for all of those years she had believed—had been led to believe—that she was merely a distant poor relation of the Sulbys.

Someone who had been foisted upon them and whom they had taken into their household only because there was nowhere else for her to go, no one else who wanted her…

Sir Barnaby was her *uncle*? Truly her uncle? By blood? Had been Janette's older half-brother?

'Drink, Jane.'

She looked up dazedly at the Duke as he stood in front of her, holding out a glass of what looked to be brandy, knowing by the compassion she could read in his gaze that he too realised the deception that had been practiced upon her all these years. That he pitied her for that deception.

First obligation.

And now pity.

Neither emotion was what Jane wanted from him.

And she was sure, once Hawk had heard the whole story of her claim to existence, those would probably no longer exist either!

'Thank you.' She accepted the glass and took a restorative sip of what was indeed the finest brandy, her fingers remaining curved about the cut glass as if even its delicacy might give her the strength she needed to continue this conversation. 'I did not know of the connection, My Lord,' she informed the Earl dully.

'You did not know…?' The Earl frowned darkly. 'But how can this be? How can you not have known, Jane?'

Her smile contained no humour, only sadness. 'For the simple reason that no one ever thought to inform me.'

'That makes no sense, Jane.' The Earl looked angry now.

'It does if you are acquainted with Lady Sulby.' Jane sighed heavily. She was sure—had no doubts—that it was at that lady's instigation that the deception had been made. That Sir Barnaby, a meek and mild man who wanted only a quiet, untroubled life, had simply been too weak to fight against his much stronger-willed wife.

Was there nothing that Lady Sulby was not capable of?

Remembering the deceptions of the last twelve years, the accusations Lady Sulby had levelled at Janette that last morning, and the lies the other woman had told about Jane concerning the theft of her jewellery, Jane truly did not believe there was…

'Dear God!' the Earl grated harshly, as he finally seemed to realise what had been done to Jane.

'Indeed.' Jane inclined her head in acknowledgement.

The Earl was very pale now. 'Jane, was Janette happy with her parson?'

'I believe she was—content,' Jane replied carefully. 'Sir, you said earlier that you know the exact date and time of day that you last saw my mother…?'

'I do indeed, Jane,' he confirmed grimly.

'And it was…?'

He frowned. 'Jane…'

'For God's sake answer her, Whitney!' Hawk interjected harshly, the tension of this conversation becoming altogether too much to endure.

He could not pretend to understand all that was taking place here, knew only that he could not bear Jane's pain a moment longer. Although he would dearly have liked at that moment to have Lady Gwendoline Sulby in his clutches!

'I— But—' The other man shook his head as Hawk continued to look at him compellingly. 'Janette was but nineteen years of age, and the existence of my marriage had never sat well with her. I had told her that I would leave Beatrice, that the two of us would go abroad, live together there. But Janette would not hear of it. She insisted that I must stay with my wife and young son— that she must be the one to go. I last saw Janette on the day she informed me that we would not meet again, that she was to—to marry a parson, a young man she had known from childhood, and retire from Society.'

'Whitney!' Hawk grated forcefully, as Jane seemed to pale more with every word the other man spoke.

'I last saw Janette at ten o'clock in the morning of the tenth of November, 1793.' Whitney's voice broke emotionally. 'I tried to do as Janette wished me to do. I tried to make a life with my wife and young son. But I could not do it. I could not, Jane! I loved Janette—was only half alive without her. And so, out of desperation, I went to Norfolk to ask for news of her. Sir Barnaby was away from home, but Lady Sulby was there. She took great delight in telling me that I was too late—that Janette was already dead. She had died after giving birth to her parson's child. You, Jane.' He looked at her hungrily.

Hawk was no longer looking at Whitney, but instead

watched as incredible joy lit Jane's features, to be quickly followed by sudden tears that brightened her eyes as she stared at the Earl.

'She lied, My Lord,' Jane told him breathlessly.

Whitney looked bewildered. 'Janette was not dead…?'

'Oh, yes, she was dead. But Lady Sulby lied,' Jane repeated forcefully, and she slowly stood up, appearing strangely delicate, almost fragile, rather than the strong-willed young woman Hawk was used to seeing. 'I believe I have some things in my bag that belong to you—that will explain…' She smiled shakily at Whitney.

Whitney looked startled. 'That belong to me, Jane…?'

'Oh, yes, I believe so,' she confirmed breathlessly, at the same time seeming unable to take her eyes from him.

Hawk felt that clenching in his chest once again as he saw the love shining in Jane's mesmerising green eyes. Not for him. But for another man.

'Some letters, My Lord,' Jane continued softly.

'Letters, Jane? For me? From Janette?' Whitney suddenly prompted sharply.

Jane nodded. 'You will wait here while I fetch them, My Lord?'

'I— Yes, of course.'

Whitney looked no less confused than Hawk felt himself and he watched Jane as she hurried across the room. She halted, hesitated once she reached the door, her face still lit with that inner light as she turned back to face them all.

But once again it was to Whitney that she addressed her next remark. 'Janette did not leave you because she wanted to, My Lord. It is my belief that she left because she felt she had to do so.'

'Had to…?' the Earl repeated dazedly.

'Had to, My Lord.' Jane nodded. 'Perhaps it will help you to understand—to realise… I believe the contents of Janette's letters will be less of a—a shock to you, My Lord, if I tell you that Janette was three months with child when she married Joseph Smith. That it was not his child she brought into the world before she died. You see, My Lord, I was born on the second of May in the year seventeen hundred and ninety-four.'

With a swirl of her skirts Jane quickly departed the room.

Hawk watched transfixed as the Earl of Whitney— a confirmed rake, a man who made no secret of the selfishness of the life he had led the last twenty years— collapsed white-faced into a chair, a look of shock upon his still-handsome face as he stared hungrily at the spot where only seconds ago Jane had stood.

'Hawk, can it be…?' Arabella had moved silently to Hawk's side. 'Is the Earl Jane's father, Hawk?'

Exactly the conclusion Hawk had just come to himself!

Chapter Sixteen

'Are you not relieved now, Your Grace, that I did not so much as entertain the idea of a marriage between the two of us?' Jane prompted teasingly a short time later, when the two of them found themselves alone in one of smaller drawing rooms at Mulberry Hall.

It was painful for Jane to realise how vicious and cruel Lady Sulby had been—both lately and in the past. But that pain was superceded by the knowledge that her father had not rejected her, or her mother. He simply hadn't known of her existence.

She had excused both the Duke and Arabella, as well as herself, from the Earl of Whitney's—her father's—presence in the drawing room, sure that he would prefer to be alone when he read such private letters as her mother's had been to her lover.

Unfortunately for Jane, once outside the library Arabella had further excused herself, on the pretext of needing to talk to Cook concerning the luncheon arrangements. Leaving Jane alone in the small room in the icily silent company of Hawk, Duke of Stourbridge. Hence the reason for the brightness of her chatter.

'Although it is perhaps as well that you had this opportunity to—to practise, Your Grace,' she continued dryly, when he remained coldly uncommunicative. 'It really was not well done, you know,' Jane added, and he at last raised one dark, arrogant brow in the otherwise austere handsomeness of his harshly sculptured face.

The Duke—for he was every inch the loftily forceful Duke of Stourbridge at this moment!—drew in a sharp breath before answering. 'In what way was it "not well done", Jane?' he encouraged coolly.

'For future reference, Your Grace?'

He gave a haughty inclination of his head. 'For future reference, Jane.'

'Very well.' She nodded. 'Firstly, I would suggest that you do not make an offer of marriage in front of any third parties. It could not be considered in the least romantic, and is more likely to end in embarassment for everyone concerned. Secondly—' she drew in a deep breath '—I do believe, no matter what your own intentions might be, that most women, of any age or temperament, would like to feel that they are at least loved a little when proposed to.'

A nerve pulsed in his jaw. 'You believe that, do you, Jane?'

It became difficult for Jane to withstand the intensity of that piercingly golden gaze, so she busied herself with straightening the skirt of her gown instead. 'Oh, yes, I think so, Your Grace.' She nodded, red curls bobbing.

'And thirdly, Jane…?' he drawled dryly, at the same time moving from his stance in front of the empty fireplace to stand beside the chaise on which Jane sat. The muscled length of his thigh in buff-coloured breeches was visible from the corner of her eye.

She looked up. 'Thirdly…?'

She should not have looked up! Should not have acknowledged how close Hawk was now standing. Her every nerve ending, her every sense of sight, sound and smell, was now totally aware of him. Of his masculinity. His sheer physical presence.

'Oh, yes. Thirdly.' She made a concerted effort to concentrate on the matter in hand rather than allowing herself to become enthralled—overwhelmed!—by Hawk's brooding proximity. She moistened lips gone stiff and unresponsive. 'Thirdly, no woman would feel happy accepting a proposal of marriage from a man who obviously makes it out of a sense of duty, of honour, rather than love.'

'I believe we have already covered the subject of love in the second piece of advice you gave me, Jane.'

Her lids fluttered nervously at what she was sure was a deceptive mildness in his tone. 'Oh, I would not presume to offer you advice, Your Grace!'

'No?' That dark brow rose once again. 'Then perhaps it is only that you mean to help ensure that any marriage proposal I might make in future will not be met by the same rejection?'

'I did not reject you, Hawk—Your Grace.' Her hands shook slightly in her agitation, and she hurriedly laced her fingers together so that he might not see their trembling. 'You were not sincere in your suggestion of marriage to me.'

'Was I not?'

'No!' She eyed him exasperatedly. 'You merely felt bound by a sense of—of—'

'Duty and honour?' he put in helpfully.

'Yes, duty and honour.' She nodded quickly. 'Although quite how you would have explained to your family, let alone the ton, how your future bride came to be accused of theft, I cannot imagine,' she continued, with some return of her normal spirit.

His mouth thinned. 'I am sure I would have managed somehow, Jane.'

She gave an impatient toss of her head. 'In any case, it is an offer you would have had to withdraw once you were made aware of my—my illegitimate connection to the Earl of Whitney.'

Silence greeted her outburst, and Jane accepted that at last she had pierced Hawk's aloof superiority.

How could she not have done when she had just made it clear that any doubts he might have harboured in that direction were completely unfounded? That she was indeed the illegitimate daughter of Janette Sulby and the Earl of Whitney!

Her heart still ached as she recalled the way in which the Earl had taken Janette's letters from her. How he had cradled them tenderly against his chest, almost as if they were Janette herself. How the tears had begun to fall down his cheeks as soon as he had begun to read the first of those letters.

'Jane?'

She swallowed hard, almost undone by the husky intensity of Hawk's tone. She could not bear it if he was kind to her. Not now! Not when she was already so close to tears.

She loved this man with every fibre of her being. Had briefly, oh-so-briefly, been offered the opportunity of becoming his wife.

Could he not see that simply being alone with him like this was torture for her? Was more painful than anything that had come before?

'Look at me, Jane.'

She closed her eyes briefly, her heart fluttering in her chest. She had been almost completely undone the last time she had looked at him, and was not sure she could withstand another onslaught of the longing she had to simply throw herself into his arms and beg to stay in his life in any guise he wished!

'Jane, I insist that you look at me!'

Her eyes flashed deeply emerald and she raised her head sharply, her chin high. 'You insist, sir?'

Despite the gravity of the situation, Hawk once again felt the familiar twitch of his lips as he recognised the indignant anger in Jane's face. The anger he had deliberately incited…

He gave a mocking inclination of his head. 'May I now be permitted to make several claims in my own defence, Jane?'

She blinked. 'Your defence, Your Grace?'

'Certainly, Jane.' He grimaced. 'For I have surely been as judged and found wanting, as you accused me of doing with you earlier this morning.'

'Oh, but—' She frowned, her expression one of increasing puzzlement as she gave a slow nod. 'You may proceed, Your Grace.'

'Thank you, Jane.' He moved to sit beside her on the chaise, at once able to feel the warmth of her thigh only inches from his own. 'Firstly,' he began determinedly, 'you misunderstood my intentions when we spoke earlier this morning.'

'When you accused me of being a liar and a thief?'

His mouth thinned at her too-sweet tone. 'When I offered my sympathy and understanding that you had felt compelled to strike back at Lady Sulby by removing her jewellery before you left Markham Park!'

'It is no more flattering to be accused of spite than of being a liar and a thief!'

Hawk sat forward tensely. 'Why do you continue to deliberately misunderstand me, Jane?' he demanded impatiently. 'It was because you learnt of the existence of those letters to Whit—to your father from your mother, that you felt compelled to leave Markham Park so suddenly, was it not, Jane?' he added gently, remembering how distraught she had looked that morning when she had pleaded with him to take her away with him in his carriage.

That Gwendoline Sulby was capable of such cruelty he had no doubts. That he intended dealing personally with Gwendoline Sulby at the first opportunity was also in no doubt!

'I learnt much more than that, Your Grace.' Jane's voice was flat. 'Until Lady Sulby took such pleasure in informing me otherwise, I had no idea that Joseph Smith was not my father. That I was the bastard daughter of my mother's previous lover!'

Oh, yes, Hawk intended dealing *very* personally with Gwendoline Sulby!

He drew in a ragged breath. 'This morning, Jane, after receiving news of the Sulbys' actions following your disappearance, I was furiously angry—'

'No doubt at the thought that you had almost made love to such a creature.'

'At the thought that the Sulbys, after all their previous cruelties to you—cruelties that I am only now beginning to appreciate fully—could do such a thing as demand your arrest and apprehension for a few baubles that I am sure can be of little real value anyway!' Hawk stood up in his agitation. 'Do you really have so little faith in my perception of people, Jane? In my perception of you?' he rasped harshly. 'For if you do then you were right to turn down any idea of marriage between us!'

Jane breathed shallowly as she stared up at him uncomprehendingly. Could it really be that he had *not* believed her capable of stealing Lady Sulby's jewellery? That his anger this morning had not been directed at her but at the Sulbys?

Towards her aunt and uncle…?

She still found it incredible that Sir Barnaby had

been her true uncle all along. And Lady Sulby her aunt by marriage. Olivia her first cousin.

For the last twelve years Jane had longed for a family. To belong. But now that she knew exactly who that family was—her father excepted!—Jane could not help but think she had been happier in her ignorance.

And Hawk, Duke of Stourbridge, must surely now realise what a lucky escape he had made when she had refused his offer of marriage…

She shook her head wryly. 'Do you not see, Your Grace, that I refused your offer for your own sake rather than my own?'

His gaze sharpened. '*My* sake, Jane…?'

She gave a weary sigh. 'I am accused of being a thief, and now you have learnt—must know—that I am also the illegitimate child of Janette Sulby and the Earl of Whitney.'

'And I am the Duke of Stourbridge—and I shall marry where I see fit!' A nerve pulsed in his tightly clenched jaw. 'I shall marry whom I please, Jane,' he continued huskily. 'I shall marry where I love!'

Jane swallowed hard. 'I—where you love, Your Grace?'

'Jane, I swear that if you do not cease—' He broke off his angry tirade, breathing deeply as he brought his emotions back under control. 'You are the only person I know, Jane, who can almost drive me to my knees one moment by refusing to marry me and then totally infuriate me the next by telling me that it is for my own good! Yes, I love you, Jane. I have loved you, I believe, since the moment you threw yourself into my arms upon the staircase at Markham Park.' His face was grim.

'Oh, but—'

'I loved you when you wore that hideous yellow gown. I loved you later that evening, when you stood amongst the dunes with the wind rippling through your glorious hair and the moon reflected in your eyes. I loved you when you burst into my bedchamber the following day. I loved you even more when you appeared at the inn that evening.' He allowed a brief smile to curve his lips. 'I loved and adored you when I held you in my arms and made love to you. Like Whitney with his Janette, I have loved everything about you in every moment of every day since the moment I first laid eyes on you, Jane!'

This could not be happening! Hawk could not have just told her that he loved her—not once, but several times!

She breathed raggedly. 'Hawk, I—'

'Please do not interrupt, Jane,' he instructed her curtly. 'Allow me the privilege of making a complete and utter fool of myself when I get down on my knees and beg you to reconsider your decision.' He suited his action to his words and knelt on the rug at her slippered feet, taking both her hands in his. 'Will you not marry me, Jane? Will you not forgive and forget the clumsiness of my earlier proposal? Will you not accept that I meant no insult by it? That I merely wished to secure you as my own before another minute had passed? That when I discovered you gone this morning my first and only wish was to see you returned to Mulberry Hall so that I might never let you out of my sight again? Jane, will you please agree to become my wife, my Duchess!'

Hawk loved her! He truly, truly loved her!

Nothing else mattered at that moment. Nothing!

'I love you too, Hawk!' She launched herself into his arms, knocking them both off balance so that they fell onto the rug before the fire. Jane rested lightly on his chest as she looked down at him, her face glowing. 'I have loved you since before we met on the staircase—for you see I saw you out of the window as you arrived. You quite took my breath away! And I have loved you ever since, I am sure.' She smiled down at him tremulously. 'I truly, truly love you, Hawk!'

'Oh, Jane…Jane!' he groaned achingly, and his fingers became entangled in her hair as he tilted her head down to receive his kiss.

It was a kiss completely different from any other they had shared, as Hawk sipped and tasted, claimed and then conquered.

'Am I a wanton to want you in this shameless way?' she murmured some time later, with Hawk's arms like protective steel bands about her waist.

Hawk's chest moved convulsively beneath her cheek as he chuckled. 'It is not wanton to want, to desire, to love in the way that we love each other. Darling Jane, you are warm and loving—and if that means you are a wanton then I thank God for it!'

She was Hawk's wanton. Wanted no other man but him. Never had and knew she never would.

'I am glad of it,' she murmured happily. 'You know,

I am not sure it is completely proper for the Duke of Stourbridge to be romping on the rug with his sister's companion!'

This time Hawk's chest reverberated with his chuckle. 'As it is something that I intend to happen frequently once we are married, it would perhaps be as well for me to issue a new instruction to the household—that no one is to enter a room in which the two of us are alone without first knocking and being bade to enter!'

He claimed her lips once again, and Jane was rendered breathless when the kiss finally ended. 'I am sure it is all well and good that we love each other—'

'Well and good?' Hawk repeated teasingly as he rolled over so that she lay beneath him on the rug. 'It is wonderful, Jane! It is miraculous to feel so much love and know that you are loved in return!'

'Well. Yes. But—'

'Why do I have the feeling I am not going to like what you are about to say…?' His face was serious above hers, his gaze searching. 'Jane, whatever obstacle you see in our path, preventing us from being together, I advise you to put it firmly from your mind. Now that I know you love me too I will not allow anyone or anything to keep us from marrying each other.'

'But I am still accused of theft by Lady Sulby—'

'You may safely leave Lady Sulby to me,' he assured her grimly. 'And I am sure that your father, the Earl of Whitney, will also have some things he wishes to discuss with that lady!'

'But that is my next point, Hawk.' Jane looked up at

him concernedly. 'How can you—how can the Duke of Stourbridge—possibly marry the illegitimate daughter of the Earl of Whitney? Perhaps it would be better if we were to just—?'

'Do not even suggest it, Jane!' he interrupted harshly, his arms tightening about her. 'You will not besmirch or belittle the love we feel for each other by suggesting that there can be anything less than marriage between us! Not even for my own sake will you suggest such a thing, Jane,' he added warningly. 'I am the Duke of Stourbridge, and your father is the Earl of Whitney. Between the two of us we will manage something that is acceptable.'

Jane believed him. Utterly. Completely. For he was the omnipotent Duke of Stourbridge. And he loved her.

Hawk, the Duke of Stourbridge, and the adopted daughter of the Earl of Whitney, Janette Justine Long— for the had learned from the church register in Somerset that Jane's full name was indeed Janette, for her mother, Justine, for her father—were married one month later in St George's church in Hanover Square. All of the St Claire and Whitney families were in attendance, as well as the ton, as they all wised the Duke and his new Duchess well.

'Do you still believe that "love has nothing to do with marriage"?' Jane teased her husband, even as she snuggled into his arms as the carriage drove the two of them away for their wedding trip.

'Minx!' Hawk chuckled softly. 'I was arrogant, ridiculous, in that assertion.'

'You were,' Jane concurred, even as she sat up to kiss along the arrogant line of his jaw. 'Oh, Hawk, I wish that everyone could be as happy as we are!'

'I too, my love,' Hawk assured her gruffly, knowing that he held all his future happiness in his arms.

'My father's family have been wonderful.' Jane glowed up at him. 'And Arabella is already like a sister to me—'

'And Sebastian and Lucian like brothers, I hope?' he growled possessively.

Jane laughed softly. 'Sebastian is the dearest—and did you find occassion to ask Lucian how he came by his bruised knuckles?' she prompted frowningly, as she remembered Arabella's distress earlier when she'd seen the bruises upon her brother's hand.

Tall, dark-haired and wickedly handsome, Lord Lucian St Claire had stood as witness for his older brother.

'He claims to have scraped it upon a wall.' Hawk's frown echoed Jane's.

Jane's eyes widened. 'And you believe him?'

'No, of course I do not.' He grimaced.

There had been no chance this last month to see or talk to his brother, following Arabella's concern.

There had been the wedding to organise—once he had Whitney's permission Hawk had allowed nothing to delay those arrangements. There had also been Lady Gwendoline and Sir Barnaby for them to visit in Norfolk—a most unpleasant interview, to say the least.

Most of all, there had been Jane!

At Whitney's behest Hawk had accepted that it was better if the Earl and Jane were to stay with her aunt, Lady Pamela Croft, on the estate that adjoined his until after the wedding. The arrangement had allowed Jane to become better acquainted with her father and his family, but had also allowed Hawk to see Jane every day. To talk with. To walk with. To make love with!

Hawk had not believed it possible to love Jane any more than he already did, but that had not proved to be the case. Jane was now everything and all things to him.

But the arrival of Lucian at their weddng today, sporting bruised knuckles and an expression that dared any to question the reason for it, was definitely a cause for concern.

A concern that would now have to wait until after Hawk and Jane had returned from their honeymoon trip to Europe.

'I will deal with Lucian when we return in six weeks.' His arms tightened about her. 'Not, Jane, I forbid you to think or talk of any other man but me—at least for the duration of our honeymoon!'

'You "forbid" me, Your Grace…?' she echoed softly.

Hawk kissed her long and deeply. 'I forbid you, Jane,' he repeated challengingly. The lure of the seat opposite was proving too much of a temptation. There was something about Jane and the privacy of an enclosed carriage…!

The mischievous glow deepened in those wonderful green eyes as Jane easily read his intent. 'I bow to your superior authority, Your Grace,' she murmured throatily as she gave him a deceptively demure look from beneath lowered lashes.

Hawk chuckled softly as he lifted her in his arms an moved with her to the seat opposite. 'I have no doubt you are going to lead me a merry dance, Jane!'

Jane looked up into the face of the man she loved aboce and beyond all things. 'You are dissatisfied with your wide already, Your Grace?' Once again she deliberately used the title she knew infuriated him. Usually into making love to her!

'Never, Jane!' Hawk assured her fiercely, even as his arms tightened about her and his mouth claimed hers.

His Duchess.

Janette St Claire.

But most of all and always, his beloved Jane.

MILLS & BOON
Super Historical

On sale 1st May 2009

A DANGEROUS LOVE
by Brenda Joyce

A DANGEROUS OBSESSION

Wealthy and powerful, Viscount Emilian St Xavier is haunted by whispers of his Romany past. When his comfortable world implodes with the news of his mother's murder, he is determined to avenge her death – and Ariella de Warenne is the perfect object for his lust and revenge…

A DANGEROUS PASSION

Ariella's heritage guarantees her place in proper society, though she scorns the frivolous pursuits of the *ton*. Then she finds herself drawn to Emilian, the charismatic leader of the gypsy camp at Rose Hill.

Though he warns her away, threatening to seduce and destroy her, she stubbornly refuses – just as determined to fight for their *dangerous love*…

MILLS & BOON

Historical

On sale 1st May 2009

Regency

LORD BRAYBROOK'S PENNILESS BRIDE
by Elizabeth Rolls

Miss Christiana Daventry will do anything to keep
from the streets – and the insufferably attractive
Lord Braybrook urgently needs a governess! Headstrong,
tawny-haired Christy is so deliciously endearing that Julian
quickly forgets how scandalous it would be to yield to this
attraction for his penniless governess…

Regency

A COUNTRY MISS IN HANOVER SQUARE
by Anne Herries

Debutante Susannah Hampton is confused by dashing
Lord Harry Pendleton's attentions. Arrogant, but undeniably
attractive, he is not the spouse she had in mind – but this
innocent country miss is determined to inflame her new
husband's passion – and melt the ice around his heart!

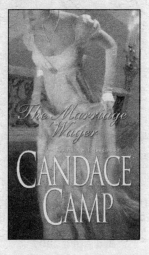

Regency

High-Society Affairs

Rakes and rogues in the ballrooms – and the bedrooms – of Regency England!

6th March 2009
A Hasty Betrothal by Dorothy Elbury &
A Scandalous Marriage by Mary Brendan

3rd April 2009
Desire My Love by Miranda Jarrett &
The Rake and the Rebel by Mary Brendan

1st May 2009
Sparhawk's Lady by Miranda Jarrett &
The Earl's Intended Wife by Louise Allen

5th June 2009
Lord Calthorpe's Promise by Sylvia Andrew &
The Society Catch by Louise Allen

8 VOLUMES IN ALL TO COLLECT!

www.millsandboon.co.uk

M&B

2 FREE

BOOKS AND A SURPRISE GIFT!

We would like to take this opportunity to thank you for reading this Mills & Boon® book by offering you the chance to take TWO more specially selected titles from the Historical series absolutely FREE! We're also making this offer to introduce you to the benefits of the Mills & Boon® Book Club™—

- ★ FREE home delivery
- ★ FREE gifts and competitions
- ★ FREE monthly Newsletter
- ★ Exclusive Mills & Boon Book Club offers
- ★ Books available before they're in the shops

Accepting these FREE books and gift places you under no obligation to buy, you may cancel at any time, even after receiving your free shipment. Simply complete your details below and return the entire page to the address below. You don't even need a stamp!

YES! Please send me 2 free Historical books and a surprise gift. I understand that unless you hear from me. I will receive 4 superb new titles every month for just £3.79 each. postage and packing free. I am under no obligation to purchase any books and may cancel my subscription at any time. The free books and gift will be mine to keep in any case.

H9ZED

Ms/Mrs/Miss/Mr ....Initials ....

BLOCK CAPITALS PLEASE

Surname ....

Address ....

....

....Postcode ....

Send this whole page to:
UK: FREEPOST CN8I, Croydon, CR9 3WZ